NOT SINCE EWE

COMMON THREADS BOOK #4

SUSANNAH NIX

WWW.SMARTYPANTSROMANCE.COM

COPYRIGHT

CHAPTER ONE

TESS

"Do you know what time it is?" I asked when I walked into the shared break room of my office co-op. It was empty except for one person, my work friend Marie, a freelance journalist who rented the office across from mine.

She looked up from her yogurt and broke into a grin when she saw me holding my phone in my hand. "Is it time to play How Many Dick Pics?"

"You guessed it." I already had my cynicism pants on as I opened the FindUr-Partner app. Not literal pants, mind you. My cynicism pants were purely metaphorical. They matched the metaphorical chip on my shoulder and provided protection from the metaphorical bitter pills waiting in my inbox.

As a single woman in my late forties who'd been online dating much of my adult life, I'd developed a cynical attitude about it. All my efforts had ever won me was some temporary companionship, a few brief but ultimately unsatisfying relationships, and more bad dates than I cared to remember. I no longer had any expectation that the dating apps I dabbled with would lead to any sort of meaningful connection.

And yet I couldn't quite give them up. It was almost an addiction at this point. I knew I'd probably never hit the jackpot, but I couldn't quit feeding nickels into the damned slot machine.

At least it provided some amusement. Marie and I always had fun laughing at the social ineptitude of the men who messaged me. As conversational overtures went, sending a photo of your junk to a stranger was about as clever as prank calling them to ask if their refrigerator was running.

"Place your bets," I said as I refilled my coffee mug. "How many dick pics from prospective suitors will I find in my direct messages today?"

Marie closed her eyes and pressed her fingertips to her temples with the gravity of a Jedi Master. "I'm sensing a lot of dicks in the Force today. Feels like…three —no—four." Her eyes popped open and she nodded, satisfied with her prognostication. "Definitely a four-dick day."

"Bold guess." I tended to average one or two daily dicks, although my all-time record currently stood at five.

Honestly, how were there so many grown men in the world with the interpersonal skills of twelve-year-old boys? How did they manage to navigate other areas of their lives? Feed themselves? Dress themselves? Hold down jobs? It was one of those unfathomable mysteries of the world. Neil deGrasse Tyson should do an episode of *The Inexplicable Universe* on it.

Marie offered a shrug as she licked berry yogurt off her spoon. "I don't control the dicks, Tess. I only predict them."

"All right, here goes. There are seven new messages waiting for me this morning. Let's see how many of them include a penis."

"I'm on the edge of my seat." Marie scooched her butt forward on her stool. "Literally."

I sipped my coffee as I opened the first message—which turned out to be a grave mistake because I nearly spit the hot liquid all over my phone.

Marie snickered as I covered my cough. "That bad?"

"Well…" I winced as I squinted at it. "He used the mirror filter so it looks like a dick growing out of a dick."

"Ohhh, lemme see." Marie hopped off her stool, then stopped and shook her head. "No, never mind. I don't want to see it." She frowned. "Or do I?"

"It's your call."

Sighing, she flapped her hand. "Lay it on me." I held the phone up, and her nose wrinkled as she studied it. "Is he trying to be artistic, do you think?"

"Beats me. Maybe he's trying to imply he has two penises like a snake."

Marie's eyebrows raised as she transferred her attention from the dick pic to me. "Snakes have two penises?"

I nodded as I blocked and reported Mr. Double Penis. I blocked and reported every unsolicited dick pic I received, and yet they still kept coming. Like a snowstorm or a zombie horde. There seemed to be an unlimited supply of men eager to send photos of their genitals to total strangers. Which went a long way to explaining why I was still single at forty-eight.

"They're called hemipenes," I said, referring to the snake penises. I was a voracious reader, which meant I'd collected a lot of weird and useless information that I enjoyed trotting out like a party trick when the opportunity arose. "They've got one connected to each testis. Fun fact: they can choose which penis they want to use when they have sex. And female snakes have two clitorises called hemiclitores."

"That just sounds like a lot of extra trouble." Marie brushed her blonde hair off her shoulder with a sniff. "If that's what this guy is going for, it's not as appealing as he thinks it is."

"Penises rarely are." I made sure to swallow my coffee *before* opening the next DM to avoid further spit takes. "Message number two…also a penis, but an uninspired one." This was a standard-issue shot of a standard-issue penis: bad lighting, awkward angle, poor composition, unflattering background. *Yawn.*

Marie went to the sink to rinse her yogurt cup and spoon. "At least the last guy gets credit for trying something."

"I don't get why so many men think we're dying to see their trouser snakes. Don't they know women pass these pictures around to their friends and laugh at them?" I moved on to the next message, which contained only two words: *Hi dear.* Having been at this for so long, I instantly recognized it as the trademark salutation of spammers, scammers, catfishers, and volatile old men. Delete.

"My friend Sandra is a psychiatrist, and she says unsolicited nude photos aren't about sex—they're a way of exerting power and control."

"Like catcalling and indecent exposure." I'd read something to that effect myself.

"Exactly." Marie frowned thoughtfully as she leaned up against the counter. "But honestly, I have a hard time understanding how these desperate randos spamming out their sad beans and wieners think they're exerting any power by inviting our mockery."

I shrugged as I deleted an obvious phishing scam trying to get me to click on a link to a malware site. "Apes and male monkeys commonly display their erect penises to indicate sexual interest to females."

"So what you're saying is all these men dropping their weens into women's DMs is what happens when you give an ape access to a smartphone?"

"Makes sense to me. And we're up to three dicks now." More bad lighting and awkward composition. The poor guy had posed his pecker next to a TV remote —for size comparison, I could only presume.

While I didn't condone body-shaming, I did feel free to judge their poor photography skills and lack of imagination. If you were going to hang your entire seduction technique on a photo of your hairy hot dog, at least put a little effort into it.

"How many messages left?" Marie asked.

"Just one. If it has a dick in it, you win."

She held up a hand with her fingers crossed. "Come on, dick!"

"Here goes." I made a dramatic show of clicking on the message. "And we have a dick!"

"Woo hoo!" Marie did a little victory dance in front of the break room fridge. "My dick Spidey sense is second to none."

A twentysomething man wearing bright orange Beats headphones—the sole occupant of the coworking space outside the break room—looked up from his laptop to cast a curious glance at us. I offered him an apologetic smile for our rowdiness, and he returned it with a careless shrug before bending his head to his laptop once more.

The demographics of our office co-op skewed fairly young, and most of them didn't start filing in until later in the morning. I was one of the oldest members, and even Marie, who I estimated to be at least ten years my junior, was older than most.

When I'd first gone out on my own as a product marketing consultant seven years ago, I'd tried working from my apartment, but I'd found it isolating and less than ideal for my mental health. My small rented office in the downtown Chicago co-op allowed for a much-needed change of scenery and afforded me an opportunity to interact with actual human people I might not otherwise get to know—like Marie.

"You've got a real gift," I told her when she'd completed her victory celebration. As I squinted at the last dick pick, I let out a sigh. "Now that's just sad."

"What?" Marie leaned in for a look. "Awww. It looks like a naked mole rat peeking out from under a blanket."

It was a full-body selfie from the neck down. The gentleman had removed his pants, but elected to leave on his gym shoes, tube socks, and a shapeless beige sweater.

"Does he honestly think this is a sexy look?" I wondered. "Not that any dick pics are sexy."

Marie tilted her head to one side. "I don't know. I think a dick pic can be sexy if it's from the right person in the right situation—prior consent obviously being a prerequisite."

"You know what's sexy?" I said as I blocked and deleted the sweater-clad mole rat. "*Forearms.* Why don't men send us pictures of their forearms?"

"God, yes," Marie agreed with a nod. "With the sleeves rolled up? Holy yumcakes!"

"Right? I'm getting sweaty just thinking about it." At least I hoped it was thoughts of sexy male forearms making me sweaty rather than a pre-menopausal hot flash. You never knew at my age.

The corners of Marie's mouth hitched. "But dicks can definitely be sexy."

I wrinkled my nose. "I can't say I've ever found one attractive enough that I'd want a picture of it."

As soon as I said the words, a random memory popped into my head of a long-lost dick from my youth. I'd been enamored enough at the time that I might actually have coveted a photo of the dick in question. Alas, that had been back in the days before digital cameras ushered in the dick pic boom.

Even more unfortunately, the dickhead who owned that sexy phallus dredged up a lot of unpleasant recollections, so I stuffed him and his accursed penis back into the locked memory vault where they belonged.

Marie offered me a shrug. "Speaking for myself, when I love the man, I love the penis. It doesn't even matter what it looks like or if it gets all weird and wrinkly when we're old. I'm always going to love it."

Of course she'd say that. She was newly married and madly in love with her hot nerd husband. Not all of us were so lucky.

Although I'd dated plenty of men over the years, never once had I felt tempted to make a lifelong commitment. My longest, most serious relationship had lasted two years before he was offered a job in another city. Faced with an ultimatum—follow him to Seattle or let him go—I didn't even think twice before wishing him well in his new life. And I certainly hadn't felt any particular attachment to his penis, if that was meant to be some sort of litmus test for true love.

I smiled at Marie as I sipped my coffee. "It sounds like the penis itself doesn't matter as much as the man attached to it."

"Physical attraction definitely increases as you fall in love. Matt wasn't at all my type when we first met—it wasn't until I got to know him better that he started to ring my bell. But I suspect there might also be a Pavlovian element at work. When you've had *really* excellent sex with a particular penis, I think it can create a conditioned response, so the mere sight of it can blow your panties right off." Her eyebrows waggled suggestively. "Even just looking at a picture."

I snorted. "I'll have to take your word for that."

"Come on, Tess. You've had sex that's rocked your world, right? I'm talking rattle the windows, break the bed, forget your own name kind of sex."

"Sure." There'd been a rare few men I considered gifted in the bedroom, though they'd been the exception and not the rule. "Just never with anyone who was interested in sticking around—or who I was interested in keeping around."

Marie gave me a knowing nod. "Hot dirtbags, right? Great sex, but nothing at all going on between the ears?"

"Something like that." I took another sip of my coffee as I thumbed my phone screen to open up my email.

"I'll bet if you saw one of those window-rattling dicks again, it'd get your engine revving though." Marie snapped her fingers. "Just like that. I'm telling you, your body has stored data on every great orgasm you've ever had."

I nodded absently as my attention caught on an email from LineagePlus, the DNA testing service I'd used several years ago to learn more about my genetic health risks. Apparently, I had a new private message. A tremor of unease shot through me as I tapped to expand the email.

As I read the message, a band wrapped itself around my chest, and my extremities went numb. Distantly, I was aware of a loud crashing sound, but all I could focus on was what I'd just read in the email.

"Tess?" Marie's face loomed in my field of vision. "Tess, what's wrong?" She clamped onto my shoulders, shaking me out of my trance.

I opened my mouth to answer, but I couldn't catch my breath to speak. Nothing came out but a choked wheezing sound.

"Breathe," Marie said as I started to panic. "Come sit down." She led me to a chair and I sank down on it, fighting to draw air into my lungs. "Here, bend over and put your head between your knees."

I did as directed, and Marie laid her hand on the back of my neck, exerting steady but gentle pressure as she calmly instructed me to inhale and exhale. After a few moments, the painful band constricting my chest loosened enough that I was able to breathe normally again.

"I'm okay," I said, pushing myself upright.

"Tess, you're white as a sheet. What happened?" Marie's concerned gaze shifted from my face to the phone still clutched in my hand. "Did you see something on your phone that upset you?"

I looked down at it, then quickly away again as my stomach clenched up. Coffee and shattered ceramic littered the floor where I'd been standing a minute ago. I'd dropped my favorite mug, shattering it to pieces.

Marie dragged a chair over next to mine. "What did you see that scared you so much? Was it a message on your dating app?"

I shook my head and swallowed. "No. Nothing like that."

"Then what? You can talk to me."

I hadn't talked to a single living soul about this in almost thirty years. It hurt too much, even decades later. The grief and guilt had scabbed over with time, but if I poked at the wound, it still felt brand-new.

Now it had been ripped open again, and I didn't know how to process the news I'd just gotten.

Marie was kind and sensible and one of the few friends I talked to regularly. I knew I could confide in her—and I should—but I couldn't make the words come out.

With shaking hands, I unlocked my phone and silently passed it to her.

She took it and peered at the screen. As she scrolled through the message, I reread it over her shoulder.

Dear Teresa,

My name is Erin, and I hope this message is not too distressing for you. I was born October 10, 1989, at Chicago General Hospital and put up for adoption. I've never known anything about my biological parents, so I signed up for LineagePlus to learn more about my ancestry and genetic health profile. LineagePlus matched your profile to mine as a very close relative. According to our DNA test results, you and I share almost 50% of our DNA, which means there is a high probability you are my birth mother.

My apologies if this information comes as a shock. I don't wish to disrupt your life, but I would very much like to know more about my family medical history. I would also be interested in learning more about you and my birth father if you're willing to share that information with me.

I understand if you need time to process this news. If you're open to communicating with me, you can send me a message through the LineagePlus app or contact me directly at the email address below.

Warmest regards,
Erin

Marie looked up at me, her big blue eyes soft and compassionate as they searched mine. "Tess? Is she right? Could she be your daughter?"

I nodded numbly. "Yes."

"Oh honey." Marie put her arms around me and pulled me into a hug. "I had no idea."

"I don't usually talk about it." I sat stiffly in her embrace, appreciative of the comfort she was offering, but unaccustomed to receiving it. I wasn't a big hugger, and Marie and I were only casual friends. Or we had been up until now. Before I'd shared my deepest, darkest secret with her.

She leaned back and studied my face. "How do you feel?"

"I don't know. I think I'm in shock."

"That's understandable. Were you looking for her?"

I shook my head. "I signed up for the genetic health screening."

"But with these testing services, you have to opt in to allow your DNA profile to be searchable by other users. You must have opted in."

I had. It was one of dozens of questions I'd had to answer when I registered my DNA test kit. And I'd clicked yes without hesitation.

"That sounds like you were hoping she'd find you," Marie said gently.

I supposed I was.

And now she had.

The baby I'd given up for adoption thirty years ago wanted to talk to me.

CHAPTER TWO

TESS

I'd gotten pregnant my senior year of high school, a few months before graduation. I'd already sent off all my college applications and was eagerly waiting to hear back from my top-choice schools to see where I'd be going in the fall.

I was an overachiever in school, a straight A student involved in as many extracurriculars as I could squeeze into my schedule. Student council executive committee, first-chair clarinet in the Eagle marching band, volleyball team captain, and class valedictorian, as well as an officer in about a dozen other after-school clubs to round out my transcript.

I wasn't the sort of girl who was supposed to get pregnant. I was a study warrior. Responsible and hardworking. A compulsive rule-follower. I didn't even date that much. My eyes were firmly fixed on my future, not on the boys at my school.

Except one boy: Donal Larkin. He was an honors student like me, in most of the same classes and extracurriculars. We'd known each other since elementary school and were part of the same friends group, but we were almost frenemies more than friends. Through all of high school we competed for the same extracurricular leadership and student government positions, butting heads over and over again.

Despite the similarities in our transcripts, we were nothing alike. Donal was popular and easygoing, whereas I was studious and uptight. I had to work my ass off for my good grades, but Donal never seemed to work for anything. He managed to coast on his likable personality, innate intelligence, and knack for performing well under pressure. He coasted so well, he nearly beat me out for valedictorian.

It infuriated me. Everything about Donal Larkin infuriated me, but the thing that infuriated me most was that I'd secretly had a crush on him since eighth grade. I couldn't help myself. He had these twinkly blue eyes and a smile that warmed you like the sun. No matter how much he annoyed me, when he focused those damned eyes on me and turned on his smile, my knees went weak, my senses got muddled, and I made bad decisions. Like trusting him.

Donal was chronically unreliable. You know the type—one of those people who never carried his weight on group projects and let others do the bulk of the work (usually me). He also had a bad habit of volunteering for things and bailing at the last minute. Or he'd make bargains and "forget" to fulfill his half. Again and again I'd been burned by him, but I still kept coming back for more because those twinkly blue eyes made me want to believe the next time would miraculously be different.

The first time he broke my heart was in tenth grade after he offered to give me a ride home from a basketball game. Naive, fifteen-year-old me was so foolishly excited, I let myself hope it was a sign he liked me. A hope that was crushed when he forgot all about me and left me on my own at a school halfway across the city at ten o'clock at night. I'd had to get myself home on the "L" in twenty-degree weather, and later I found out he'd blown me off to go to a party and hook up with a member of the cheerleading squad. He was a real prince charming, that guy.

I held a grudge over that for a long time, let me tell you. But I didn't learn my lesson. Eventually, I gave him another chance to hurt me, and boy did he ever.

Halfway through our senior year, we were practicing a skit we'd been assigned for English class and somehow one thing led to another and we ended up making out in my parents' basement. After that, we started meeting up regularly—not dating or anything, just messing around.

Donal made that abundantly clear early on. It was the second time he broke my heart. The first week after we'd started seeing each other, I overheard one of our friends ask him if he had a girlfriend who'd been keeping him busy. Donal looked right at me and said no.

I should have had the self-respect and good sense to walk away from him then and there, but I was too proud to let him know he'd hurt me. We'd always been fiercely competitive with one another, and it felt like losing to admit I wanted more. So I pretended to like the secrecy, even managing to convince myself it made it more exciting. If being his dirty little secret was what it took to keep him, then fine. I told myself it was worth it.

We'd be heading our separate ways in the fall anyway—I was hoping for Northwestern, and Donal had already been accepted at Yale. It was too late for us to have anything serious, even if Donal had wanted that with me. Why not enjoy what I had while I had it?

Our covert make-out sessions continued, and pretty soon I'd lost my virginity in the back seat of Donal's Chevy Citation. We used protection, of course. We were young and stupid but not *that* stupid.

In those days the local pharmacies kept their condoms locked up behind glass—unconscionable at the height of the AIDS epidemic (or any other time, for that matter)—and not many teenagers were bold enough to hunt down a pharmacist and ask him to fetch you a box of prophylactics. Fortunately, Donal had acquired some from a friend's older brother. Only apparently they'd been sitting around too long, or maybe they weren't very high quality, because I ended up pregnant anyway. *Oops.*

It felt like the end of the world. I had plans for my life that didn't include marrying Donal Larkin and becoming a mother at the age of eighteen. Not that he offered to marry me. When I told him, he totally freaked out and started ranting about his future plans and how this was going to mess up everything.

Yeah, no shit.

He basically acted like I'd ruined his life—as if my plans wouldn't be ruined right along with his. Then he told me he needed time to think and promised to come to my house so we could talk about what we were going to do.

He didn't. Quelle surprise. I didn't hear a word from him all that weekend.

It was clear he was avoiding me, so I cornered him Monday at school. Once I got him alone, I told him I'd decided to give the baby up for adoption and didn't want or need his help. By then I knew better than to expect a guy like Donal to take responsibility. He wasn't someone you could rely on to come through for you. I was in this on my own.

The only thing I asked from him was that he keep my secret. Amazingly, he did. He was so relieved to be let off the hook, he was happy to pretend none of it had ever happened.

We barely spoke for the rest of the school year. Lucky for me, baggy clothes were all the rage in the late eighties, and I was able to hide my pregnancy until graduation. I was five months pregnant when I gave my valedictorian speech, but no one could tell under my graduation gown.

My dad and stepmom did their best to be supportive, although I'd forever be haunted by their looks of disappointment when I broke the news. It didn't help that I'd been the result of an unplanned pregnancy. My mother's unhappiness at being saddled with a husband and baby she'd never wanted had driven her to leave us when I was ten. My determination not to end up like my mother was a major factor in my decision to give the baby up for adoption.

I deferred my acceptance to Northwestern for a year, told everyone I was visiting my grandmother in Michigan for the summer, and sequestered myself in my parents' house for the next four months. I cried when they took the baby away, and I cried on and off for the next two months, convinced I was a horrible, selfish person for giving my daughter up. But after my hormones leveled out, I picked myself up, dusted myself off, and took a full load of community college classes to get a head start on my undergraduate credits.

Eventually, my life went back to normal. Except for the fact that I thought about my daughter almost every day. Even now, thirty years later, I still thought about her all the time, wondering what she looked like, where she'd grown up, if she was happy and loved, if she had kids of her own.

I finally had the answer to one of those questions. She'd uploaded a picture to her LineagePlus profile. I'd been staring at it for hours, ever since I got home.

After my panic attack in the break room, Marie had cleaned up my broken coffee mug for me. Then we'd gone into my office, closed the door, and I'd unburdened myself on her sympathetic shoulders. She'd listened to every word, then gently reminded me to use commonsense precautions before sharing any personal information with a stranger. She'd done a lot of research on social engineering and phishing scams for a story she'd written recently, and described some red flags I should watch for in my correspondence with Erin. She even offered to talk to a friend of hers who owned a security firm if I wanted to have a background check done on Erin.

I politely declined. Marie was a wise person and good friend. She was right to be paranoid, and I intended to heed her advice. But I knew in my bones this wasn't a scam.

Erin was the daughter I'd given up for adoption.

Now I was at home, alone in my apartment, and I couldn't stop staring at the picture of Erin in her LineagePlus profile. She was beautiful. A golden complexion to go with her golden brown hair, a heart-shaped face, and a smile as bright as her eyes.

She looked so much like her father it made my chest hurt.

Crap.

Her father.

She wanted to know about him. That meant I'd need to contact Donal.

Although we'd crossed paths occasionally thanks to mutual friends and our involvement in our high school alumni association, we'd mostly avoided speaking face-to-face. Since I was still nursing a mother of a grudge and Donal was still a self-centered asshole, our limited interactions had been terse and unpleasant.

It seemed unlikely Donal would take this latest news well. He had a family of his own now, and he might not want anything more to do with Erin than he had thirty years ago. I'd need to feel him out before I put her in touch with him.

But first, I needed to respond to her message.

CHAPTER THREE

DONAL

My stomach made a noise that sounded like a fork in a garbage disposal. It was a noise so loud and unholy, it startled me out of my concentration on the contract I was reviewing.

Damn. I'd forgotten to eat lunch.

Again.

And I had a meeting in fifteen minutes.

Pushing my chair back from my desk with a sigh, I stood and tried to stretch some of the kinks out of my back. I'd been hunched over my computer, so fixated on redlining this damn contract, I'd barely moved in the last three hours. I seriously needed to make time for the gym tonight, or my back and shoulders were going to lock up on me completely. I'd wake up tomorrow morning creaking like the Tin Man and begging for a squirt of oil to loosen my rusty joints.

I walked across my office and opened the door. "Debra?"

My secretary swiveled her chair around and wordlessly held up a protein bar.

"How do you do that?" I asked, gratefully accepting her offering.

She shrugged as she spun her chair back around. "You skipped lunch."

Debra was a godsend. She'd been my legal secretary for the last ten years, and I pretty much worshipped the ground she walked on. The woman singlehandedly kept my life from collapsing around me like a Jenga tower. If she retired before me, I'd be lost.

I unwrapped the protein bar and gnawed off a bite. It tasted like ground-up shoe leather that had been dipped in the abstract idea of chocolate. Whatever. As long as it kept my stomach from growling. "Are the packets for the Fulton meeting ready?"

The phone on Debra's desk rang, and she held up a finger for me to hold my horses while she answered it. "Donal Larkin's office."

I chewed off another bite of protein bar while Debra listened to whoever was on the other end of the line. Cradling the phone between her ear and shoulder, she pulled the packets I needed out of a stack on her desk.

Thank you, I mouthed, taking them from her and heading back into my office.

"Hold on," she said to the person on the phone. "I'll ask him."

I halted and turned on my heel, eyebrows raised.

"It's the lobby receptionist," she said. "Someone's downstairs asking for you."

That was unusual enough to get my attention. We didn't get walk-ins at a firm like this. "Who?" I asked around a mouthful of protein bar.

"She says she's a friend of yours. Tess McGregor?"

I let out a groan and scrubbed my palm over my face. "Jesus, really?"

Tess had emailed me twice in the last week, asking if we could talk, and I hadn't gotten around to answering her yet. I assumed it was more trivial bullshit to do with our upcoming high school reunion that I neither had the time for nor gave a damn about. Unbelievable that she'd actually showed up at my fucking office over alumni association drama.

"Want me to take care of it?" Debra offered, her expression brightening at the prospect of going to battle on my behalf.

I looked at my watch and shook my head. "No, I'll go down and see her." Might as well deal with Tess now that she was here. The meeting I had in a few minutes would save me from having to talk to her for too long.

"He's on his way down," Debra said into the phone.

I handed the packets back to her. "Can you make sure these get to the conference room for the meeting?"

Shoving the last of the protein bar in my mouth, I sent up a prayer for strength and forbearance before I headed downstairs to deal with Tess fucking McGregor, who was apparently never going to stop making my life miserable.

I saw her as soon as I stepped off the elevator. Standing by the reception desk in a tailored red coat and tall black boots, not a hair out of place despite the windy April weather outside. Even though she had her back turned, my eyes zeroed in on her as if pulled by a magnet. Same upright posture, same proud tilt of her head, same athletic frame. Same Tess.

She turned around, and a band pulled tight around my chest as our eyes met.

Interacting with Tess always brought up a lot of complicated, messy, unpleasant emotions that I'd tried hard to repress. We'd been friends growing up, but our senior year of high school we'd hooked up for a while and...let's just say it had ended badly.

Extremely badly.

Although we still corresponded about alumni stuff occasionally via email and social media, I'd managed to avoid seeing her in person since our last high school reunion ten years ago.

She looked good, dammit. Gorgeous, in fact. The observation caused an unsettling sensation in the pit of my stomach.

Or maybe I was still hungry. Hopefully, that was all it was.

Her hair was blonder and straighter than it had been in high school, hanging in smooth waves that reached her shoulders. She had more wrinkles than the old days, but they added character that looked great on her. Her dark eyes were as sharp and intent as ever, and as I came through the security barrier they glinted with hostility.

That was familiar as well. I girded myself for a disagreeable conversation.

"You haven't responded to my emails," she said, stepping forward to meet me as I approached.

"Hello to you too." I guided her away from the reception desk to an empty corner of the lobby where we hopefully wouldn't be overheard. "Why are you at my office?"

"Because you wouldn't respond to my emails."

I tried to keep my tone placating, something I'd gotten good at during my marriage. "I'm sorry, Tess, I don't have time to get involved in the reunion planning this time around. Email me the invite when it gets closer to the day, and I promise I'll try to show up."

"I'm not on the reunion committee anymore."

I couldn't help my irritated sigh. "What do you want me to do about that?"

Tess had managed to create so much strife over the reunion planning that I'd been fielding complaints and pleas for assistance from various members of our graduating class for the last twenty-five goddamn years. If I'd known I'd be saddled with responsibility for organizing the high school reunion committee for the rest of my life, I never would have run for senior class president.

"I'm not here because of the fucking reunion," she ground out.

I drew back a little, studying her with increased wariness. I was used to Tess being contentious, but dropping f-bombs in the lobby of a prestigious downtown law firm was out of character for her. "What is it you want from me, then?"

"I need to talk to you about something."

I checked my watch. "You've got five minutes before I have to get back upstairs for a meeting."

"This is more than a five-minute conversation."

"Fine, then I'll have my secretary email you to set up a time for us to get coffee next week." That was the best I could offer, and even that was more time than I wanted to devote to whatever nonsense Tess had gotten herself into a lather over now.

"It's not the sort of conversation you want to have in a Starbucks." Tess's eyes locked onto mine, and I saw something that looked like anxiety flicker in their depths. "Trust me."

An uneasy prickle crept down my spine and pooled in my stomach. "What sort of conversation is it?"

"The kind you want to have in private."

"Tess?" I was legitimately alarmed now. "What is this—"

"In private," she repeated, shaking her head. "Please. It's important."

It was the word *please* that really unsettled me. That and the way her voice shook a little when she said it. "Does tonight work?"

She gave me a curt nod. "Tonight would be good."

"Where?"

"I'll email you my address." She shot me a sour look. "Assuming you'll read the email this time."

"I'll be there," I said, giving her a sour look of my own. "As soon as I can get away from here. Which probably won't be until at least seven."

"Fine. I'll see you then." Without another word, she turned and walked away.

I watched her push through the glass revolving door and disappear into the stream of pedestrians on the sidewalk outside. A glance at my watch told me I had three minutes left to get to my meeting upstairs.

And four hours to worry about what Tess wanted to tell me tonight.

CHAPTER FOUR

DONAL

Tess lived in a modern, high-rise building in the Loop that turned out to be only a short walk from mine. I was a little unnerved to discover we'd been living so close to each other. Did we frequent the same coffee shop? Get takeout from the same restaurants? Jog the same route along the Riverwalk? How many times had I passed her on the street without even noticing?

The doorman sent me up to Tess's seventh floor apartment, and I paused on her doorstep to shrug off my coat, taking a second to collect myself before knocking.

She opened the door dressed in workout clothes—a white athletic jacket over a light blue top and matching leggings—with her hair pulled back in a neat pony-tail. "Thank you for coming," she said as she took my coat and hung it on a rack by the door. "I wasn't sure you'd show."

The dig about my lack of dependability needled at my already brittle nerves. "I *said* I would," I shot back in irritation.

"Would you like a drink?" she offered, ignoring my peevishness.

"No, I'd like you to get to the point."

She gestured to the couch. "Sit down."

Her apartment was small and tidy, with floor-to-ceiling windows that offered a view of the surrounding high-rises. The living room held two upholstered chairs and a pristine white sofa arranged around a compact oval coffee table.

I did as requested, perching on the couch and rubbing my hands on my thighs. I'd come straight over after work without changing, and the combination of the brisk walk and my nerves had me sweating inside my wool suit jacket. I considered taking it off, but I dearly hoped I wouldn't be here that long.

Tess sat in one of the chairs across from me, her posture even more rigid than usual and her hands folded in her lap as she rubbed her fingers over her knuckles. She was nervous, I realized as she regarded me without speaking. Trying to work herself up to saying whatever she'd asked me here to say.

My attitude softened in the face of her apparent difficulty even as my anxiety increased. "Is this about what I think it's about?"

She nodded, looking relieved that I'd been the first to acknowledge the elephant in the room. "A few years ago, after my father was diagnosed with Alzheimer's, I signed up for one of those DNA testing services that assesses your genetic health risks. But they also offer family tree tracing that can match you with relatives who share a common ancestor." She paused, letting this sink in and giving me time to prepare myself for what was inevitably coming next.

I swallowed around the lump that had formed in my throat. "Go on."

"Last week, I received a message from someone who said my DNA profile had been matched to hers as a probable close relative. Her name is Erin. She was born in October of 1989 and put up for adoption." Tess hesitated, pressing her lips together. "We're her birth parents."

"It was a girl?" My voice cracked, and I cleared my throat. "The baby was a girl?"

Tess looked surprised by my question. "Yes."

My shoulders sagged as I let out an unsteady breath. "You never told me that."

She lifted her chin, her eyes narrowing in accusation. "You never asked."

I gave her a long, hard look before responding. "You made it pretty clear you didn't want me to ask."

When Tess didn't say anything in response to this, I got up and walked to the window, turning my back on her as I rubbed both my hands over my face. "Do you think I could have that drink after all?"

"Of course." I heard her get up and walk into the kitchen. "Would you like wine? Or something stronger?"

"Something stronger, please." I unbuttoned the collar of my shirt and yanked my tie loose.

A minute later she appeared at my side and handed me a tumbler of brown liquid.

"Thank you." I sniffed it as she sat back down. "Irish whiskey?"

"Teeling."

I gulped down a mouthful before taking my seat on the couch again. I ran a hand through my hair. "I'm sorry, I'm just—I didn't think I'd be this emotional when it happened."

She looked surprised again. "You expected this to happen?"

"I knew it was a possibility. Especially after Illinois unsealed original birth certificates in 2011. I've always wondered if one day a child I'd never known would come looking for me."

"I didn't realize you ever thought about it."

My eyes snapped to hers. "Of course I did. For Christ's sake."

Once again, Tess didn't say anything. Her expression was as cool and impassive as a polished stone wall. It was impossible to tell what she was thinking.

"So what did the message say?" I asked finally. "What does she want?"

"Right now, she just wants to know more about us."

I nodded. "All right."

"Does that mean you're okay with it?"

I let out a wry laugh as I rubbed my forehead. "There are so many fucking things about this that I will never be okay with. But getting to know my daughter isn't one of them."

"I wasn't sure how you'd feel. Especially since you have your own family now. I didn't know if you'd want the disruption of another child you never wanted."

I cut a glare at her. "You don't have the slightest idea what I wanted or didn't want."

Tess's mouth snapped shut. We traded glares for a lengthy moment before she cleared her throat. "I've been messaging with her since last week, and I've told her a fair amount about myself already. But I haven't told her anything about you yet. I said I needed to talk to you before I revealed any personally identifying information."

"So what's the next step? What do we do now?" My voice came out gruff, but there wasn't anything I could do about that. I was barely holding it together.

"I'm meeting her in person for the first time on Saturday. We're having coffee."

"I could come with you." Now that our daughter had found us, I was impatient for the next steps to happen. I needed to meet her. To *know* her. To finally get the answers to the unknowns that had haunted me for the last three decades of my life.

Tess frowned. "I don't think that's a good idea. This is a lot for all of us to process, and I don't want to overwhelm her. It might be better if she meets us one at a time."

I swallowed a bitter surge of resentment. Rationally, I could see the wisdom in Tess's position. But I couldn't help feeling she was shutting me out all over again. Just like thirty years ago, she was insisting on doing everything on her own. Yet again, I'd be stuck on the outside wondering what was happening.

But Tess held all the cards, like always. And our daughter's feelings were the only ones that mattered right now. It was probably true that it'd be easier for her to meet us one at a time.

"Fine," I agreed. "If that's what you think is best. You can answer whatever questions she has about me and tell her how to get in touch with me herself if she wants."

"You're okay with me telling her you're married and have kids?"

"I'm divorced now, but you can tell her I have two kids. She'll probably want to know she has an eighteen-year-old half-sister and a fifteen-year-old half-brother.

Let her know I welcome the chance to get to know her." I wasn't sure how my kids were going to take the news they had an older sister they didn't know about, but I'd cross that bridge when we came to it.

"I'll tell her," Tess said. "I didn't realize you'd gotten divorced."

"A year ago." I took out my phone. "I'm emailing you my cell number and home address so you can give them to her. You can also use them yourself if you need to get in touch with me for any reason."

"I appreciate that." Tess extracted her phone from a pocket in her leggings.

I sipped my whiskey as I watched her tap her thumbs on the screen. "You said her name was Erin?" I asked, getting used to the sound of it.

"That's right."

"Is she happy? Did she have a good childhood? Good parents?"

Tess's brow creased as she looked up at me. "She hasn't revealed much about herself yet. I know she was adopted as an infant, but otherwise she's said very little about her parents or her childhood. She's been careful how much personal information she shares with me, which is smart, considering I'm a total stranger."

"It is. I'm glad she's protecting herself." My phone vibrated next to me on the couch. Tess had sent me a text so I'd have her cell number.

"She did tell me she's a science teacher. But I don't know what grade or anything."

"Really? A teacher." I smiled as I tucked my phone into my jacket pocket. "She must get that from you."

The corner of Tess's mouth tugged upward. Our eyes caught and held, and as the moment stretched out, something that felt like kinship passed between us. Whether we liked it or not, the two of us were bound together by what had happened thirty years ago.

And now we were connected by our grown daughter. God, what a thought.

I cleared my throat. "I don't suppose you have a picture of her?"

"I do, actually." Tess got up and came over to sit beside me on the couch. She pulled up a photo on her phone and passed it to me.

My hand shook a little as I took it. "That's her?" The tightness in my throat made my voice rough. Erin's face looked so familiar it took my breath away.

"She looks just like you," Tess said, leaning in closer to gaze at the photo with me. "It's uncanny, isn't it?"

"She looks exactly like my sister at that age." Both my other kids, Jack and Maddy, took after my ex-wife. I couldn't get over the fact that I had a daughter I'd never met who looked so much like me. She'd been out there all these years, walking around with my smile on her face. "My mom's going to love her—assuming Erin wants to meet her, that is."

"I have a feeling she probably will eventually." Tess cut a glance at me. "Do your parents know about her?"

I shook my head. "I never told anyone, like you asked."

It was the only thing Tess had let me do for her back then, and I'd made damn sure I didn't fuck it up. I'd never told a single living soul about Tess being pregnant or the baby she'd given up for adoption. Not my parents, not my twin sister, not even my wife years later. I'd kept the secret for Tess like she'd wanted, which meant I'd never been able to talk about it or unburden myself to anyone. I'd carried it deep inside me all these years like a wound that had never fully healed.

As I stared at the picture, something loosened in my chest. For the first time, it didn't feel so much like a wound anymore. It felt like a miracle.

I set my glass down on Tess's coffee table and reached up to wipe my eyes. "I can't believe it's really her. That's our daughter."

Tess laid her hand on my arm. "I know." Her voice sounded as rough as mine.

I covered her hand with mine, tangling our fingers together, and we leaned against each other as we looked at the miracle we'd made.

CHAPTER FIVE

TESS

On Saturday, I walked into a coffee shop in Edgewater and laid eyes on my daughter for the first time in twenty-nine years and six months.

She was sitting at a table by herself, her chin resting in her hand as she gazed down at the mug in front of her. As soon as I recognized her, I froze in panic, wishing I'd accepted Donal's offer to come with me.

He was so much better at this kind of thing than I was. You'd never know it by the way he usually acted toward me, but he could be incredibly disarming. People tended to take an instant liking to him. Me, not so much.

If I was being honest, that was partially why I hadn't wanted him to come with me today. I was afraid of being overshadowed by him. I was the one who'd nurtured Erin in my body for nine months and endured the side effects of pregnancy and the pain of childbirth to bring her into the world. All Donal had done was have an orgasm and fuck off to Yale without a care in the world. I deserved this chance to get to know my daughter without being outshone by him.

Admittedly, I had felt a little bad about rejecting his offer when I saw how much it hurt his feelings. I hadn't expected him to be so emotionally invested in all of this. He'd been so hostile when he first showed up at my apartment, I'd expected him to say he didn't want to have anything to do with Erin. But there'd been actual tears in his eyes when I showed him her photo. And the way his whole body had sagged when he found out I'd had a girl…it was like he'd been given the answer to a question he'd been searching for all his life.

Maybe he had, in a way I hadn't appreciated. I hadn't been in the best place, mentally or emotionally, in the weeks following the birth. Which he would have known, if he'd ever bothered to check on me. He'd known my due date. If he'd wanted to find out how things had turned out, he could have taken five minutes to call and ask. But he'd been too busy enjoying his freshman year of college, I guess.

Whatever. He had his own kids now, so he must be more into the whole dad thing these days.

Come on, feet, you can do this. One in front of the other. Pretend it's free cookie samples over there instead of a terrifying conversation I've been waiting thirty years to have.

I was still trying to pep talk myself into moving when Erin looked up and saw me. The first time our eyes met, I felt it like a jolt of electricity.

She got to her feet, and I finally managed to propel myself forward. "Are you Tess?" she asked as I approached. Her voice was as beautiful as her face.

I smiled, blinking away the sting of tears in my eyes. "That's right. You're Erin."

She nodded, looking every bit as nervous as I felt.

Wanting to ease her discomfort, I widened my smile and extended my hand. "It's nice to meet you, Erin."

My heart did a weird pitter-patter in my chest as we shook hands. It felt like a litter of puppies were scampering around in there. This was the first time I'd touched her since I'd given birth to her, and I was struck by an overwhelming urge to wrap my arms around her and clutch her to my chest. But something told me I shouldn't do that. It was too soon. Or maybe it was too late. Maybe she wouldn't ever want anything like that from me. If so, that would have to be okay. Whatever she wanted, I was determined to be okay with it. My heart puppies would just have to settle down and take a nap.

I made myself let go of her hand. "I hope you haven't been waiting long."

"I got here ten minutes early. I was a little anxious, I guess."

"Me too," I admitted. "I was afraid you might change your mind about wanting to meet me."

Her laugh was soft and restrained. "I was afraid *you* might change *your* mind."

"But here we are—both of us early and neither of us having changed our minds." My smile felt awkward.

"I guess we really are related."

There went my heart puppies again, cavorting all over the place.

I draped my jacket over the chair opposite Erin's. "I'm going to go get a drink. Do you want anything while I'm up there?"

She declined my offer, and I went to the counter, grateful for the opportunity to regroup and compose myself. The last thing my jangling nerves needed right now was caffeine, so I ordered myself a bottle of water and carried it back to the table where Erin waited for me.

We regarded each other silently for a moment after I sat down. I detected wariness in her expression, but also curiosity. Curiosity was good. I could work with curiosity. And it was a heck of a lot better than the resentment I'd anticipated.

"You look just like your birth father," I said, because I knew she was interested to know more about him.

As expected, her interest piqued. "I do?"

"He has a twin sister who looks exactly like him, and you're the spitting image of her."

Erin's eyes widened at this information. "He's a twin?"

"Dizygotic twins are twice as common as monozygotic twins and more likely to run in families, so that's probably something you should be aware of if you plan to have children." I looked at Erin. "Do you have any children?"

She hesitated as if she was reluctant to answer.

"You don't have to tell me," I said quickly. "I completely understand if you'd rather not share too much personal information with me."

"It's not that." Her eyes dropped to her coffee mug. It wasn't coffee, I noticed. It was herbal tea. "I'm pregnant, actually."

I blinked, momentarily rendered speechless.

The baby I'd had was going to have a baby. Which meant…I was going to be a grandmother. *A grandmother*. Holy smokes.

"It's my first," Erin continued, filling my shocked silence. "I'm only ten weeks along, so we haven't told that many people yet."

I finally recovered my wits. "Wow. That's wonderful. Congratulations."

"Thank you. We're pretty excited."

"You're married?"

"Yes." She toyed with the string on her herbal tea. "He actually tried to talk me out of messaging you."

"He did?"

"Ever since we found out about the baby, he's been a little overprotective. He was worried it might be too stressful."

I nodded in understanding. The circumstances of Erin's conception were pretty innocuous, but how many people went searching for their birth parents only to discover they were the result of infidelity or something even worse like sexual assault? I could only imagine how upsetting that would be.

"It must have been a little scary, not knowing what you'd discover or who we'd turn out to be."

She offered me a smile. "It hasn't been too bad so far—as long as you're not about to tell me my birth father is a serial killer or something."

I laughed. "No, just a lawyer. His name is Donal Larkin. I talked to him, and he gave me permission to share his contact information with you. He'd like to meet you when you're ready. And he wanted you to know you have an eighteen-year-old half-sister and a fifteen-year-old half-brother."

Erin's mouth tugged into a small smile as she took this information in. It looked so much like Donal's smile it made my chest hurt. "What are their names?"

"I don't know, I'm sorry. You can ask him. I'm sure he'd love to tell you."

"So he's married?"

"Divorced, apparently." I remembered Donal's wife from our last reunion. She'd been dark-haired and curvy, with an easy smile and a bubbly personality. Basically the polar opposite of me. I'd avoided speaking to them, but I'd watched them from across the room. I hadn't been able to help myself—I'd wanted to know what kind of woman he'd picked to settle down with and start a family.

Erin looked thoughtful as she sipped her tea. "I've never had a sibling before."

"You're an only child? Me too." I hoped she'd volunteer more about her childhood and the family who'd raised her. Every atom in my body was starved for more information about her, but her guardedness made me reluctant to push too hard.

"Are your parents still alive?" she asked me instead.

I opened my mouth, but didn't speak immediately. It wasn't a simple question for me to answer. "My mother died about five years ago, but I hadn't seen her for a long time before that. She left when I was a child and we didn't have much contact."

Erin digested this information in silence. The glaring parallel between my mother abandoning me and the way I'd abandoned Erin sat between us like a big, hairy mole no one wanted to acknowledge out loud.

Tucking my hair behind my ear, I pushed on. "My father remarried a few years after my mother left us. My stepmother and I…" Words failed me as I struggled to adequately describe our relationship. Her death was recent enough that it still hurt to talk about it. I'd been aching for Sherry's advice and comfort ever since I'd first heard from Erin. "We were very close. She was like a mother to me…but she passed away nine months ago. My father's still alive, but he has late-stage Alzheimer's. He's been living in a residential memory care facility for the last year."

"I'm sorry," Erin said quietly. Her expression was pensive, and I sensed disappointment in her. Perhaps she'd been hoping for more extended family.

I shared her disappointment. It seemed cruel that I'd effectively lost both my father and Sherry before Erin found me, and now they'd never be able to know each other.

I cleared my throat. "They would have loved to meet you. Sherry—my step-mother—she was in the delivery room when you were born. She would have been thrilled to see how beautiful you grew up to be."

In a way, it had been my pregnancy that had brought Sherry and I together. Before that, I'd been wary of her and obstinately standoffish like teenagers are sometimes prone to be. But Sherry had stepped up in my time of need and supported me in a way my well-meaning father hadn't been equipped to do.

Erin's gaze dropped to the table, and she rubbed her fingers over her knuckles. "You said you were in high school when you got pregnant with me."

"That's right. It was our senior year." In the emails we'd exchanged before today's meeting, I'd only shared the essentials—that Erin's birth father and I had been high school students, unprepared to be parents—without going into too much detail.

"Were your parents upset when they found out?"

"Mostly they were shocked—and pretty disappointed with me, although they tried to hide it. I was an honors student, only a few months away from heading off to college. I think they'd assumed I was too responsible to end up a pregnant teenager and blamed themselves for trusting me too much."

Erin nodded, looking like she wanted to ask something else but was trying to work up the courage.

"You can ask me anything." I smiled to show her how unbothered I was. "I promise to try and answer as honestly as I can." It was the very least I could do for her. She'd reached out to me for answers, and I was here to give her whatever she wanted.

"Did they pressure you to give me up? Because they wanted you to go to college?"

She was basically offering me a "get out of jail free" card. An opportunity to shift responsibility onto my parents and their high expectations, absolving myself of at least some of the blame for my choice.

I'd be lying if I said I wasn't tempted to take the out, though the momentary impulse made me ashamed. It wouldn't be fair to my parents. It wouldn't honor their memories to lay the blame at their feet for a decision I'd made myself.

Nor would it be fair to Erin. I'd promised her honesty, and that was what I owed her. Even if it was more painful for both of us.

"I made the decision on my own. My parents would have supported me no matter what." I paused, trying to make my thoughts orderly. "I told myself that giving you up was the best thing for you, that you'd be better off with more mature, financially stable, married parents who wanted to have a child. But I also did it for selfish reasons. I didn't want to be a teen mother. I wanted to go to college and have the life I'd been working so hard for."

Erin nodded, and I wondered if she'd been hoping I'd say something else. She was staring down at her hands, rubbing her fingers over her knuckles again.

"I do that too," I said, tipping my chin at her hands. "I rub my knuckles in the exact same way when I'm nervous."

"Really?"

"It's funny, isn't it? How random little things like that are written into your DNA."

She smiled faintly. "I wonder what else I inherited from you."

"Hopefully not my crooked teeth. I had full headgear for most of middle school."

"I had braces, but it wasn't quite that bad."

As I watched Erin's smile wane, I felt the need to say something more. "I don't want you to think it was easy for me to give you up. I agonized over it before and after. There hasn't been a single day these past thirty years I haven't thought about you and wondered if I did the right thing. I don't know what kind of mother I would have been, or what kind of family you ended up with instead, but I wanted to believe you were better off without me. I hope I wasn't wrong about that. I hope you were always safe and loved."

Her expression softened into something that looked like compassion. "I was. I am. I had good parents and a good childhood. It all worked out okay."

As I exhaled, a painful knot loosened in my diaphragm, one that had been there for so long I'd forgotten what it felt like to breathe without it. "I'm glad."

"What about my birth father? Did he know about me?"

"I told him when I found out I was pregnant. But the decision was all mine." Regardless of my feelings about Donal, I couldn't cast the blame on him for something that had been my choice. If Erin harbored any resentment, it rightfully belonged to me and me alone.

She observed me in silence a moment, her expression inscrutable. "Were you in love?" she asked finally.

I hesitated, taken off guard by the question. I'd promised to tell her the truth, yet I wasn't comfortable admitting I'd merely been Donal's dirty little secret—and I wasn't certain she wanted that level of detail. If she'd been hoping for a fairy tale about high school sweethearts, we weren't it.

"We were friends all through school," I told her, choosing my words carefully. "But it wasn't until our senior year that…I guess you could say we got carried away, and for a little while we were more than friends. But there was never any possibility of us getting married and raising a baby together. No one would have been happy with that arrangement."

Donal's reproach the other night came back to me. *You don't have the slightest idea what I wanted or didn't want.* The resentment in his voice still mystified me —and pissed me off. He'd made it pretty clear he didn't want anything to do with me or my inconvenient pregnancy. How dare he act as though he was the aggrieved party when I'd done him a favor by absolving him of responsibility?

"Will you tell me about him?" Erin asked, leaning forward in her seat, her eyes wide and hopeful. "What's he like?"

CHAPTER SIX

DONAL

I'd been climbing the walls of my apartment all day, but I lasted all the way until seven o'clock before breaking down and calling Tess. Her meeting with Erin had been hours ago, and she hadn't answered any of the texts I'd sent her. I was fed up with cooling my heels on the sidelines waiting for her to dole out the smallest crumbs of information.

"Hello?" Tess's voice sounded muzzy when she answered the phone, like she was surprised to hear from me.

"You haven't answered any of my texts." I was too fired up with righteous indignation to care that I had no right to claim the moral high ground after I'd ignored her emails last week.

"I was going to call you tomorrow."

I paced across my apartment, squeezing my phone in a white-knuckled grip. I'd practically worn a path in the carpet, I'd been pacing so much today. "Did you meet her?"

"Yes."

I stopped pacing and sank down on the couch while I waited for Tess to elaborate. "Well?" I said impatiently when she didn't. "How did it go?"

"Fine. It was fine."

My jaw clenched as I tried to keep my annoyance in check. "That's all I get?"

"Can we talk about this tomorrow?" Something about her tone sounded off. It was oddly quiet and lacked her usual edge of irritation.

"Is everything okay?"

"Yes, it's fine. Everything went fine, and I'll tell you all about it tomorrow." The fact that she'd said the word "fine" four times in the last ten seconds didn't do anything to put me at ease.

"Why can't you tell me now?" I wasn't letting her blow me off. Not when I'd been waiting all day to hear how the meetup had gone.

"Because I'm exhausted, and I'm not ready to talk about it yet."

"Why not? What happened?"

"Nothing. Nothing happened. It was just…" I heard her suck in an unsteady breath. "It was a lot, okay? I need some time. *Please.*" Her voice, which had grown increasingly shaky, broke completely on the last word.

I stood up and ran a hand through my hair. "Can I come over and see you?"

"No, I told you—"

"Tess, you shouldn't be alone right now." I was already putting on my shoes. Fuck waiting until tomorrow.

"I'm fine."

"Repeating the word 'fine' over and over won't make it true. It's obvious you're not fine, and pretending nothing's wrong isn't going to make it any better. Trust me on that. You need to talk to someone, and I'm the only one who understands what you're going through. Let me come over." I snatched my keys and wallet off the counter while I waited for her answer.

I heard her sigh, followed by a sniffle. "Fine."

———————

I could tell Tess had been crying as soon as she opened the door. She'd tried to hide it by washing her face, but there was no mistaking the telltale red blotches staining her pale complexion.

"You didn't have to come," she said, sounding resentful.

She could be hacked off at me if she wanted. I was used to it by now. I could barely even remember a time she didn't hate my guts.

After hanging my jacket by the door, I followed her into the apartment, which was messier than the last time I'd seen it. A large cardboard box sat on the living room floor, while clothes and papers and other random objects littered the couch and coffee table.

"What's all this?" As I gestured to the mess, I noted the bottle of whiskey and half-full glass sitting in the midst of the clutter.

"Memories."

I looked more closely at the items sitting out. There were some old journals and spiral notebooks that looked like they might have been from high school, a bunch of clothes, a half-finished pile of knitting, and one of those plastic hospital wristbands.

Then I realized. These were the things Tess had saved from when she was pregnant. No wonder she'd sounded so odd on the phone.

She stooped to retrieve her whiskey glass from the coffee table and downed the remaining contents before waggling it at me. "You want some?"

"No thanks." At least one of us should probably stay clearheaded.

"Suit yourself." She dropped onto the couch and reached for the bottle of Teeling to refill her glass.

Shifting some things from the couch to the coffee table, I made a space so I could sit next to her. "Today was hard, I take it?"

"You could say that." She looked like she was carrying the weight of the whole world on her shoulders. Typical Tess, thinking she had to do everything by herself. But this wasn't something she should have to deal with alone any more than she should have had to do it back in high school.

"Did Erin say something to upset you?" I'd been worried she might be angry at us for giving her up, especially if her life with her adoptive parents had been less than ideal. There was no telling what she'd been through or how much she blamed us for it.

I was relieved when Tess shook her head.

"No, nothing like that. She was lovely. Really…" Her chest hitched as she drew in a breath. "She's perfect, actually. So beautiful and kind and smart. She's amazing." Choking on a sob, she scrubbed away a tear that had slipped down her cheek. "She's just this amazing, perfect person."

I'd never seen Tess cry before. She'd always been so strong-willed, so completely in control of herself and everyone else around her. My brain didn't know how to process a Tess who cried. Fortunately, after twenty years of marriage and two kids, I'd gotten pretty good at offering comfort when faced with tears, and my instincts took over.

Settling my arm around Tess's shoulders, I drew her toward me. She stiffened initially, like she was about to pull away. But when another sob racked her body, she sagged against me. Carefully, I took the glass out of her hand and set it on the coffee table before wrapping her up in my arms.

"She looks so much like you," Tess mumbled into my chest. "It's unbelievable. It's like I was just the incubator for your clone."

I stroked my hand over her hair. "Is that what you're upset about?"

"No. I mean, yes, it pisses me off. But no. That's not what this is about."

"Then what?"

"I don't even know what I'm so upset about." She shifted in my arms, tucking herself more firmly against me.

A strong protective instinct overwhelmed me as I held her. Instead of the bitterness I usually felt around Tess, all I could think about was how much I wanted to keep her close and shield her from anything that could hurt her.

I should have offered her this kind of comfort when she was pregnant. We'd both been a couple of terrified kids—no older than my daughter Maddy was now. We should have supported each other through it instead of turning on one another.

Tess sniffled into my shirt. "I'm just feeling too many things right now, and it's all so overwhelming."

"You're allowed to feel overwhelmed under the circumstances."

Every difficult emotion I was having right now, Tess had to be feeling ten times more. Maybe even a hundred times. She'd not only been the one to carry Erin and give birth to her, she'd been the one who made the decision to give her up. As much as I'd hated being shut out, it meant I wasn't the one carrying the responsibility for that choice. I still *felt* responsible, but not as much as if the decision had actually been up to me.

"I thought I didn't have any regrets, but..." She exhaled an unsteady breath. "Meeting her today and seeing the amazing woman she grew up to be, it made me realize how much I've missed out on. I thought I'd be relieved to see she was safe and healthy—and I am—but now I know exactly what I gave away."

Before I could say anything, she pushed out of my arms as if she suddenly felt the need to distance herself from me.

She sat on the edge of the couch, leaning forward to press her fists against her eyes. "Shit. I didn't mean to dump all this on you."

"Tess—"

"Don't." She jerked away when I tried to touch her. "Don't say anything, okay? I don't expect *you* to understand."

I reared back, stung. "Why do you think I wouldn't understand?"

"I know you never wanted to deal with any of this."

"It's not something any teenager wants to deal with, but it happened anyway."

"Yeah, to *one* of us," she shot back, her tone scathing.

"Jesus, really?" A flare of anger roughened my voice. This was the problem with being around Tess. Every time I let my defenses down, she used the opportunity to stick a knife between my ribs. Just in case I needed a reminder that my feelings had always been irrelevant to her. "You're the one that pushed *me* away, Tess."

She'd cut me out of her life after she found out she was pregnant. I'd cared about her, and she hadn't cared about me back. Not enough to want my help when things got hard.

She exhaled a dark laugh that twisted the knife a little more. "Oh, please. You were only too happy to be left out of it so you could go live your life like nothing had ever happened."

"You didn't give me a choice! You made it clear I wasn't entitled to have a say in what happened."

Her eyes burned with indignation as she glared at me. "You *weren't* entitled to have a say in what happened. It was *my* body."

I threw my hands up in frustration. "I fucking know that, Tess! I wasn't trying to tell you what to do. But it was as much my responsibility as yours, and you shut me out completely. You wouldn't even talk to me."

"I tried to talk to you! Do you remember what you said when I told you I was pregnant? Because I do. 'This is a fucking nightmare.' Those were the first words out of your mouth. Then you started babbling about how you were supposed to go to Yale and this was going to ruin your life."

"I panicked. I was eighteen and terrified. Of course I was thinking about how it would affect my future. You can't tell me you weren't thinking the exact same thing."

"The difference is that I didn't have the option to walk away."

"It wasn't my choice to walk away," I ground out, fighting to keep my temper in check. "You made that decision for me. Or did you conveniently forget about the part where you said you didn't want to see me anymore?"

"You couldn't get away from me fast enough! You said you needed time to process or whatever, and I gave it to you like you asked, but you never showed up. You *never* show up, because that's who you are—the guy who dodges responsibility and bails when he doesn't want to do something. I knew I was totally on my own, so no, I didn't want to fucking see you anymore!"

I battled to keep my voice even. "I was going to come talk to you just as soon as—"

"Three days," she cut in. "That's how long I waited for you to be ready to talk. I told you I was pregnant, and you disappeared on me. You left me sitting around my house waiting on you and wondering what you were thinking."

"I fucked up, okay? Is that what you want to hear? I admit it. My head was spinning and I didn't know what to do. When I said I'd come see you, I forgot we had a family reunion that weekend. I was in Lake Geneva with my mom and my sister and about a hundred other relatives."

"You couldn't have picked up the phone and told me that? Taken thirty seconds to let me know before you left so I didn't feel abandoned?"

"I should have." I dragged a guilty hand through my hair. "My mom wouldn't even leave me alone for five minutes, and it seemed easier to put it off and talk to you when I had more time. I shouldn't have. I get that it was an inconsiderate thing to do to you, but I was going to talk to you on Monday, I swear to God. I had a whole speech planned out about how I'd be there to support you no matter what you wanted to do."

It had been seriously shitty of me, leaving Tess hanging like that. I hadn't appreciated how shitty at the time. I hadn't appreciated a lot of things. Selfishly, I'd been focused on my own feelings and hadn't given enough thought to what Tess must have been going through. She'd seemed so calm and collected when she told me she was pregnant, I'd assumed she was coping better than me. But of course she wasn't. How could she have been? She was just better at pretending.

"I wasn't going to leave you to deal with it on your own, Tess. I never would have done that. I might have been a dumbass teenager, but I wasn't a complete dickhead. Fuck, I was even prepared to put off college and marry you if that was what you wanted." She might not have thought much of me, but goddammit, I'd been nuts about her in my incompetent, blundering way. I would have done whatever she asked.

She stared at me in stark incredulity. "You actually expect me to believe you would have stuck around to take care of a baby?"

"*Goddammit, yes!*" I yelled back, her unconcealed contempt snapping the fraying thread of my temper.

Tess went still, her eyes widening at the intensity of my outburst.

"Fuck." I dropped my head and pressed my palms against my forehead. "Fuck. I'm sorry."

What the hell was I doing? I'd come over here to comfort her, and instead, I was shouting at her like an asshole. This wasn't who I wanted to be, but I always seemed to turn into this angry, defensive person around Tess. She kept poking at my sore spots until she brought out the worst in me.

"Is that true?" she asked after a lengthy silence. "Did you really want to be involved?"

I turned my head, giving her my eyes so she'd be able to see I was telling the truth. "Yes."

"But you never said anything."

I fought to keep my voice steady, to keep the old pain from breaking loose again. "I was going to, but then you basically told me to get fucked. What was it you said? 'The only thing I want from you is to stay the hell away from me and never tell anyone about this.' I mean, Jesus, Tess. What was I supposed to do? Ignore your wishes? Force my presence on you even though you didn't want it?"

She'd been so cold. Emotionless. Like I didn't mean anything to her. Like I was dispensable. Extraneous. *Insignificant.*

She wasn't emotionless now. She was staring at me as if my words had shocked her. When she spoke, her voice was barely above a whisper. "I was so angry at you. I thought—I thought you didn't want anything to do with me. It was all so much to deal with and…" Her lip trembled, and she sucked in an unsteady breath.

"I know." I reached for her hand and was relieved when she didn't pull away. "I know it was. I'm so fucking sorry I wasn't there for you. You have no idea." She really hadn't had any idea, had she? All this time I thought she'd rejected me, and she'd thought I abandoned her. What a goddamn mess.

"I really thought that was what you wanted."

She probably had. Tess always thought she knew better than everyone else, which I couldn't even blame her for, because most of the time she was right. It was one of the many completely aggravating things about her.

But when it came to me, she'd always assumed the worst. Yes, I'd fucked up and let her down a few times, but she only ever seemed to see my mistakes. I'd worked so hard to get her to give me a chance, but right when it felt like I'd finally started to earn her trust, she'd gotten pregnant and everything had gone to shit.

Now I was forever cemented in her mind as the asshole who'd fucked up her life. I could understand why she felt that way, but it still hurt every single goddamn time she let me know what a low opinion she had of me.

"I thought it was what *you* wanted," I said despairingly.

Her face crumpled as her eyes welled with fresh tears. "I had no idea."

I pulled her into my arms again. "You did what you thought you had to. You were just a scared kid. We both were."

The way her arms wrapped around my waist felt significant. She might never fully forgive me, but the fact that she was holding on to me like this had to mean something. I wanted to believe it was her way of saying she regretted that things had gone bad between us.

I knew better than to expect anything would ever be simple or painless with the two of us, but it sure would be nice to think maybe she needed me a little after all.

CHAPTER SEVEN

TESS

I hated how good it felt to have Donal's arms around me. I hated that he smelled so nice, and that I could feel muscles underneath his T-shirt. I hated that his hand was rubbing comforting circles on my back and I didn't want him to stop. I hated that I liked it so much I couldn't make myself let go of him.

I hated that I didn't hate being close to him, and that I couldn't properly hate him anymore.

I'd made a hobby out of hating Donal. Hating him had gotten me through a dark time in my life. I'd clung to my hate to keep me sane. For the last thirty years, I'd been lugging my hate around with me like a piece of battered old carry-on baggage with a glitchy wheel.

Was it possible I'd misinterpreted his intentions? Did I bear some of the blame for pushing him away? Would he really have stuck by me if I'd given him the chance?

I found it difficult to believe. But it was tempting to give Donal the benefit of the doubt when I was lying in his arms like this. The seductive power of his embrace had always clouded my judgment. It was how we'd gotten into this mess in the first place. It was impossible to think rationally with his warm body next to mine and his fingertips stroking gentle patterns over my back, inducing a dreamy sense of calm…

Maybe it would be best to let all those bad feelings go, once and for all. Wipe the slate clean and leave the past in the past where it belonged.

Only I couldn't. Not yet. I hadn't asked him what he wanted thirty years ago, but now I needed to know.

"If it had been up to you, what would you have wanted me to do?"

He tensed at my question, his hand stilling on my back. "I would have wanted whatever you wanted. Only I would have wanted to be right there with you through all of it, whatever you decided to do."

"Don't cop out. If I'd left the decision completely up to you, what would you have wanted to do? Would you have wanted me to get an abortion?"

I felt him flinch. "Shit, Tess. I can't—" He drew in a long breath and let it out again. "I would have paid for it and driven you to the clinic if that was your choice, but I never would have told you to do that."

"Would you have wanted to keep the baby? To raise her ourselves? To marry me?"

Ever since I'd met Erin today, I hadn't been able to stop thinking about what-ifs. What if Donal and I had tried to stay together and kept her? Would we be one big happy family today? Had I thrown away the chance to turn our mistake into something wonderful?

A deep sigh rumbled through his chest. "I honestly don't know. My first instinct was that I had to marry you and take care of you and the baby. But I think that was coming from a sense of duty rather than what I actually wanted. I'm not convinced it was the right instinct either. I mean…can you even imagine us married?" The way he said it made it clear he couldn't.

I huffed out a laugh, pretending that didn't hurt. "No."

"I doubt we would have made a very happy family—or very good parents. Especially at that age. Jesus, I was such a dumbass at eighteen."

"Are you implying you're not anymore?" The instinct to tease him was automatic, but this time there was no venom in it. It was how we'd always been with each other. That competitive push and pull, goading one another, came as naturally as breathing. It was only when things had fallen apart that it turned toxic.

When he laughed, it vibrated through his body and mine. "I'll have you know I'm a much more experienced dumbass now."

"Glad to hear you've grown."

"All I'm saying is maybe the way it worked out was for the best." His hand smoothed up and down my back again, and I closed my eyes, surrendering to the sensation. "Do you think she had a good family who gave her a happy childhood?"

The anxious concern in his voice brought a faint smile to my lips. "I think she did. She seems well-adjusted and comfortable in her own skin."

"There you go. Who knows how badly we would have screwed her up."

I remembered I hadn't told him the big news yet. What with all the fighting, I'd almost forgotten. "She's pregnant, by the way."

Donal's hand stilled on my back. "Pregnant?"

"She's still in the first trimester, due in November. Her husband's a software engineer. It's their first child."

"You know what that means? We're going to be grandparents. Fuck me. That's crazy."

"Yeah, I know. Can you imagine?"

"Yeah, actually. I can." The smile in his voice was unmistakable. "What else did you find out?"

I shifted, getting more comfortable on Donal's chest. He lifted his arm while I squirmed, then draped it back over me once I'd settled. "She grew up in Deerfield."

"Hey, that's not bad. Probably nicer than the neighborhood we grew up in."

"Her parents are both still alive, but they divorced when she was thirteen. She said her mother is a science teacher also." I chewed on my lip. "That must mean they had a good relationship, right? If Erin wanted to be a teacher like her mother?"

Donal's arm tightened around me. "Yeah. It sounds like she had a pretty okay life without us."

"She asked me a lot of questions. She seemed really curious to know more about us."

"What'd she want to know?"

"All about you, of course."

"Yeah?" He sounded pleased.

"She seemed interested to hear you had a twin. And I think she was especially excited to find out she has half-siblings because she was an only child. She also wanted to know about my parents." As always, the thought of my parents caused my chest to tighten painfully.

Donal squeezed my shoulder. "How are your parents? You said your dad has Alzheimer's?"

"That's right." I slipped out of his arms and sat up to retrieve my whiskey glass from the coffee table.

"Tess?" Donal's voice was soft with concern.

I washed away the burning in my throat with a swallow of whiskey and cradled the glass in both hands. "We had to put him in a residential facility last year."

"That must have been hard. How's your stepmom taking it?"

"She, uh, she passed nine months ago." Goddammit, I hated being this emotional.

Donal sat up. His hand stroked my back again as he pressed a kiss against my temple. "I'm sorry. I didn't know."

"How are your parents?" I asked, desperate for a change of subject.

"They're good." He let go of me and shrugged. "Both of them are retired now. My dad got remarried a while back. My mom's as busy as ever with church and volunteering and everything."

"How's Shannon doing? I haven't talked to her since the last reunion." I'd always liked his sister, who I remembered as a slightly more subdued and intense version of Donal.

His mouth twisted. "My twin sister continues to outshine me. Currently, the State Department has her assigned to the US embassy in The Hague." He took the glass out of my hand and helped himself to a sip of my drink.

Now that we were sitting side by side where I could look at him up close, I could see how much silver there was at his temples and in the stubble along his jaw. I hadn't noticed it before, because it blended with his light brown hair. He had deep lines in his forehead as well, and lots of crinkles around his eyes and mouth, but they only made him look more handsome. Distinguished. Sexy, even. It was so unfair, the way men got better-looking as they aged.

Donal glanced at me, and his eyebrows lifted when he caught me staring.

I took my whiskey back and tried to pretend I hadn't been blatantly ogling him. "Does Shannon have kids?"

"Three. She's beating me at that too, as my mother delights in reminding me— although now I suppose technically we're tied." His lips spread in a slow grin.

Wow. His smile was still as intoxicating as ever. Other than a slightly sad, half-hearted smile the other night, Donal hadn't smiled around me in a very long time. I wasn't used to being confronted by the full force of it anymore, and it caught me unprepared.

A squirmy, ticklish sensation erupted in my stomach. It had been so long since I'd felt anything like it that it took me a second to realize it wasn't a sign of impending stomach upset, but rather the fluttery feeling that accompanied a crush. The fact that this particular man had triggered it was deeply unnerving.

Get a hold of yourself, McGregor. Under no circumstances are you allowed to be dazzled by Donal Larkin's smile.

Fun fact: that butterflies-in-the-stomach feeling is a side effect of your body's fight or flight response. When it senses danger, the sympathetic nervous system releases adrenaline and cortisol to divert blood away from your digestive system and into your heart and leg muscles in order to help you flee. Hence the fluttery tummy as the blood flow to your stomach suddenly drops. I'd always found it amusingly apropos that our bodies considered the appearance of a potential mate as much of an emergency as a ravening predator snapping at our heels.

Tearing my eyes away from Donal and his stupid smile, I took a large gulp of my whiskey, praying it would dull the electric boogaloo my nervous system had set off in my stomach. "That means Erin has cousins."

Donal nodded as he took the glass back from me. "But they're all in the Netherlands. I haven't even seen them in..." He tilted his head, squinting as he thought about it. "Two years?"

All this talk about his family brought home how much more he had to offer Erin than I did. He could give her siblings, grandparents, cousins, and an aunt who looked just like her. Whereas I had no family left except a father who no longer recognized me and barely spoke anymore. If Erin was looking for family connections, Donal had me beat by a long shot.

I reclaimed my glass and finished it off. When I reached for the bottle to refill it, Donal leaned forward and picked up the yellowed hospital wristband sitting out on the table.

After Erin's birth, I'd packed everything that reminded me of the pregnancy into a box and carried it down to the basement of my parents' house. I'd found it again when I was going through the house after my stepmother's death. I hadn't been able to bring myself to get rid of it, so I'd brought it to my apartment and shoved it in the back of my closet. But I hadn't opened it until today.

My head had been reeling and my emotions in chaos when I got home from meeting Erin this afternoon. I'd dragged the box out of my closet and thrown myself a pity party for one, picking through it and crying over all the memories I'd tried so hard to forget.

That was what I'd been doing for the last two hours when Donal called and insisted on coming over.

His expression grew pensive as he ran his thumb over my old hospital wristband. After a moment, he set it down and poked through the other mementos lying out. He picked up a cassette tape with a handwritten label and looked at me in surprise. "I gave you this."

It was a mixtape he'd made of his favorite songs. At the time, I'd wanted to believe it meant something, that he'd intended it as a romantic gesture. I'd secretly hoped it was a sign he wanted us to be more than just a dirty little hookup.

But then I'd gotten pregnant and…yeah. So much for that.

A smile hovered at the corner of his lips as he read the song list on the insert. "You kept it."

Everything that reminded me of Donal had gone into the box with the pregnancy stuff. I'd been trying to purge the memories, not preserve them. Although…if I'd really wanted to get rid of them, I supposed I would have set the box out with the trash instead of burying it like a time capsule in the basement.

"We used to listen to this in my car, remember?" Donal seemed to be enjoying the trip down memory lane. "God, that old Citation I had was such a piece of shit."

I remembered it well. I'd lost my virginity in the back seat of that car while listening to that very mixtape.

I looked away and took another drink. "Erin asked me if we were in love."

"She did?" Donal's voice sounded choked, as if Erin's question had thrown him as much as it had thrown me. "What'd you say?"

"I told her we were friends who got carried away."

"Why do you think she wanted to know?"

"I couldn't say. She asked a lot of questions. Maybe she's just curious about everything."

"Do you think it matters to her?" He was still holding the mixtape, running his fingers over the scratched-up plastic case. "Would it make any difference if we'd been in love?"

"I don't know."

He set the mixtape down and shuffled some papers aside, unearthing a sonogram photo.

I watched him closely as he picked it up. We'd stopped speaking by the time I'd had my ultrasound, so he'd never seen it. It hadn't occurred to me he might have wanted to. I'd been so full of anger and resentment by that point, I wasn't sure I would have shown it to him even if he'd asked.

As his eyebrows drew together, I wondered again if I'd been so wrong about him and his interest in being a father. The way he was looking at the sonogram photo made me think yes. Except I'd never be able to forget the look of horror on his face when I told him I was pregnant. It was burned into my memory like a scar.

More likely, the passage of time and his more recent experiences with fatherhood were tinting his perception with a paternal sentimentality he hadn't felt back then.

He set the sonogram photo down and ran his hand over the back of his neck. "I know you and I haven't always gotten along…"

"Understatement," I said with a snort.

Even back when we'd been friends, we'd argued and poked at each other constantly. The two of us were like oil and water. No, scratch that, we were more like vinegar and baking soda that erupted into a volcanic mess when you put us together.

Donal's lips compressed. "I think it's fair to say we've both said and done things we regret." He raised an eyebrow, apparently waiting for me to disagree. When I didn't, he continued. "It's too late to change the way things turned out. But we've got a chance now to change the future and build a relationship with our daughter. I don't know about you, but I'd really like to meet my first grandchild in November and be a presence in that baby's life. I don't want to do anything to mess that up."

"Agreed." I'd already spent thirty years wondering how my daughter was doing. I didn't want to spend the next thirty wondering the same thing about a grandchild. Not if I could help it.

"If Erin's willing to let us into her life, it's likely you and I will be seeing a lot more of each other going forward. Holidays, birthdays, and hopefully a lot more occasions in between. In light of that, I'd like to make a proposal."

I narrowed my eyes, Donal's eminently reasonable lawyer voice putting me on my guard. "What?"

"From here on out, you and I try to act like a team. For Erin's sake, and for the sake of the grandchild I want to be allowed to spoil rotten."

"You want us to pretend to like each other?"

A muscle ticked in his jaw. "I'm suggesting we make a concerted effort to get along. We're going to be grandparents together—don't you think it would be better if we weren't at each other's throats? I'm guessing Erin will be more likely to want us in her life if we can avoid becoming those nightmare relatives who turn every family gathering into a battleground for our airing of grievances."

I smiled despite myself. "I suppose that's true."

"I just think this whole situation will be easier on everyone if we can figure out a way to put up with each other. It's liable to bring some pretty big changes to our lives, and it would be nice if we could navigate them like functional adults." He paused, holding my gaze for a beat. "And maybe even try to support each other through it a little."

My knee-jerk instinct was to argue that he was asking for the impossible. Combativeness had always been our default with one another. Even during the brief period when we'd let our libidos get the better of us, there'd been an underlying edge of competition to our physical relationship. The sparks that had ignited between us had been fueled as much by friction as teenage hormones.

Supporting each other wasn't in our playbook. The first real crisis we'd faced had driven us apart and provoked three decades of bad blood. Did Donal seriously expect us to magically come together now in some kind of rah-rah kumbaya spirit after years of dysfunction?

And yet...we'd already taken the first tentative steps toward a truce. Yes, we'd fought tonight, but it had felt more like excising an old wound than inflicting new ones. We'd actually managed to talk a little without lashing out, and said some things we should have said years ago.

Maybe we could build on that. It was possible we'd both changed enough that what he was asking was possible. Wasn't it worth a shot? If I wanted Erin in my life, Donal would have to be part of it as well. As long as we were stuck with each other, we could at least make an effort to get along.

"Since when are you so emotionally mature?" I asked him, feeling uncomfortably out of my depth. Being around him made me feel like an insecure kid again, so desperate to be the best at everything and afraid to show any imperfections or weakness.

"People grow up, Tess." There was a sharp edge to his voice—regret but also a touch of hurt.

"Apparently they do," I said more gently.

He accepted my mea culpa by inclining his head, a ghost of a smile touching his lips. "Does that mean you're on board?"

"Sure. Fine." I rolled my eyes, following it up with a smile to let him know it was meant in good humor. "I'll try if you will."

"Deal." Donal's dimples came out as he offered his hand to seal our verbal contract.

I accepted, fitting my palm against his to shake on it. When his fingers tightened around mine, the room swooped as if I'd drunk too much whiskey.

"I'm holding you to it." His eyes twinkled as he kept his grasp on my hand. "Teammate."

Oh no. It wasn't the whiskey making my stomach lurch and my heart race. It was Donal.

If I couldn't get these wayward feelings in check, I was in for a world of trouble.

CHAPTER EIGHT

DONAL

I received an email from Erin the day after her meeting with Tess. I wrote back right away, attaching a recent photo of myself as well as one from high school. We exchanged several emails over the course of that week, and Erin agreed to meet me for lunch the following Saturday.

The first thing she said to me when we saw each other for the first time was, "Wow, we really do look alike."

I'd thought I was prepared for it, but the way my heart lurched at the sight of her said otherwise. Seeing a photograph couldn't compare to looking someone in the eye for the first time. No wonder Tess had been such a wreck after their meeting.

"There's definitely no doubt we're related." I experienced a moment of uncertainty as I stood to greet Erin. Should we hug? Or would that be presumptuous?

She settled the question for me by extending her hand. Her smile was wide, but her fingers trembled a little as they grasped mine, which made me wish I'd taken the initiative and hugged her like I'd wanted to.

We sat down and traded small talk for a few minutes as we perused our menus. It should have been awkward, but instead it felt strangely comfortable to be talking to her. More like talking to an old friend I'd lost touch with than a total stranger.

I congratulated her on the pregnancy, and she told me about the morning sickness that troubled her early on but thankfully passed. She asked me about my job, I asked about hers, and that carried us through until the waiter came back to take our orders.

"Sorry if I stare at you," Erin said after the waiter had departed. "I've never met anyone I looked like before."

"Stare away. I'll probably be doing some staring myself."

"Do your kids—your real kids—er, your other kids—" She winced, and we shared a smile over the bizarreness of the situation. "Do they look like you?"

"No, they both take after their mother. Here…" I pulled up the lock screen photo on my phone and handed it across the table. "That's Maddy and Jack."

Erin examined it closely. While she studied them, I studied her. She did look a hell of a lot like me, but I noted subtle differences between us. Her nose was rounder and less prominent than mine, her face slightly more heart-shaped. It was her eyes that struck me the most, however. Instead of my deep-set gray-blue, Erin's eyes were wide and greenish brown. Exactly like Tess's.

"Would you like to meet them sometime?" I asked, trying not to sound overeager.

Erin looked at the photo for another second before handing my phone back with an uncertain frown. "Do you think they'd want to meet me?"

"I don't see why not."

"Do they know about me?"

"Not yet, but I'm going to tell them next week." We were supposed to have dinner on Monday, and I'd decided to tell them about Erin then.

"You don't think it'll upset them? Finding out they have a surprise half-sister they never knew about?" The probing look Erin gave me was one hundred percent Tess.

"It might at first, but once the initial shock wears off I suspect they'll be curious about you. They might even be excited about it." I hoped so, anyway. Jack was a pretty easygoing kid, but Maddy was a different story. Things between the two of us had been difficult lately, but I wanted to think she wouldn't take her issues with me out on Erin.

There was a lengthy moment of silence as Erin seemed to think about it. My fingers gripped the edge of my chair until she finally nodded. "If they're comfortable with it, I'd like to meet them."

I exhaled my relief. "After I talk to them, we'll see if we can't set something up. My mother will definitely want to meet you as well, if you're willing."

My neck itched at the prospect of telling my mom about Erin. I could already feel the weight of her disapproval pushing the oxygen from my lungs. God have mercy, she was going to give me the guilt trip of all guilt trips. On the bright side, Mom was going to love her to death, especially when she found out she was expecting. Hopefully, the prospect of becoming a great-grandmother would temper some of her disappointment in me.

A faint smile curved Erin's lips. "I'd really like that."

"I wish you could meet my sister Shannon and your cousins, but they don't get back to the States very often."

"What's your sister like? I mean, besides the fact that she looks like you."

"She looks like *us*," I said, and was pleased to see Erin smile. I scratched my temple as I considered how to describe my twin. "She's more serious than me and a little quieter—more thoughtful, I guess. She doesn't always say everything she's thinking, which is probably what makes her a good diplomat. But she can be funny when she lets loose."

Erin's eyebrows lifted slightly. "Are you implying you're not serious or thoughtful?"

I fidgeted with my knife and fork, lining them up so they were perfectly parallel with the napkin. "I'm better than I used to be, but I've always been more impulsive than Shannon. I don't always think things through, and it sometimes gets me in trouble."

Erin's slow nod triggered a suspicion.

"Tess said something about me, didn't she?" I'd been expecting it, so I wasn't surprised. I just hoped she hadn't badmouthed me too much before Erin had a chance to make up her own mind about me. "Let me guess: she called me unreliable."

Erin blinked, startled by my question. "No. She didn't say anything like that. She only had complimentary things to say about you."

"Oh." *Well, fuck.* Now I felt like a shit for assuming Tess would run me down behind my back. I should have known that wasn't her style. She was much more of an "insult you to your face" type of person.

"Did she think you were unreliable? Is that why…" Erin clamped her lips shut and shook her head. "Never mind. You don't have to answer that."

I shifted in my seat, eager for a change of subject. "Can I ask…what made you decide to try and find us?"

Erin's gaze dropped to her water glass, where she was rubbing her thumb over the condensation. "I've always wondered about my ancestry and medical history. It nagged at me every time I went to the doctor and had to leave the family medical history questionnaire blank. Or when people would say, 'Oh, I'm X percent this and X percent that,' and I had no idea what percent of anything I was. I used to come into the city and see all the different neighborhoods, and I'd wonder, 'Am I Polish? Am I Irish? Am I German?' I think I felt a little disconnected, like I didn't know where I belonged because I didn't know who my people had been."

"For the record, you're about as Irish as they come," I said. "At least on my side, and I think Tess's family is similar. My mother could give you the whole history of our family, tell you exactly who immigrated when, what town in Ireland they came from, and list all the family we still have in the old country—if you're interested in that level of detail."

Erin's smile grew. "I'll definitely ask her about it."

The waiter reappeared, and there was a pause in the conversation as he dropped off our entrées before bustling off again.

"Getting back to your question," Erin said, picking up her fork, "I decided to sign up for LineagePlus when I found out I was pregnant because I wanted more information on my ancestry and genetic health risks. Initially, I didn't even think about the fact that it could help me find my birth parents. It was only after I'd sent off my DNA kit and went on the website that I saw the relative matching service. I knew when I opted into it there was a possibility it would turn something up, but it wasn't like I decided to actively go looking for you. That wasn't something I'd ever seriously considered doing before."

"Why's that?" I asked as I stirred around the salmon, brown rice, and vegetable bowl I'd ordered.

Erin frowned at her plate as she cut a piece of her chicken kebabs in half. "I guess I was worried my parents would think I was trying to replace them, and I didn't want to hurt their feelings."

"Do your parents know you've been in contact with us?"

"My mom does. I told her as soon as the DNA match showed up, before I worked up the courage to message Tess."

"How did she take it? Was she upset?"

"No, she was great." Erin smiled as she sipped her water. "At first I wasn't sure what to do about the match—I didn't know if I actually wanted to make contact —but my mom didn't put any pressure on me one way or the other. She let me decide for myself, and once I had, she helped me write the message to Tess."

It was a huge load off my mind that Erin's mother didn't begrudge our presence in her life. Also that Erin seemed to have such a good relationship with her mother. "Sounds like you two are close."

"We are, yeah. Although we didn't always get along so well—you know how teenagers can be."

I exhaled a long sigh as I stabbed a piece of broccoli with my fork. "Yes, I do."

"Now that I'm older, my mom and I get along really well. Things got a lot easier once she didn't have to parent me anymore."

"What about your dad?" I'd noticed Erin hadn't mentioned him at all.

A wrinkle formed between her brows as she pushed her cucumber salad around. "We don't talk as often since he moved to Florida ten years ago. He's not really a phone person, so it's hard to stay close."

Perhaps it was unfair of me, but I couldn't help judging him. I'd been doing everything I could to stay connected with my kids since the divorce. It wasn't always easy—especially with Maddy—but that didn't stop me from trying.

She might resent me and every minute of time she was forced to spend with me, but at least she knew I wanted to be part of her life. If I'd had the chance to be a father to Erin, I liked to think I wouldn't have let her drift away from me.

"Was it hard for you when your parents split?" I asked.

"It's always hard, isn't it? I can always tell when one of my students is going through a divorce at home. It upends everything you thought would stay the same, and for a little while it feels like the ground will never feel solid again. But then you get used to it, and it becomes your new status quo." She lifted one of her shoulders as she glanced up at me. "Tess mentioned you were divorced."

I nodded as I swallowed the bite of salmon in my mouth. "My wife and I only split a year ago, so it's still pretty new."

"How are your kids adjusting?"

"Jack—he's the younger one—seems to be rolling with it okay. Maddy's another matter. The two of us used to be really close, but more recently we've been..." I hesitated, reaching for my water glass. "Things have been difficult between us. I think she blames me for the divorce."

Erin didn't say anything. She was too polite to pry, but I could see the question in her eyes.

I cleared my throat, trying to decide how honest I wanted to be. "I let my job turn me into a workaholic, and I wasn't around for my family as much as I should have been. So Maddy's got good reason to blame me."

It had been a real wake-up call when Wendy asked me for a divorce. Until that moment, I hadn't realized how much I'd been taking her for granted. I'd let her carry too much of the load on her own while I buried myself in work, and I wasn't around for her or the kids nearly as much as I should have been.

It was unsettling to think Tess had been right about me. I hadn't made a very good husband or father after all.

I reached for my water again to wash away the bitter taste in my mouth. I could feel the weight of Erin's gaze on me, but I avoided meeting it, afraid of what I'd see in her eyes. "Anyway, I've been making an effort to be more present for Jack and Maddy since the divorce. It's harder now that I don't see as much of them, but I want to show them they're my number-one priority even if we don't live together anymore."

"I think that's great," Erin said softly. "It sounds like you're doing the right things to help them through it."

I glanced at her and winced at the sympathy in her expression. "I'm sorry. It's probably hard to hear about this, considering I was never there for you at all."

"No, it's okay. It's actually…" When she hesitated, I leaned forward, curious to hear how she'd finish the sentence. "This probably sounds bad, but it's sort of reassuring."

"You mean knowing that I would have been a crappy father?"

"No." She frowned at me. "I don't think you are—and as a teacher I've gotten good at spotting the bad ones. But it's a useful reminder that no one's perfect."

I huffed out a wry breath and rubbed my forehead. "I'm definitely not that."

"It's just that when I was younger, sometimes I'd get upset with my parents and fantasize about my biological mom and dad, imagining that I would have been better off with them." Her cheeks pinked with embarrassment as she lowered her eyes.

"That sounds like a pretty normal thing for a kid in your position to think about."

She nodded absently and brushed at a crumb on the table. "I almost didn't message Tess because I was afraid of finding out something bad about my birth parents—but I think I might also have been afraid of finding out something too good."

"What do you mean?"

"Sometimes I'd watch movies like *The Princess Diaries* or *What a Girl Wants*— you know, where the main character finds out the parent she never knew was royalty or rich and famous?"

"I'm familiar." I'd watched both movies with Maddy when she was younger.

"It's supposed to be some kind of wonderful revelation, but I always thought I'd be upset if I ever found out something like that. Like, I could have had this incredible alternate life, and instead I missed out on all that awesomeness and had to settle for my boring, ho-hum life in the suburbs."

I couldn't help laughing a little. "Well I'm definitely not a prince—or Colin Firth—so you didn't miss out on anything that incredible."

"Exactly. I traded one ordinary life for another. My adoptive parents might not have been perfect—or royalty," she added with a grin, "but I was lucky to have them."

My smile faded as I held her gaze. "I don't know your parents, but from what you've said about them, they probably did a better job raising you than Tess and I would have at that point in our lives. Historically, eighteen-year-olds don't tend to win parent of the year competitions."

The conversation came to a halt as our waiter reappeared. Erin hadn't eaten much and I'd eaten even less, but we both indicated he could take our plates away.

"Can I ask you something?" she said once he'd gone.

"Anything."

"You knew about me, right?"

"Yes."

"Did you ever think about me?"

"All the time," I told her, feeling an echo of the ache I'd carried around for most of my life. "For the first five years or so, I probably thought about you every single day, wondering where you were and if you were all right. Over time, the not knowing receded from an acute pain to a dull one, but it never went away. And then it got worse again for a while after Maddy and Jack were born. Having them reminded me of everything I'd missed out on with you—and everything I'd failed to do for you."

"So it's okay that I found you?" Her hopeful, uncertain expression cracked my heart wide-open.

"It's better than okay." I reached across the table, offering my hand, and a lump formed in my throat when she slipped her fingers into mine. "I'm really, genuinely grateful you did. You have no idea what a relief it is to know you grew up safe and cared for."

She squeezed my hand before releasing it. "But you never wanted to look for me?"

"I thought about it." Frowning, I dropped my gaze to the table where our hands had been joined a moment ago. "But I wasn't sure Tess would want me to, and I didn't know any of the details of your birth, so I would have had to talk to her."

"I gather you two weren't in touch before I came looking for you."

"Not so much, no." I chewed the inside of my lip as I fought a pang of regret. "I think what really stopped me from looking for you was that I was afraid you wouldn't want me turning up out of the blue and forcing my way into your life. If you were happy with the way things were, I didn't want to disrupt that."

"Do you think Tess—" Erin stopped and pressed her lips together. "No, never mind."

"What?" I couldn't help pressing, my curiosity piqued. "I said you can ask me anything."

"But this isn't a question about you. I'm not sure it's fair to ask for your opinion about her under the circumstances." Erin stared at her hands, rubbing her fingers over her knuckles in a way that reminded me of Tess.

"I used to know her pretty well," I offered. "If you want my advice, all you have to do is ask."

She seemed to consider this for a moment before making a decision. "Do you think she minds that I tracked her down?"

"Of course not," I answered automatically. "Obviously it's a huge development, but only in the best kind of way. Why would you ask that?"

"No reason, really. She's been lovely. It's just, she doesn't have kids, which makes me think she never wanted them, and here I am, the child she gave away" —Erin's eyes met mine as she repeated my words back to me—"turning up out of the blue and forcing my way into her life."

"You're not forcing anything," I assured her. "If Tess hadn't wanted to know you, she wouldn't have let anyone or anything pressure her into answering that message from you. Trust me."

"Okay, good."

As I watched Erin chew on her lip, I debated how much I should interfere in her relationship with Tess. I knew Tess well enough to know how hard she could be to read—and the more nervous she was about a situation, the more impenetrable she became. I could guess how difficult Erin was finding it to interpret her vibe.

"Listen." I leaned forward and rested my forearms on the table. "The thing you should understand about Tess is that she's not someone who easily expresses emotions or affection, but that doesn't mean she doesn't *feel* emotions and affection. I know she's as glad as I am to have found you, even if she comes across a little reserved."

She seemed to relax. "That's helpful. Thank you for telling me that."

"You're welcome."

"It sounds like you two were pretty close."

"For a while we were—a long time ago."

"But you didn't stay that way?"

"Things didn't exactly end well between us." A fresh lance of regret stabbed through me at the memory of my conversation with Tess last weekend.

I couldn't believe all this time she'd actually believed I hadn't wanted anything to do with her or the baby. At least her hostility made more sense now. No wonder she'd hated me. She'd thought I'd turned my back on her willingly, which couldn't have been further from the truth. I'd been devastated to lose her. The only reason I'd walked away was because she'd told me to. And I'd spent the last thirty years resenting her for it.

God. We really had been idiots back then. Both of us.

I cleared my throat, uncomfortably aware of Erin watching me. "Tess mentioned that you asked if we were in love when she got pregnant. Why did you want to know? Does it matter to you?"

Erin's gaze lowered as her cheeks pinked with embarrassment. "It's just something I used to wonder when I was younger and I'd make up stories in my head about who my birth parents were. I guess I was curious to know what the real story was. I didn't mean to make either of you uncomfortable by asking."

"No, it's fine." I rubbed my thumb across my palm. "We hadn't been seeing each other very long when Tess got pregnant."

"She said you were friends."

"We were. All through school. But being more than that was still new when she found out she was pregnant. I can't speak for Tess—I don't really know how she felt about me back then—but I cared about her. A lot. I thought…" I had to take a breath before I could say it. "I thought I loved her."

I'd never told anyone that before. Tess hadn't just been a hookup for me. I'd wanted more, and I'd been working my way up to telling her that, but something had held me back. Fear of scaring her off maybe. She'd seemed so adamant about keeping our relationship a secret, I hadn't been convinced she saw me as serious boyfriend material. And the way things shook out, it seemed pretty clear I was right. But I'd wanted to make Tess my girlfriend, and I'd been planning to ask her to prom. Foolishly, I'd even begun toying with the possibility of going to Northwestern instead of Yale to stay close to her.

"Shit." I rubbed my forehead, embarrassed by my confession. "I don't know why I told you that."

"Did she know?" Erin asked.

I shook my head. "I never got around to telling her."

"Because of me."

"No." I lifted my head, frowning as I met her gaze. "Not because of you. Because of *me*. Because of problems between me and Tess that had nothing to do with you."

"But if she hadn't gotten pregnant, then maybe—"

"The problems were already there. They would have bubbled up one way or another. I'm just sorry that…" I shook my head, not really sure how to put all my regrets into words Erin would be able to understand. "I'm sorry that you came along at a point in my life when I wasn't able to be a father to you."

"It must be strange, knowing you've got a child who was raised by someone else."

"It is. It feels like I failed you."

"You shouldn't feel like that." Her smile was unbearably kind. "My dad's great —the dad who raised me, I mean."

I nodded to show her I understood. "He's your real dad. I'm just the DNA donor."

"I had a good father, so you didn't fail me. I had everything I needed growing up." This time she was the one who reached across the table, and I slid my hand gratefully into hers. "But I'm glad that now I have you too."

CHAPTER NINE

TESS

I was dying to know how Donal's lunch with Erin had gone. I'd offered to go with him, but of course he'd declined. Which—fine. I recognized it was only fair after I'd rejected his offer to come along when I met her. Didn't mean I liked it. There were too many things that could go wrong.

For starters, what if Erin liked Donal more than she liked me? That one wasn't so much a worry as an inevitability. Everyone liked Donal more than they liked me. He was easygoing and personable, while I generally came off as unapproachable and uptight. I'd tried my best to be warm and welcoming when I'd met Erin, but I wasn't a naturally effusive person. I'd never beat Donal in a personality contest.

In addition, he had parenting experience I lacked. He'd raised two kids and knew how to be a father and therefore knew how to relate to his children on a level I could never fathom. I didn't know the first thing about being a mother, and I had no idea how to act around Erin, or any innate sense of what she needed from me.

There was no changing these essential facts of the situation. Erin would instantly be charmed by Donal's open, friendly manner and respond to his natural paternal instincts. From this day forward, he'd be her favorite biological parent.

And that was without even getting into the fact that I was the one who'd made the decision to give her up. If Erin was going to resent anyone, it would be me. While Donal once again got off scot-free.

What if they ganged up on me? Donal could tell Erin his version of events and paint me as the villain who'd kept them apart. There would be nothing I could do to prevent it. If he chose to throw me under the bus, I'd be stuck to the tire treads like a pancaked frog.

I was torn between believing it was exactly what I deserved and resenting that I was at Donal's mercy. He'd said he wanted us to act like a team, so presumably I was supposed to trust he wouldn't do anything to undermine my relationship with Erin. That sounded great in theory, but in practice I found it difficult to trust him.

Sure, he'd seemed sincere the other night, but I'd been down this road before. He always *seemed* sincere—so sweet and genuine that anyone would want to believe him. Convincing people of his good intentions was his superpower. Only after he'd lured you into lowering your defenses did the real Donal come out— the one who was forgetful, irresponsible, and self-centered. How many times had he made promises, then left me or others in the lurch back in high school? Whether accidentally or intentionally, the result was the same.

So no, I didn't trust him to have my back now. No matter how sincere he'd seemed. Historically Donal wasn't someone who followed through on his commitments.

Knowing this about him made me even more anxious about his relationship with Erin. I'd been terrified he was going to stand her up for their lunch date today. I'd texted him first thing this morning to remind him about it, again a half hour before to make sure he'd left on time, and then a third time to confirm he'd actually made it to the restaurant.

I didn't doubt he'd been annoyed by my nagging, but would he have made it there if I hadn't checked up on him? What if he'd stood Erin up and left her sitting in that restaurant alone thinking he didn't care about her? It'd be just like that time he'd left me stranded at the basketball game. Or the time he'd promised to meet me at the library to work on a project for Latin class and never showed. Or that other time he was supposed to help me transport donations for the food drive and I'd ended up hauling everything by myself.

It was one thing for Donal to let me down—I was used to it and entertained no illusions about him. But if he got Erin's hopes up and disappointed her, so help me God, I would kill him. Literally, I would murder him with my bare hands if he hurt her in any way.

Fortunately, he seemed to be taking this seriously so far. But I hated not being in control of a situation, and being forced to rely on Donal was even worse. He wanted us to be a team, but I knew what it meant to be on Donal's team—me doing all the hard work while he got all the glory.

I checked my phone for the millionth time as I paced around my apartment. What I really wanted to do was text him and ask how the lunch had gone, but I'd already annoyed him by texting so many reminders today. If I pushed him too much, he might shut me out completely. Besides, they might still be at lunch. I was reluctant to interrupt if it was going well. Erin might think I was intruding on her time with Donal and decide I was pushy and overbearing.

I *was* pushy and overbearing, but she didn't need to know that yet. In high school people had called me Bossy Tess behind my back because of my tendency to step in and take charge. It wasn't as if I enjoyed doing all the work myself. I only did it when other people wouldn't. They were happy to let me make all the decisions until it came to the one decision out of a hundred they actually cared about —then suddenly I was being bossy because I'd tried to take over a task no one else had been willing to do.

That was fine. Being bossy had made me good at my job, even if it hadn't won me many friends. My clients appreciated my bossiness and paid handsomely for it, because it meant shit got done.

But I was trying extra hard not to be pushy and overbearing with Erin. She'd figure it out eventually, but I wanted to put it off as long as possible because I wanted her to like me.

Why hasn't Donal texted yet, dammit?

I sank down on my couch and glared at my phone. Was he punishing me for nagging him? I wouldn't put it past him.

Casting my phone aside in frustration, I surveyed the clutter that still covered my coffee table. I hadn't yet put away the box of old pregnancy memories. It wasn't like me to leave a mess sitting around, but every time I thought about packing it all away again something stopped me.

I leaned forward and picked up the cassette tape Donal had given me. On the spine of the tape he'd simply written *Songs for Tess* in his messy, teenaged boy scrawl. As I read the faded list of song titles scribbled in ballpoint pen, I couldn't help smiling. They were all love songs. Not slow songs or mushy ballads, but every single song was about love, attraction, or sex. It seemed so obvious now, but at the time I'd been unsure, hesitant to believe Donal had those kinds of feelings for me.

And yet here I was, holding the evidence in my hand. It had been staring me right in the face back then and I'd refused to see it.

Maybe I was being too hard on Donal now. I should probably make more of an effort to give him a chance. I had to keep reminding myself he wasn't a teenager anymore. He wasn't the same boy who'd made me this tape, or the boy who'd left me at that basketball game in tenth grade. He was a middle-aged man, a partner in a big downtown law firm, a father, and an ex-husband. Those experiences had changed him in ways I couldn't understand, just like the last thirty years had changed me.

As I set the cassette down, my eyes fell on the baby blanket I'd started knitting when I was pregnant. I'd had this fanciful idea that I could give it to the baby so she'd have something to remember me by. I didn't even know if they would have let her keep it, and anyway I never finished the stupid thing.

I picked it up, running my fingers over the stitches. I hadn't knit in years—not since I'd abandoned this blanket, in fact. If I closed my eyes, my hands could almost remember the motions. But I didn't have the needles anymore. My stepmother had taken them back and transferred the blanket to stitch holders before I put it in storage. I didn't have the pattern anymore either. I couldn't even remember where I'd gotten it from. Probably one of Sherry's pattern books, which I'd given away with all my parents' other possessions.

As I sat there holding the blanket, squeezing the ancient acrylic yarn between my fingers, my phone chirped on the couch beside me.

Donal had texted me finally.

Do you want to come over tonight? If you bring pizza I'll give you a million dollars.

"No mushrooms, right?" Donal eyed the pizza box in my hand as he admitted me to his condo. He might have changed since high school, but his pizza preferences hadn't.

"Oh sorry, did you say *no* mushrooms?" I blinked at him innocently. "I thought you wanted *extra* mushrooms."

"You're messing with me, aren't you?" His eyes narrowed as he took the pizza box from me. "You'd better be messing with me."

He wore jeans and a plain blue polo shirt that fit his body immaculately. So many men our age still favored the same pleated pants and Obama mom jeans that had gone out of style twenty years ago. Not Donal. His jeans were casually fashionable and hung low on his hips in a way I found inconveniently distracting.

It was an effort not to stare as he carried the pizza into the kitchen. Instead, I set my purse on a table by the door and went to admire the view from his living room windows. His building was only a half mile from mine and nearly the same distance from the Riverwalk, but his corner unit was higher, more spacious, and afforded a view of Lake Michigan, whereas mine faced away from the waterfront.

"Oh, thank God," Donal muttered from the kitchen after opening the special deep dish I'd picked up from Giordano's on the walk over. "For a second I was scared you'd totally fucked me over."

Turning my back on his spectacular view, I wandered toward the kitchen and leaned against the doorframe. "I might be a heartless bitch, but I'm not a monster. I still remember how you feel about mushrooms."

His mouth pulled into a frown as he cut a glance at me. "You're not a heartless bitch."

"I have a few former coworkers and an ex-boyfriend who'd disagree with you there." Smiling, I tilted my head and lifted my shoulders to show I didn't care.

I'd learned to embrace my badass boss bitch reputation—I even had a coffee mug that touted the title. As long as I claimed it openly, it couldn't be used as an insult against me.

"Your boyfriend didn't actually call you that, did he?" Donal looked appalled.

I waved his concern away. "No, he was too polite for that. I think the words he used were cold, unfeeling, and passionless, but it amounts to basically the same thing."

"Anyone who thinks you're passionless doesn't know you at all."

I stared at him in surprise, unsure how to respond. It had sounded like a compliment, and the way he was staring at me made my stomach do an uncomfortable flip.

His eyes lingered on mine for what felt like a long moment before he shrugged and turned to pull open the fridge. "Sounds like you're better off without him. You want a beer?"

Swallowing, I forced myself to answer. "I'd love one."

"All I've got is an imperial stout. Hope that's okay." He got out two bottles and rummaged in a drawer for a bottle opener.

"What, no Milwaukee's Beast?" I asked, raising my eyebrows at the expensive craft beer.

He snorted as he handed me one. "Jesus, the Beast. I can't believe I used to drink that swill. Sláinte."

I clinked my bottle against his and took a long pull of my beer. It was dark and rich—like Guinness but stronger and sweeter—and I squinted at the label, looking for the ABV. "So your taste in beer has matured with age, but you still hate mushrooms with a burning passion?"

"Mushrooms have the same consistency as diced slugs." He shuddered dramatically as he opened a cabinet and got down two plates. "Why would anyone want to put that in their mouth? Why?"

I accepted one of the plates and helped myself to a slice of pizza and a paper towel. Donal piled three slices on his plate before gesturing toward the living room.

"You seem like you're in a good mood," I observed, taking another sip of beer as I followed him. It was so strong I could already feel the alcohol chipping away at the tension I'd been carrying all day. "I hope that means your first meeting with Erin went well."

"It went great." He smiled as he dropped down on one of the two couches and set his beer on the round glass coffee table. "Thanks for the pizza."

I took a seat on the other couch and balanced my plate on my knees. "I'm dying to hear all about it."

Donal had just crammed a big bite of pizza in his mouth, and I had to wait for him to finish chewing. After he'd swallowed, he reached for his beer and took a long sip. "You were right. She's amazing." He shook his head slightly, a smile playing on his lips, and I was struck anew by how handsome he was. "It was a good lunch. We talked a lot. About…a lot of things."

I waited for him to elaborate, but instead he fell silent as he gazed thoughtfully out the window. "Like?" I prompted.

He shook himself out of whatever trance he'd been in and aimed a sideways look at me. "A lot of things. Me, her. My family, her family." His shoulders twitched in a shrug and he took another huge bite of pizza.

"That's all I get?" I downed another mouthful of beer while I waited for him to finish chewing.

"You can't expect me to repeat everything we talked about."

"I told you everything we talked about when I met her."

"I appreciate that, but it was the first time either of us had met her and I hadn't even had a chance to make contact with her myself. The circumstances are different now."

"Of course they are," I muttered. "So much for being a team." *Typical fucking Donal*. He got what he wanted from me, but as soon as it was his turn to reciprocate, he didn't want to play ball anymore. I set my plate on the table with a loud *thunk* and got to my feet. "Enjoy the pizza."

"Tess, dammit. Come on." Donal jumped up and scrambled to follow me. His hand closed around my wrist as I reached the door. "Can you just wait, please?"

"What?" I snapped, pulling my hand out of his grasp as I rounded on him. "What else do you want from me?"

"I want you to hear me out for once without making me into the bad guy."

"I'm not making you into anything. You're doing that all on your own."

"Fuck." He sagged back against the wall, tilting his head to the ceiling as he scrubbed his hands over his face. "Why does it always have to be like this with us?"

"Like what?"

"Like we're enemies." He dropped his hands and gave me a pleading look. "I don't want to be your enemy. I swear to God, I'm trying here. If you could just give me the smallest fucking benefit of the doubt instead of automatically assuming I'm out to get you."

"Fine." I crossed my arms and glared at him. "You want me to listen? I'm listening. Say whatever it is you have to say."

He sighed and pushed off the wall so he was facing me. "We're both trying to build a relationship with Erin. I want us to support each other in doing that, but that doesn't mean we should necessarily share everything Erin says to us. She needs to feel like she can trust us—like she can have a separate, unique relationship with each of us. Independently. That's what parents do."

I bristled at the implication that he knew more about parenting than I did, but bit down on my reflex to snipe back. As much as I resented that he was throwing it in my face, it was true—he did have more experience with this than I did.

It was possible he even had a point. *Dammit.*

He eyed me warily, waiting for me to respond. When I didn't, he relaxed a little and continued in a gentler voice. "I'm sorry if you feel like I'm holding back on you, but I don't feel comfortable revealing every detail of a conversation we had in confidence."

"She told you things in confidence? Did she say something about me?"

"Not everything is about you!" he shot back with a sudden flare of anger. "Did you ever consider I might have told Erin things *I* don't feel like sharing with you?"

I recoiled at the intensity of his reaction. "Oh."

He squeezed his eyes shut with a grimace and turned his back, pacing a few steps away from me. "I'm sorry. Fuck." His shoulders hunched as he rubbed his face again. "I keep screwing this up."

Some of my anger dissipated at the sight of him so obviously struggling. It was replaced by something else. Something softer and warmer that might have been compassion, but felt more like tenderness. Maybe even affection.

I moved to Donal's side and laid a conciliatory hand on his arm. "I'm sorry. You're right. I'm making this all about me, and it's not."

"I shouldn't have said that." He shook his head, wincing. "I can't seem to control my fucking mouth around you."

"That makes two of us." I started to pull my hand back, but he covered it with his, exerting warm pressure as his eyes found mine.

"If you want to know what Erin said to me, you should talk to her. Ask her questions. Open up to her about yourself. Establish your own rapport with her. She wants to know you, but you've got to build that relationship with her yourself."

I nodded, swallowing thickly. "I will."

I'd been trying, in the emails I'd been exchanging with Erin, and we'd been talking about getting together again for dinner soon. But I couldn't help feeling like Donal had swooped in from behind and gotten further in two hours than I'd managed in two weeks of steady effort. As per usual.

"I'm just nervous." Admitting that to Donal took a lot of effort. "Opening up to people isn't exactly my strong suit, and I'm taking my insecurity out on you."

He surprised me by pulling me into a hug.

Wow. The man really knew how to give a hug. I wasn't generally a big hugger, but just like the other night when he'd held me in his arms, I didn't hate it.

In fact, it felt amazing. A few more hugs like this, and I'd be a dedicated convert to the holy sacrament of hugging. I'd be going door to door proselytizing on the spiritual benefits of embracing physical embraces.

"I promise I'm on your side." Donal's voice was low and rough, his breath a warm caress against my hair. "I'm not going to say or do anything to damage your relationship with Erin. You've got to trust me on that."

It was difficult to talk with my heart lodged in my throat and my face pressed against his astonishingly firm chest. "I want that for you too. I'll try to be a better teammate."

He pulled back to look at me, and my stomach did another one of those unsettling flips under his up-close scrutiny. "We're really bad at this, aren't we?"

I was so flustered, I thought he was making fun of my poor hugging skills and stiffened. "I—what?"

"Being friends."

Oh. There went my heart, right into my throat again. "Is that what we are?"

"I'd sure like us to be." His eyebrows notched up a few millimeters. "Wouldn't you?"

Damn the man for being so likable. How was I supposed to protect myself when he kept being all vulnerable and appealing?

And handsome. Don't forget the handsome.

Shit, did I really want to be friends with Donal Larkin again?

Yes.

Even with our poor track record, I wanted that. Maybe it could be different this time. We were both mature adults now. Surely we could handle it. We wouldn't make the same mistakes.

"I'd like that too." I sounded out of breath, like I'd just done a hill ride on the stationary bike.

"Good." Donal's shoulders sagged in relief. "Can we go sit down and eat now? Because I was too nervous to eat much at lunch, and I'm seriously hangry."

CHAPTER TEN

TESS

We both sat down again, and I picked at my pizza while Donal inhaled his three slices like a vacuum cleaner. I couldn't help wondering what he'd confided to Erin that he didn't want to tell me. Something about his children, perhaps, or maybe his divorce.

"Can I ask you something?"

Donal froze mid-bite, his eyes growing wary as they flicked in my direction. I wasn't the only one of us with trust issues to overcome.

I held up my hand in a peaceful gesture. "I'm not trying to be combative, I promise."

His guarded posture relaxed a fraction as he lowered his plate. "What?"

"Why did you invite me here if you didn't want to talk about your lunch with Erin?"

"Because I wanted to see you." Before his gaze dropped to his lap, I caught a glimpse of embarrassment in it. "I didn't want to be alone tonight, and you're the only person who knows what I'm feeling."

Well fuck. I was the asshole, wasn't I? If this was one of those Reddit posts, I'd be the one roasted in the comments.

Donal had been looking for support, and I'd let my insecurities get the better of me and picked a fight with him. I'd been fooled by his apparent good mood, but I should have guessed he'd be feeling raw tonight. I'd been an absolute wreck last weekend after my own meeting with Erin. And Donal had shown up at my apartment to offer a shoulder to cry on. I'd assumed he'd come over to interrogate me and satisfy his curiosity, and maybe that was part of it, but it wasn't the only reason. His concern then had been as genuine as his need for company was now.

This was what he'd meant by being a team. It was my turn to reciprocate and fulfill my duty as a teammate.

Or friend, apparently.

"If you need to cry it out, feel free to let 'er rip. I can take it." I was half joking, half serious. Donal didn't appear to be on the precipice of tears, but if he was, I stood ready and willing to lend a sympathetic shoulder.

The lines around his eyes crinkled in amusement. "I think I'm good, but thanks."

I patted the couch next to me. "Come on now. Turnabout is fair play. I'll let you snivel into my neck and everything. We could put on a sad movie if it would help get you started. Or maybe play some Adele? I understand that works for a lot of people."

He laughed and reached for his beer. "If you really want me to cry, you'd be better off playing the clarinet for me."

"Ouch." I stifled a smile as I feigned a wounded look.

"Come on, you know they're the most useless instrument in the marching band. Nothing but fillers." His eyes were warm and teasing, and my smile broke free at the old, familiar argument.

"You only think that because you and your stupid trumpet section had the dynamic range of an air raid siren."

He cracked a grin. "Now I am going to cry."

A warm feeling settled in my chest as we smiled at one another. I'd forgotten how much I used to enjoy our bantering and teasing.

As Donal's gaze lingered on me, I was reminded of something else—how much I'd liked the feel of his eyes on me before they'd turned cold and unfriendly. He used to have this way of looking at me that tricked me into thinking I was something special and amazing.

Donal was looking at me that way right now, and I felt my face heat. I took another long drink of beer, silently cursing the Irish complexion that transformed me into a human tomato at the slightest provocation.

"How much alcohol is in this?" I asked, hoping I could blame my lightheadedness on the beer.

The dimple beside his mouth deepened. "It's ten percent ABV."

Sheesh. That explained why I felt buzzed off half of one measly beer.

"You want another?" he asked, pushing himself to his feet.

"No thank you." A second one of these would have me under the coffee table singing "Don't Worry, Be Happy" before the night was out.

Donal went into the kitchen and came back with a fresh one for himself. "I almost forgot, I've got something to show you. Hang on."

While he disappeared into the back of his apartment, I slipped my shoes off and pulled my feet up underneath me, getting more comfortable. A minute later, Donal came back carrying four large hardbound books.

"Oh, my God," I said when I recognized our old yearbook covers. "Are those what I think they are?"

"Go Eagles." Grinning, he sat down next to me on the couch, so close that his thigh was pressed up against mine. As he leaned forward to set his beer down, I took the topmost yearbook from him and opened it across my lap.

"Wow. Look at that." Of course, the page I'd opened it to happened to be the band photo. I bent my head, squinting at the rows of familiar faces from our past.

"There I am." Donal leaned in and pointed. His chest pressed against my arm, and his hair grazed my cheek as his finger moved across the page. "And there you are."

It was like looking at a stranger. I still felt young inside my head—like a youthful twentysomething trapped in the body of a forty-eight-year-old. But staring at this seventeen-year-old version of myself, I could feel every single second of the years that had passed.

Donal flipped to the next page, and I was confronted by a photo of the two of us. We were sitting side by side on the floor of a classroom with notebooks propped on our legs—studying for Academic Decathlon according to the caption. Donal was grinning up at whichever one of our friends on the yearbook staff had taken the picture, while I appeared irritated by the interruption.

"God," he murmured. "Were we ever that young?"

"I can't believe I thought that spiral perm was a good idea."

"I thought it was cute." He pressed his fingers to the page, flattening the spine for a better look as he let out a wistful sigh. "I miss having that much hair."

I swiveled my head to study him. "You've still got plenty of hair." It was a little thinner on top, and his hairline might have risen a centimeter or two, but compared to most men he was doing extraordinarily well for his age.

His mouth twisted into a grimace. "You wouldn't believe how much I'm spending on Rogaine and hair pills to delay the inevitable, but every year I lose more of the battlefield."

"I use Botox," I confessed as I flipped to the next page.

"Really?" He sounded surprised, and I felt the sweep of his eyes over my face like a physical touch.

"With my resting bitch face?" I tried to sound flippant, hoping he wouldn't notice how much his scrutiny affected me. "I'd be able to hold a pencil in my forehead wrinkles by now if I didn't."

He didn't laugh. "She has your eyes, you know."

"What?" The abrupt subject change threw me.

"Erin. You said she was my clone, but she has your eyes. They're the exact same color."

"Really?" I hadn't even noticed Erin's eye color. She looked so much like Donal in every other respect, I'd assumed her eyes were blue like his.

He touched his fingertips to my chin, swiveling my face toward his. "Brown with subtle depths of green and gold at the center. I've never seen anyone else with eyes quite like yours. Until today."

I swallowed as he studied my face. His words, his touch, and his soft, thoughtful expression made me feel unmoored and off-balance. Pulling out of his grasp, I directed my attention back to the yearbook in my lap and tried to ignore the way my skin felt feverish where his fingers had touched me.

"Oh, wow," I breathed as I flipped the page to our senior class superlatives.

Best Looking, Most Athletic, Cutest Couple. And there in the middle of the page was another photo of me with Donal, his arm slung casually around my shoulders, under a banner that read *Most Likely to Succeed.*

"Huh." He propped his arm on the couch behind me as he bent closer. "I forgot all about that."

I inhaled a shaky breath at the sensation of being surrounded by him. His arm was at my back, his chest pressed against my shoulder, his lightly stubbled cheek mere inches from mine. The problem wasn't that it made me uncomfortable being this close to him. It was that it felt *too* comfortable.

Physical affection rarely came naturally to me. My parents had been loving, but not demonstrative. They'd showed how much they cared with their thoughtful gestures and steadfast support rather than hugs and kisses and verbal *I love you*s.

Outside of explicitly sexual contact, I shied away from unnecessary touching. I only hugged friends when failing to do so risked hurting their feelings, and I'd never been into holding hands or cuddling with boyfriends.

And yet, the warm solidity of Donal pressing against me felt like heaven. Inexplicably, my instinct was to lean *toward* him rather than away. Something about his physical presence felt natural enough to make me crave more.

It was unnerving. And nearly overpowering.

Retreating like a spooked deer, I plucked my beer off the table while I tried to get a handle on my confused thoughts, which were shouting bizarre, imprudent instructions like *Snuggle him!* and *Press your face into his neck so you can snort him like a scratch 'n' sniff sticker!*

I tried to remember the last time a man had gotten to me this much and came up blank. What was it about Donal Larkin that his mere proximity still had the power to turn me from a levelheaded adult into a dizzy, twitterpated teenager?

Seemingly oblivious to my plight—thank all the powers that be—he rescued the teetering yearbook from my lap and leaned back against the couch with it. While I gulped down a reckless amount of the strong beer meant for sipping, he stared at the yearbook he'd propped on his legs.

"They should have voted for Dave Pang instead of me. That tech company he started is valued at like five hundred million now." Donal aimed a glance at me, his forehead creasing. "I just realized, I don't even know what you do for a living."

"Product marketing. I started up my own consulting business a few years ago." I smiled faintly as I picked at the label on my beer. "I've actually done some contract work for Dave Pang's company."

"Your own business?" His mouth quirked faintly. "I'll bet your employees are terrified of you."

"I'm sure they would be if I had any, but it's only a one-woman shop." I leaned back on the couch and propped my socked feet on the coffee table next to his. "Going out on my own was more about practicality than ambition. After my dad's Alzheimer's diagnosis, I needed more flexible hours so I could help my parents out more."

"How long ago was that?"

"Seven years." Out of the corner of my eye, I saw his head swivel toward me.

"How's he doing?" Donal asked quietly. "Really?"

I stared straight ahead, fighting to keep the emotion out of my voice as I spoke. "Physically, he's still pretty strong, although he has difficulty walking so he uses a wheelchair. Mentally, he's not really there anymore. When I visit him, he doesn't even look at me and rarely speaks. It's been a long time since he recognized me."

Donal didn't say anything, but his hand closed over mine where it rested between us on the couch.

The back of my throat burned, and I swallowed thickly. "I haven't talked about it with anyone since Sherry died."

I wasn't sure why I'd admitted that. My personality didn't naturally invite close friendships or emotional intimacy, so I wasn't exactly teeming with bosom buddies. Marie was probably the closest friend I had at this point, and we weren't all that close. As kind as she was, I doubted she considered me part of her inner circle of friends.

I never used to feel lonely—I'd always been happy on my own. But since my stepmother's death, I'd become more aware of how solitary my existence was. Sherry and my dad used to be the people I turned to when I needed companionship or help. Not having them as a support system anymore meant I didn't have a support system at all. I didn't even have anyone to put down as an emergency contact these days. How sad was that?

I really *was* alone now.

"You don't have to talk about it if it's painful," Donal said gently. "I didn't mean to upset you."

"It's okay." I turned my hand over and interlaced my fingers with his, struck anew by how natural it felt. "My dad doesn't even know Sherry's dead. His mind was already too far gone by the time we lost her. He used to ask for her all the time, but he doesn't even do that anymore. I can't imagine what it's like for him. He must be so scared. He has no idea where she is or why he's surrounded by strangers. He must think she's abandoned him."

Donal held my hand even tighter. "What happened to her?"

"Pneumonia. But really I think she died of a broken heart." I took a deep breath, feeling the loss of her like a physical pain. "She insisted on keeping Dad at home with her for as long as possible—much longer than she should have, probably. It was hard on her, physically and emotionally. Once she finally admitted she couldn't take care of him anymore and we moved him into a residential facility, she seemed to give up. It was as if her life wasn't worth living if they couldn't be together. Three months later she was gone."

"Imagine loving someone that much." Donal's gaze was caught on our hands as his fingers stroked mine.

"I suppose it's beautiful, in a way. A beautiful tragedy."

"They were lucky. Endings are always painful, but all the years they had together —all the love—most people never get to experience anything like that."

It hadn't occurred to me to think of them as lucky, but Donal was right. How many people managed to find a love strong enough to last to the end of their life? I'd pretty much accepted I'd never have anything like that. Even Donal was divorced now and living alone. He might still find it with someone new, the way my dad had with Sherry, but then again he might not.

My parents *were* lucky to have found each other and stayed together for as long as they did. There was comfort in focusing on the blessings they'd had instead of the pain of what they'd lost.

"You're the one it must be hardest on." Donal's voice was soft and sympathetic. "You've lost your only family."

"I'm fine." Hot pressure filled my sinuses, and despite my best efforts my voice betrayed a slight wobble. Slipping my hand out of his, I sat up and reached for his beer, helping myself to more of the numbing liquid.

Behind me, Donal stayed silent, likely sensing I needed a minute to pull myself together.

My gaze traveled over his living room. It was expensively furnished but sparsely decorated. Other than a few framed photos of his kids, there was very little that felt personal about it. A giant flat-screen TV dominated the wall across from the sofa where we sat, and my attention snagged on the collection of cords and electronics sitting out on the console below it.

"Are those game controllers?" In a million years, I wouldn't have taken Donal for a gamer.

Sitting up, he reclaimed his beer from me and took a drink. "It's for my son."

Right, he had teenagers who probably stayed here sometimes. That made sense.

Except…other than the game system, it didn't look like an apartment frequently inhabited by teenagers. It didn't look like an apartment that was inhabited much at all.

"I'm telling my kids about Erin on Monday." Something in his voice made me turn and look at him. Instead of meeting my eyes, he took another swig of beer.

"How do you think they'll take the news?"

He wiped his mouth with the back of his hand. "I haven't got a clue. I'm pretty nervous about it, actually."

"Do your kids come stay with you often?"

"Not as much as I'd like." Lines of sadness etched his face as he stared at the game console across the room. "They're at that age where they've both got a lot going on. Between school and extracurriculars and everything, it doesn't really work out for them to stay over much. I try to take them out to dinner once a week, but it's not the same."

"You miss them."

Donal took another drink of beer before offering me the bottle again. When I shook my head, he tipped it back one more time before setting it on the table. "I started playing Final Fantasy XIV as a way to spend more time with Jack. It's his favorite game, and you can play it with other people online, so I figured it would help me stay part of his life."

It was unbearably sweet—and exactly the kind of thing my own father would have done. The thought brought a fresh pang of sadness, but I shoved it back down. "And has it?"

"Yeah, actually." He slumped back against the couch again. "I'm crap at it, but he's nice enough to let me tag along with him and his friends sometimes. Teenagers are different around their friends than they are with their parents— more talkative and less guarded—so it's been nice to see him in that element. I know more about what's going on with him now than I ever did when we lived in the same house."

I twisted to face him, pulling one leg underneath me and propping my arm on the back of the couch. "What about your daughter?"

Donal's gaze dropped to his lap, where he was rubbing his thumb across the palm of his hand. "She's been harder to connect with. I wish I could find something like video games that would give me a way into her life, but Maddy's a tough nut to crack."

He fell into a pensive silence, and I waited to see if he'd say more. After a moment he did.

"When she was little, I was Maddy's favorite person in the whole world. Wendy used to complain about how unfair it was that I was the favorite parent when she spent so much more time with the kids than I did, taking care of their every need. I was a junior associate at my firm, expected to work seventy- or eighty-hour weeks, so I wasn't around for the kids as much as she was."

Having spent much of my life cast into similarly thankless roles, I felt a bone-deep swell of empathy for Donal's wife. Being the one who did most of the work without getting the glory was pretty much my personal brand.

"As soon as I walked in the door, Maddy would always come running to greet me." A smile curved Donal's lips at the memory. "She'd glue herself to my side, chattering nonstop about everything that had happened to her that day. If I was home, I was the only one she wanted to give her a bath, read her bedtime stories, and tuck her in at night. I used to feel like the center of her universe."

Listening to Donal talk about his daughter's early years was like getting a glimpse into an alternate reality. It wasn't a huge stretch to imagine things would have played out similarly if we'd tried to raise Erin together.

Donal would have been the fun parent who wasn't around enough, and I would have been the one who shouldered all the thankless responsibilities and eventually grew to resent him over it. I couldn't just picture it, I could *feel* it—exactly what we would have been like in a parallel universe where we'd tried to stay together.

"Maddy used to look at me like I walked on water." Donal's smile faded into an expression of such sorrow it brought a lump to my throat. "And I squandered all that affection by taking it for granted. It happened so gradually, I don't know exactly when everything changed—maybe around the same time she hit puberty. Maddy became more withdrawn and didn't want to talk to me anymore. Getting her to tell me about her day was like deposing a hostile witness. I thought it was simply teenage moodiness at first, but she grew closer to Wendy as she pulled away from me."

My hand itched to reach for his as I watched his eyes grow sadder and more faraway. But something held me back. I hadn't fully embraced the hand-holding life yet. I wasn't ready to be the initiator.

Donal cleared his throat before continuing. "It was only after Wendy and I split up that I understood the source of Maddy's resentment and how much of it had built up. Every night I hadn't come home until after she'd gone to bed, every weekend I'd worked through, every missed school function and special event—every disappointment had caused her to retreat farther from me and put up walls between us so I couldn't let her down anymore."

I rubbed my chest, brokenhearted for both of them. Having felt the sting of Donal's neglect a time or two myself, you'd think my sympathies would lie wholly with Maddy. But the pain I saw in his face stirred a possessive tenderness in me. Donal's remorse was so palpable my bones ached with it. Yes, he'd made mistakes, and he was paying for them now. But at least he was taking responsibility and trying to make amends.

He stared straight ahead, his eyes remote and unseeing. "Maddy blames me for the divorce even though Wendy was the one who asked for it. She was old enough to see how I made her mother so unhappy for so many years that I drove her to it. And she's right. It was my fault for being such a terrible husband and father, for being so absent and self-involved that I didn't even notice I was losing my family until they were gone." His throat moved as he swallowed, and his eyes shifted toward me without quite meeting mine as his voice turned harsh. "At least you can feel good knowing you were right about me all along."

The cold reproach in his tone struck a nerve. All the old hurts still hovered right under the surface, ready to bubble up at the slightest provocation, and my defensive retort slipped out before I could think better of it. "You must think I'm a real cunt if you think anything you've just said would make me feel good."

He flinched, and his face crumpled with regret. "I'm sorry. I didn't mean it like that. I don't think anything of the sort. I only meant you and Erin were better off without me."

I did reach out for him then, surprising myself when my hand darted out to touch his chest. "I don't think that's true either."

His eyes held mine hostage, his expression so torn open and vulnerable that I grew self-conscious and started to pull my hand back from his chest—but his fingers caught mine before they could retreat.

My throat tightened with an emotion I was scared to name. Barely six inches separated our faces, and I was acutely conscious of every square millimeter of surface area where his skin touched my skin, the contrasting areas of warm softness and rough calluses, and the shivery sensations zipping up my arm.

Holding my palm against his heart, he offered me a ghost of a smile. "Thank you."

I tried to swallow, but my mouth had gone dry. "For what?"

"For listening." He stroked my fingers before loosening his hold on me.

I took a steadying breath as I brought my hand back to my lap. It was still tingling from his touch, and I squeezed it into a fist, trying to chase away the phantom feelings as I refocused on the matter at hand. "You'll win your way back into Maddy's affections. It just might take some time."

Donal's head dipped forward until his chin hit his chest. "I hope so. I can't lose her."

"What about your wife?" I asked, perhaps unwisely. "Have you thought about trying to win her back?" If things could be fixed with Maddy, maybe they could be fixed with his ex-wife as well. If he was willing to put in the work and honestly trying to change, he might be able to put his whole family back together.

His expression shifted from sadness to resignation. "It's way too late for that," he said with apparent matter-of-factness. "Wendy's moved on, as she should. She's with someone else now, and I'm happy for her."

I studied him, trying to discern if he was telling the truth or saying what he wanted the truth to be.

Propping his arm on the back of the couch, he leaned his head against his hand and met my gaze openly. "You know what I felt when I found out about her new boyfriend? Nothing at all. That's how far past its expiration date our marriage was. The kids were the only thing holding us together—that and force of habit, I guess."

As far as I could tell, he meant what he was saying. I shouldn't have been pleased about that, but hearing he wasn't hung up on his ex gave me an excited flutter I wasn't proud of.

"That's pretty fucking sad, isn't it?"

"It is sad," I agreed. "But I don't think it's that uncommon." I knew several people whose marriages had devolved into a similar state of apathy. It made me feel better about remaining single. Sure, I might feel lonely occasionally, but was

I any lonelier than someone trapped in a loveless marriage? At least I hadn't structured my whole life around someone I no longer had feelings for.

Donal dragged his fingers through his hair before resting his head against his hand again. "There was a time I was convinced Wendy was the love of my life. But when I try to reach for that feeling now it's just...not there anymore. I still care about her—she's the mother of my children and I want good things for her, but..." He trailed off with a shrug.

At least he'd felt that kind of love for a while, even if it hadn't lasted. Looking back over my own romantic history, which included a few short-lived infatuations and two failed attempts at more serious relationships, there'd never been anyone I felt inspired to declare "the love of my life."

I couldn't even say with confidence that I'd ever loved anyone outside of my family. I'd never even experienced the sort of platonic best-friend love so many people seemed to find. I'd had friends, some closer than others, but none so close they'd been indispensable. They'd either remained casual, friendly acquaintances —like Marie—or drifted away over time.

Was the dearth of love in my life the result of bad luck? Or a sign there was something wrong with me? Did I drive people away before they could love me? Or did I simply not feel things as deeply as other people?

Maybe my ex had been right when he called me cold and unfeeling. Maybe I was fundamentally incapable of giving my heart to another person or letting anyone into mine.

Donal gently tapped my temple, bringing me back to the present. "What's going on in there? You've got that frown you always get when you're thinking hard about something."

I ducked my head, not wanting him to guess where my thoughts had taken me. "It's nothing. That's probably just a side effect of the Botox."

"Liar." He touched a fingertip to the underside of my chin, tipping my face toward his again.

My pulse thudded under his shrewd examination, but I was too transfixed by his blue eyes to turn away. They were so beautiful. They always had been. Mesmerizingly so.

The corner of his mouth twitched as he finally dropped his hand. "Should I be scared? Are you plotting my demise or someone else's?"

"Neither." I chewed on my lower lip, trying to figure out how to ask what I wanted to know. "I was just wondering…"

"Yes?" he prompted when I fell silent again.

"The way you feel about Erin—how does it compare to the way you feel about your other kids?"

He raised his eyebrows. "Wow. You're really bringing the heavy questions tonight."

"You're the one who asked what I was thinking."

"You're right. I should know better." His mouth twitched again, almost but not quite a smile. "Tell me why you want to know, and I'll tell you my answer."

I shook my head, losing my nerve. This wasn't a conversation I wanted to have after all. "Never mind. Forget I said anything."

"Hey." His hand smoothed down my arm. "Talk to me. Tell me what's on your mind." When he reached my wrist, he placed his palm against mine and laced our fingers together.

I stared at our linked hands, unable to meet his eyes. "You obviously love your children, and I was wondering if that was a feeling that built slowly over time, or if it was something you felt right away. Was it learned, or was it an immediate biological response?"

He took a long time to answer, giving it serious thought. "It's different with Erin than it was with Maddy and Jack. Infants are so helpless, I think there is something instinctive that kicks in. The first time they place that tiny wriggling creature in your arms, it triggers a biological imperative to protect it."

"I read once that babies release a pheromone that creates a dopamine response in our brains. That's why people think they smell good." Although personally, I'd never felt babies smelled all that good. Further proof that my human skills were defective, maybe.

"Can I ask…" Donal tugged on my hand to draw my eyes to him. "Did you get to hold Erin when she was born?"

"They wouldn't let me." I could remember craning my head to try and get a look at her, but I'd only caught a brief glimpse before they'd taken her to another room.

His fingers squeezed mine. "They didn't want you to get attached."

"So you're saying I missed my chance to form that bond?"

"No, because that's not the only way to form a bond with your child. Think about all the parents whose babies spend weeks in the NICU, or military fathers serving overseas when their children are born—not to mention adoptive parents."

"And stepparents," I said, thinking of Sherry, who'd loved me better than my own mother.

Donal nodded. "They all missed those first moments, but it doesn't stop them from forming that bond later."

"Like you missed it with Erin," I said, and watched his brow crease. "Do you love her now that you've met her?"

His frown deepened, and he blew out a long breath before speaking. "I don't know the answer to that question. She's a fully grown adult who's essentially a total stranger to me. So no, I don't feel the same way about her as I feel about Maddy and Jack."

"But you think you will, with time." It wasn't a question. I knew he would. It was obvious from the look that came into his eyes whenever he talked about her.

Searching my face, he reached up to tuck my hair behind my ear. "What are you worried about? That you won't love her as much as I do?"

"What if I can't?"

He ran his thumb over my cheek, so tenderly it made my heart stutter in my chest. "Of course you can."

"How do you know?"

A smile tugged at the corner of his mouth. "Because I know you. The way you were hassling me today to make sure I didn't miss my lunch with Erin, that was you looking out for her because you care. You're already feeling those protective instincts, just like I am."

"Is that all there is to it? Is that what love is?"

"It's one part of it. There are as many different ways to experience love as there are people in the world who deserve to be loved."

Silence stretched out between us as I turned his words over in my head, not sure what to make of them.

"Tess."

It did something to me, the way he said my name. I was used to hearing him say it in irritation, but there was no trace of irritation in his voice now. Only softness. Affection. Possibly even something deeper. It made me so disoriented I didn't know which way was up.

He held my gaze captive as his hand slipped into my hair, cupping the back of my neck. "I know you like everything filed into neat little boxes, but emotions are messy and complicated. Sometimes you just have to let yourself feel whatever you're feeling instead of trying to put a label on it." His eyes burned right through me as he paused. "Look at you and me."

My stomach tightened with a longing I shouldn't be feeling. "What about us?"

"You make me feel so many things I never thought—" He broke off, and I stopped breathing. "Tell me you're not feeling it too."

I couldn't. I was feeling so much, it was hard to make sense of anything. This was all too surreal and confusing. But despite the chaos inside me, one feeling stood out above all the others—the urge to press my mouth against Donal's.

He leaned fractionally closer, and I mirrored his movement, unable to resist the magnetic pull. We were close enough that I could count every one of his eyelashes.

When his gaze dropped to my lips, I drew in a shaky breath, caught in a dream-like state. The tightness in my stomach had grown into a low, urgent throb in my abdomen.

Donal's fingers squeezed the back of my neck as he leaned toward me. Reflexively, I moved to meet him. Our lips touched, hesitant and cautious. No more than the silky soft graze of a butterfly's wing.

My chest hitched as he drew back far enough to look into my eyes, seeking something. Permission, maybe. He seemed to be waiting to see if I'd push him away.

When I didn't, he angled his head. I caught a glimpse of a dimple before our mouths slid together. There was no hesitancy this time. Only urgent, warm pressure. My stomach fizzed with pleasure at the sensation, so rich and sweet and breathtakingly familiar. As if our lips remembered each other's shape after all this time.

I used to think about Donal's kisses a lot. I'd convinced myself I'd exaggerated their superiority, that it was just my mind romanticizing a youthful memory.

But no. I hadn't exaggerated a thing. It was every bit as wonderful as I remembered.

His tongue darted against mine, deftly teasing and exploring with the same confidence he'd had as a teenager. Drunk on the taste of him, I curled my fingers in the front of his shirt, tugging him closer as I opened wider. In response, his body curved around mine, the hand on the nape of my neck tightening possessively.

Shivers rippled down my spine as he kissed me harder and deeper. The world narrowed to the demanding crush of his lips, the greedy thrusts of our tongues, and our hot, panting breaths.

Somehow my hands had worked their way under his shirt, and I felt his muscles contract as my fingertips skated over bare skin. His own hands had gone wandering as well. He cupped my breast in one large palm as his other hand squeezed my hip, urging our bodies together.

I gasped in surprise when I felt myself being lifted, our mouths barely even parting as he maneuvered me onto his lap. Once I was straddling him, his hands grasped my hips, yanking me hard against him. We let out matching moans as my pelvis met his erection, and I couldn't stop myself from grinding against him, desperate for more friction.

But when I felt his fingers move to the clasp of my bra, the reality of what we were doing splashed over me like a bucket of ice water. Once the clothes started coming off, I knew we'd end up having sex, and the thought sent a spike of panic through me.

"Wait." I jerked back, struggling for breath as I pushed off his chest. "Stop."

Donal took his hands off me and held them up in a gesture of nonresistance. His chest heaved raggedly as he regarded me with hooded, hazy eyes. "What's wrong?"

I clambered off his lap and paced away from him, my stomach twisting itself into knots as I rubbed my forehead with the heels of my hands. "What are we doing?"

"I don't know what you were doing, but I was really enjoying kissing you."

I rounded on him, and whatever he saw in my expression wiped the smile off his face.

"Relax, okay? Just calm down." His placating tone had the opposite effect.

"This is a terrible idea. I can't believe I let you lure me into doing something so stupid."

"Hey!" Anger tinged his voice as he pushed off the couch. "I didn't do any luring. You were right there with me the whole time."

"This was a huge mistake." I couldn't believe I'd let myself fall right back into his orbit. How many times had this man broken my heart? No kiss on earth was worth going through that again.

He dragged a frustrated hand through his hair. "Tess, come on. It was just a kiss."

Just a kiss.

As if it meant nothing. As if anything between us could ever be that simple or consequence-free.

I stared at him in disbelief. He was the last person I should trust myself with. "I can't do this with you again."

He flinched but recovered quickly, taking a step toward me with his hands held out. "Okay, look—"

"I have to go." I turned my back on him and headed for the door, grabbing my purse on my way there.

"Fuck," I heard him mutter behind me. "Wait."

In an encore of our earlier argument, he scrambled to follow, arriving at the door right behind me. His hand flattened against the door beside my head before I could pull it open. I tensed, the scrabbling claws of panic in my chest increasing at not being able to escape.

"You forgot your shoes," he said flatly.

When I spun around, he held them up, his face set in hard lines of dissatisfaction.

"Thank you." Without meeting his eyes, I clutched them to my chest along with my purse. "Now let me go."

"Let me at least walk you home."

"That's not necessary." I'd been getting around the city by myself my entire adult life. I didn't need a man to escort me for protection. Especially not the man I desperately needed to get away from.

His eyes swept over my face, and I had the sense he was trying to decide if it was worth arguing the point further. I tipped my chin up, forcing myself to meet his gaze with a challenging glare.

"Fine." With a sigh of resignation, he removed his hand from the door and took a step back. "I won't stop you if you want to go."

I didn't hesitate. As soon as the path was clear I got the hell out of there.

CHAPTER ELEVEN

DONAL

Tess had been abso-fucking-lutely right about one thing. Last night had been a huge mistake.

What had I expected to happen when I kissed her? That she'd fall into my arms and we'd pick up where we left off thirty years ago?

Yeah, right. What kind of delusional fantasyland was I living in?

This was all so goddamn predictable. Tess had been an irresistible temptation back in high school, and that still hadn't changed. I was still throwing myself at her like a fool, knowing full well she could barely tolerate me. She was a bad habit I hadn't grown out of. Whenever I got around her, my good judgment went straight out the window. She'd always brought out the worst in me: my competitiveness, my impulsivity, my reckless disregard for common sense.

I didn't want to be that guy anymore. And I sure as fuck didn't need to be chasing after someone who'd never wanted me. That was some twisted, masochistic bullshit. I had enough problems without letting Tess's contempt for me get under my skin.

Like right now, for instance. I needed to keep my wits about me. Because I was about to face my Irish-Catholic mother and confess that I'd knocked a girl up in high school, kept it a secret for thirty years, and—surprise!—she had another granddaughter she'd never met.

This was not going to be a pleasant conversation.

But it was time. I was telling my kids about Erin tomorrow night at dinner. Which meant I needed to tell my mom too. And I needed to do it in person.

My mother still lived in the house I'd grown up in, a brick three-bedroom on a postage-stamp lot. Although she'd retired from her bookkeeping job a few years ago, she kept herself busy with gardening, volunteering, church activities, and generally being a busybody. My mother didn't simply know everyone in the neighborhood, she also knew their parents, all their grandchildren's names and birthdates, where they did their grocery shopping, and which church they attended. She was generous, industrious, saintly, and completely exhausting.

The front door flew open before I could ring the doorbell, and I quickly pasted a smile on my face. "Hi, Mom!"

"Hello, sweetheart." She gave me a sharp once-over before jerking her head to beckon me inside. "Nice of you to come see me. Even if I did have to miss the after-mass coffee to rush home and put the cookies in the oven."

Ah, yes. My mother's specialty: passive-aggressive guilt trips.

"I didn't mean for you to go to any trouble." I stepped over the threshold and bent to hug her, casting an uneasy look at the large crucifix hanging in the foyer. I'd lapsed years ago, a fact my mother had grudgingly made peace with, but I still felt a pang of Catholic guilt whenever I set foot in this house.

"It's not often my only son asks to come visit me, so of course I wanted to make your favorite treat." She kissed me on both cheeks before pulling back to stare into my eyes. "You look like you haven't been sleeping."

"I'm fine. You look stunning, as usual. Is that a new church dress?"

"I got it on clearance at Field's. Seventy-five percent off." Turning on her heel, she beckoned me to follow her through the house. "Come on, I'll put the kettle on."

"How've you been?" I asked as I trailed her to the kitchen.

"I'm fine." She set the kettle on the stove and waved a hand toward one of the cabinets. "Grab a plate for the cookies, would you?"

While I transferred warm butterscotch cookies from the baking sheet onto a flowered china plate, my mother kept up a steady stream of conversation, regaling me with the latest tales of her church friends' triumphs and tragedies as she bustled around gathering mugs, tea bags, milk, and sugar. In between sneaking bites of cookie whenever her back was turned, I made appropriately sympathetic or approving noises at her anecdotes.

When the tea was ready, we carried everything to the small oak kitchen table and sat down beneath the Belleek Irish blessing plate hanging on the wall next to a St. Brigid's cross my sister had made in CCD a million years ago.

My mom made the sign of the cross before fixing me with a penetrating stare. "Well? Now that I'm sitting down, you'd better tell me whatever it is that's brought you here. I'm assuming it's bad news. The kids are all right, aren't they?"

"Everyone's fine," I assured her. "It's not bad news."

She arched a skeptical eyebrow at me. "Then why do you look like you swallowed a bug?"

I rubbed my forehead, wincing. "Because I'm pretty sure you're going to get mad at me when I tell you the first part of the good news."

Her eyebrows jumped even higher as she blew across the top of her tea. "Out with it."

"Do you remember Tess McGregor? I was friends with her in high school."

She gave me an odd look. "Of course I remember Tess. Such a lovely, smart girl. You know her stepmother passed last year? Nice woman, God rest her soul. She made the most amazing lemon bars—I still have her recipe around here someplace. Tess's father has dementia, apparently. They had just put him in a nursing home when Mrs. McGregor passed." She clucked her tongue, shaking her head. "So sad."

How the hell my mom knew all that about Tess's family, I had no clue, but that was my mom for you. She kept up with my old high school friends better than I did.

"So the thing is…" I paused and cleared my throat. "Back in high school, Tess and I were a little more than friends for a while." My mom's eyes narrowed, and

I ducked my head, shifting uncomfortably under her gaze. But the only way out was through. Taking a breath, I hurried through the rest of it. "Our senior year, I got Tess pregnant, and she gave the baby up for adoption."

There was a long, dreadful silence. When I couldn't take it anymore, I dared a glance at my mother. She set her tea mug down slowly, then folded her hands on the table as she focused a grim-faced gaze on me. She'd come close to joining a convent when she was younger, and I'd always thought she would have made one hell of a scary-ass nun.

"Why didn't you tell me any of this before?" she demanded, her voice pitched unnaturally low.

I swallowed, my insides churning the way they always did when I'd earned her disapproval. "Tess didn't want me to. She didn't want anyone to know."

"You should have told me. I could have helped."

"She didn't want our help. She didn't want anything to do with me after she found out."

Her eyes widened. "Jesus, Mary, and Joseph, are you saying the poor girl went through all that alone? You weren't there for her at all?"

"She wouldn't let me be there for her." The weight of my own guilt, combined with my mother's disappointment, caused my voice to break. This was the part of the story I'd most dreaded fessing up to. Not the fact that I'd had sex, or that I'd been stupid enough to get a girl pregnant, or even that I'd kept it all a secret from my mom—although that stuff was all pretty fucking bad. The thing I was most ashamed of was that I hadn't taken any responsibility for my own mistake. I'd let Tess carry the burden alone.

My mother's expression softened, and she reached across the table to give my hand a squeeze. "All right. What's done is done. Drink your tea."

I nodded glumly and did as I was told.

She watched me in thoughtful silence. "Why are you telling me about this now?"

I swallowed and set my mug down before telling her the next part. "Tess signed up with one of those DNA testing companies, and they had this relative matching service and…well, our daughter found us."

My mom pressed her hand to her chest. "A daughter?"

This was the good part of the news, and I couldn't help smiling as I nodded. "Yeah."

"Have you talked to her yet?"

"I met her yesterday for the first time."

She crossed herself again, muttering a prayer under her breath. "What's she like? Tell me everything."

"Her name's Erin, and she's great. You're gonna love her."

"Erin." A smile lit my mom's face. "That's a beautiful Irish name. Is she Catholic?"

"I have no idea," I admitted with a twinge of guilt. I hadn't even thought to ask. It made no difference to me, but my mom would be over the moon to have a Catholic grandchild, since both my sister and I had married outside the faith.

My mom's mouth tightened fractionally—just enough to let me know my guilt wasn't misplaced. "No matter. And your Erin must be—what? Thirty now?"

"In a few more months. Her birthday's in October."

"Single? Married? Kids? What else can you tell me about her?"

"She's married. Her husband's a software engineer. And she's ten weeks pregnant with their first child."

I smiled as I watched my mom's whole face break open. "My first great-grandchild. How about that?" Already I could tell she was thinking ahead to baby showers, christenings, babysitting. It had been a while since any of her grandchildren had been babies.

"She's a science teacher," I continued. "Grew up in Deerfield. Two good parents, a nice home. She's an only child."

My mom raised her eyebrows. "Not anymore she's not. She's got a brother and sister now."

"Yeah." My smile returned.

"Have you told them yet?"

"I'm telling them tomorrow. They're coming over to my place for dinner so I can break the news. You might want to say a prayer for me because I'm probably gonna need it."

My mom eyed me as she sipped her tea. "Have you told Wendy?"

"No."

"Well, you'd better tell her before you tell the kids—unless you want them to blindside her with the news."

"You're right. I will." *Shit.* I hadn't even thought of that.

"How's Tess doing with all of this? I assume you two are back in touch?"

"Yeah. She's good." A memory resurfaced of last night's ill-advised make-out session, and I reached for another cookie.

Before I could take one, my mom yanked the plate out from under my hand. "Tess is single, isn't she?"

"Yeah," I mumbled like a ten-year-old being called to account for an unsatisfactory report card.

"Never married, as far as I know. No other children. No parents to lean on anymore, poor thing. This must all be quite an adjustment for her." My mom made a sympathetic tutting sound before skewering me with another one of her formidable glares. "I hope you're doing everything you can to support her now."

"I am."

"Hmm." Her eyes narrowed distrustfully.

"I swear. We even had dinner together last night after I saw Erin." We'd done a lot more than just have dinner, but I sure as hell wasn't telling my mom about that part.

"Good." She pushed the plate back toward me. "Have another cookie."

For the next hour, I sat there while my mom grilled me with questions about Erin —and Tess—all of which I answered to the best of my ability while eating way too many cookies. Some of Mom's interest in Tess was probably just natural curiosity. My mother collected information about people the same way she collected Precious Moments figurines and spoons from around the world. But I had a strong sense she was also testing me—quizzing me about Tess to make sure I was invested in doing the honorable thing this time.

The more I talked to my mother, the more ashamed I felt about my behavior last night. This morning I'd woken up seriously pissed off at Tess—her rejection and abrupt departure had reopened old wounds and done a real number on my self-esteem—but after one conversation with my mom, my guilt far outstripped my anger. The woman was a super-powered guilt-generating machine.

I never should have kissed Tess last night. Even if she'd been an enthusiastic participant—right up until she wasn't—I should have known better than to give in to my urges. Hadn't I been the one pushing for us to act like a team and try to get along better for Erin's sake? Sticking my tongue down Tess's throat was a surefire way to blow up any chance of us maintaining civil relations. Talk about self-sabotaging.

Eventually, my mom finally ran out of questions, and I was able to make my escape. She pressed a Tupperware of leftover cookies on me and saw me off with a stern reminder to call my ex-wife before tomorrow night.

Once I was back in my car, I took out my phone and stared at my contacts. I didn't especially feel like talking to my ex right this second. But I was headed into the office to try and get ahead of the curve so I could leave early to pick up the kids tomorrow. I knew if I didn't do it now, I'd get caught up in work and forget to call Wendy.

With a sigh, I started the car, switched my phone to hands-free, and called Wendy's number. "Hey," I said when she answered. "Do you have a minute to talk? I need to give you a heads-up about something I'm telling the kids tomorrow night."

CHAPTER TWELVE

TESS

My day was going fine until the limbo contest started up.

Actually, that was a lie. My concentration had been shot long before Chubby Checker started blasting in the break room down the hall.

Ever since I'd left Donal's apartment Saturday night, I'd been distracted and out of sorts. My stomach was so twisted up in knots, I'd been chugging Maalox like it was Gatorade. No matter how hard I tried to erase the entire episode from my brain, I kept fixating on tiny details: the rough tug of his lips, the desperate, ragged sound of his breathing, the eager, possessive way his hands had moved over my body.

Unfulfilled lust was a hell of a thing.

I'd barely slept the last two nights, although insomnia was hardly a rare occurrence for me. My mind had trouble turning itself off even under the best of circumstances, and I'd gotten used to tossing and turning until my body got tired enough to overrule my brain.

What I wasn't accustomed to was the relentless and ill-advised longing I'd been feeling the last two nights. I couldn't remember the last time a little bit of kissing had left me this preoccupied and horny. Although, in my defense, this was Donal we were talking about, the man who'd preoccupied my thoughts to an unhealthy degree since I was twelve years old. And it had been more than just a little bit of kissing. We'd been a few panting breaths away from banging each other's brains out.

God, what a terrifying thought.

But also? Dangerously tantalizing.

Nope. Nope. Nope. I refused to be ruled by my libido. Falling into bed with Donal was a recipe for disaster. Of that I was certain.

There was an undeniable attraction there—apparently on both sides—but I couldn't afford to give in to it. It would be too damned easy to fall under Donal's spell again. I'd always had a weakness where he was concerned. That smile of his, in those moments when it felt like he actually cared, turned my insides to gooey marshmallow fluff.

But if I let myself be taken in by his charms, I'd only wind up getting hurt.

My God, we were both on such a hair trigger around each other, we couldn't even go an hour without arguing. It would only be a matter of time before things between us went south. Once the orgasm high had worn off, we'd be at each other's throats—and not in a sexy way, but in an angry, hurtful, destructive way.

That wasn't something I could allow to happen right now. Not with Erin in the picture. Donal and I needed to maintain civil relations for her sake. He'd been right about that much. Adding sex to the equation would only make everything worse.

This attraction I was feeling to Donal wasn't real. It was the past spilling over into the present. A combination of nostalgia and old unresolved feelings and an instinctive reaching out for comfort.

I was lonely, that was all. But Donal Larkin wasn't the solution to my loneliness. He might seem like an appealing option—he was always appealing, that was his superpower—but it would be dangerous to put much faith in him or his feelings for me.

It was good that I'd put an end to it before things went too far to turn back. Assuming they hadn't already. I'd need to talk to Donal and try to smooth things over. The thought of it made me cringe, but I knew he was unhappy about the way I'd left on Saturday.

I'd had no choice. If I'd stayed even a minute longer, I would have given in to temptation and thrown myself at him, consequences be damned.

A tap on my office door dragged me away from my thoughts, and I looked up to find Marie waving at me through the glass. I beckoned for her to come in, and a blast of Harry Belafonte entered the room with her.

In an attempt to compete with the glut of newer, trendier coworking spaces cropping up around the city, our quiet little co-op had upped its game by adding sponsored "networking" events, most of which seemed to have been planned by a frat house social chair.

The music quieted to a muffled hum as Marie shut the door behind her. "Not quite as soundproof as they advertise, are they?"

"What's the occasion today?"

"Flavored rum shots." She flashed a grin as she hooked a thumb over her shoulder. "Want me to get you one?"

"At twelve thirty on a weekday? I'll pass."

"I'm not interrupting, am I?"

"God no. I wasn't getting anything done anyway." I waved at the chairs across from the desk in my tiny solo office. "Welcome back. How was your trip?" She'd been out of town all last week, doing research for a story she was working on.

"Productive. I've got piles of notes and interviews to transcribe, which is why I'm prowling the halls in search of a distraction."

"I hear there's a limbo contest you could join."

"Ha! You're hilarious." Her expression grew more serious. "So did you have your first meeting with Erin? How did it go? I was thinking about you all last week."

Since my breakdown in the break room, Marie had been checking in on me regularly. I wasn't used to sharing so much of my personal life with a colleague. Laughing over online dating escapades was one thing, but I'd never spoken to anyone other than my parents about the baby I'd given up.

Having that panic attack in front of Marie had punched a big fat hole through my privacy barriers, and I'd actually found myself grateful for it. Marie was a good listener, and it had been helpful to have someone to talk to besides Donal, who posed his own set of problems.

I filled Marie in on all the highlights of my first meeting with Erin, telling her what I'd learned about Erin's childhood and that she was pregnant with her first child. But I refrained from any mention of Donal or the kissing incident that had sent me into a tailspin.

"She sounds lovely," Marie said. "I'm so happy for you. It seems like it's all going really well."

"It is," I confirmed. "And she is."

Marie's blue eyes narrowed, her reporter senses pricking up. "Then why am I sensing hesitation? Is something troubling you?"

I shook my head, forcing my smile wider. "No, not really. It's all just been a lot to process."

"I can understand that." She continued to study me. "What about the birth father? You haven't mentioned him much. How's it been, interacting with him again?"

Freaking journalists and their finely honed instincts. I shook my head as I floundered for words to sum up our interactions. "Complicated. Confusing. Messy."

Marie nodded sagely. "Do you want to talk about it?"

When I searched my feelings, it surprised me to find that I did. Opening up to Marie about Erin had helped me process my feelings, and I suspected talking to her about Donal would have a similar effect.

Making friends had never been easy for me, and I'd only grown more closed off with age. In part, because I'd learned through experience that I needed to smooth off some of my sharper edges if I wanted people to like me. I'd gotten into a habit of holding back rather than sharing what I was thinking and feeling.

But also, I simply hadn't made friendship a priority. For years I'd been trolling dating apps and forcing myself to go on dates in my perpetual quest for romantic or sexual companionship. But I hadn't made an equal effort to find or maintain friendships, which were equally as important—perhaps even more so. Instead of wasting my time looking for romance, maybe I should be working harder to build friendships.

"Would you like to go out to lunch?" I asked Marie spontaneously.

"I wish I could," she said, looking genuinely disappointed. "But I've got a conference call in twenty minutes." Her expression brightened. "You know what though? Why don't you come over for dinner tonight? If you're free, that is."

"I'd love that," I answered honestly. "As long as it's no trouble."

"No, it'll be fun. I'll throw some curry in the pressure cooker when I get home. Matt will be thrilled."

CHAPTER THIRTEEN

TESS

Marie's husband opened the door when I arrived at their apartment. "You're Tess," he said, giving me a perfunctory appraisal. "Marie's friend from the office co-op."

"You must be Matt." I'd seen his photo on Marie's desk, but I'd never met him before.

"Correct. I'm Marie's husband." He wore jeans and a dark red T-shirt emblazoned with the word *Rocinante* above a diagram of a spaceship. His clothes, combined with his rumpled hair, gave him a boyish appearance despite his strong, square jaw.

"Nice to meet you." I extended my hand. "Thank you for having me to your home."

He shrugged as he accepted my handshake. "I don't mind that you're here because it means Marie made coconut curry."

She'd already warned me about Matt's penchant for unfettered honesty, so I took the comment in stride. "I take it you're a fan of *The Expanse*," I said with a nod at his T-shirt.

"Do you like *The Expanse*?" he asked, focusing on me with increased interest.

"I'm only up to the third season," I warned him. "So no spoilers."

Marie appeared at Matt's side and pulled me into a hug. "Welcome. Come in."

The apartment they shared was even smaller than mine, but it had a comfortable, homey feel to it and a delicious smell that I assumed was the curry. I handed Marie the wine I'd brought and followed her through to the kitchen. She took out a corkscrew and opened the bottle while Matt got down three glasses.

"Are you staying to hang out with us?" Marie asked, flashing a teasing smile at him. "I thought you might hide in the bedroom to avoid the girl talk."

"I'm staying for the coconut curry." He stooped to peer at the display on the pressure cooker. "It's ready. Should we eat?"

Marie rolled her eyes as she handed me my wine. "The man is cuckoo for coconut."

I suppressed a smile, amused by their banter. "This is a great apartment."

"Thank you." Marie opened the pressure cooker, releasing a cloud of heavenly smelling steam, and glanced around the small galley kitchen with a grimace. "It's really too small for us, but Matt loves it for some reason."

"It's comfortable," he said, getting down bowls.

"Comfortable's a stretch. It's *barely* big enough for two, and it'll definitely be too small if we have kids."

"When," Matt corrected, smiling at her. "*When* we have kids."

"We'll see." Marie patted his arm fondly as she stirred the curry.

Matt's gaze wandered to me. "Do you have kids, Tess?"

I sensed he was hoping to find an ally, but I wasn't in a position to be much help in that regard. "I'm actually not sure how to answer that question anymore."

He frowned at my response, not so much unhappy as intrigued. "Explain."

"Is it all right to tell him?" Marie asked me as she took the naan from the oven.

"Be my guest." I'd assumed she already had. And if Erin was going to be a part of my life, I'd need to get used to people knowing the peculiar circumstances of our relationship.

While we took turns dishing up our own servings of rice and curry, Marie filled Matt in on my situation, with me jumping in to add details here and there. By the time we'd finished telling him all of it, we were seated around their small kitchen table.

Matt gave me an approving nod at the end of the story, gazing at me with something that looked like respect. "You did the right thing. You would have made terrible parents under those circumstances."

Marie cut a frown at him. "Matt."

"Am I being insensitive?" He blinked innocently at his wife, but the smile on his lips was unapologetically sassy. "Should I lie and pretend that two teenagers who were practically children themselves and had given up their college dreams to provide for a baby they never wanted would have been terrific parents? Would that be more appropriate?"

"You'll have to excuse him," Marie said to me. "His perspective on this particular subject is clouded by personal experience."

"It's all right." I assured them, feeling a kinship with Matt and his bluntness. "I felt the same way—that's why I chose to give the baby up."

Matt lifted his chin, addressing Marie. "Relevant, firsthand experience isn't a cloud. It's a hot sunny day spent on top of a mountain, in Denver, where you can see for miles."

She gave him an affectionate smile. "Anecdotal experience specific to you that's not necessarily representative of everyone else's experience."

"Were you adopted?" I asked Matt.

"No, I was an accident whose parents didn't want me, and I can tell you that no child is better off growing up like that." He said it in a very matter-of-fact way, yet I guessed from his strong feelings on the subject that it must have affected him deeply.

"It happens I was an accident too. My parents felt obligated to get married, but my mother was miserable. She left when I was ten."

His eyes met mine with a look of understanding. "There you go."

Marie shook her head as she reached for her wine. "All I'm saying is you can't claim to know what the right decision is for everyone. Every situation is different, every person is different, and there's no universal right or wrong choice."

"Sure there is," Matt said. "The right choice is the one that allows children to grow up feeling wanted. If you don't want to be a parent, it's better to let your child be raised by someone who does."

"It'd be nice if it could always be that simple, but it's not." Marie reached across the table and squeezed his hand. "You know from your work with foster children that surrendering a child doesn't always lead to a happy outcome."

"That was the hardest part," I said. "When I gave my baby up, I had no idea where she'd be going or what kind of life she'd have. Even in open adoptions there are no guarantees, because you can never really know what kind of parents people will turn out to be. I've spent every day since Erin was born worried I'd made the wrong choice."

Marie's eyes were compassionate as she nodded at me. "The sad reality is that lots of children whose parents wanted them still have negative experiences in childhood. Wanting to be a parent doesn't necessarily make you a good one."

I lowered my gaze to the table before making the same confession I'd made to Erin. "I wanted to believe I was doing what was best for the baby, but I've always been afraid my choice was actually motivated by selfishness—that I really did it because I was unwilling to put my whole life on hold to raise a child."

"The fact that you were so worried about it tells me you weren't being selfish," Matt countered softly.

"Does it?" Given his propensity for candor, I doubted he was saying it to be nice, but I still found it a difficult statement to accept.

"Was it hard to give your daughter up after you'd carried her for nine months?" His expression was openly curious.

"Yes. Very hard."

Matt nodded as if I'd proven him right. "But you did it anyway, because you believed it was the right thing to do, so it was in your situation."

"Thank you for saying that."

He shrugged off my gratitude. "If it makes you feel better, data that contributes to improved outcomes—correlational, not causational—tells us adopted children are less likely than children in the general population to live in households with incomes below the poverty threshold. They're more likely to live with two married parents and more likely to have health insurance. They're also more likely to be read to, sung to, or told stories every day as young children."

"That actually does make me feel better." I smiled at him. "Marie mentioned you work with foster children?"

He shook his head as he got up for another helping of curry. "I work in artificial intelligence."

"Matt's developing a compassionate AI to provide emotional support and stability to foster children," Marie explained, directing a proud look at her husband.

"You mean a robot companion?" I asked. "Like Baymax in *Big Hero 6*?"

"Sort of," Matt said, smiling at me. "Sort of—hopefully—exactly like that."

The rest of the meal was spent talking about Matt's work, a subject I found fascinating, especially in light of his own upbringing. After we'd all eaten our fill, Matt volunteered to handle the cleanup, leaving Marie and me to move into the living room with our wine.

As I settled onto the love seat, I noticed a bundle of knitting sitting on the table beside me. "Are you a knitter?"

"I sure am." Reaching across me, Marie scooped it off the table and laid it out between us. "Are you?"

"No. I used to know how, but I haven't done it in years." My eyebrows lifted as I ran my fingers over the edge of Marie's knitting. "A baby sweater?"

"It's for a friend's baby. I'm racing against the clock to finish it before she outgrows it."

"It's lovely." I glanced up at Marie. "Do you not want to have kids?"

She took a sip of wine, looking troubled. "I don't know, honestly."

"Matt sounds awfully enthusiastic about it."

"He is now, but when we first met he felt pretty strongly that he never wanted to have children." One of her shoulders lifted as she tilted her head. "Of course, he also told me he didn't want to fall in love or be in a relationship, and look how that turned out."

"But now you're not sure if you want kids?"

Her gaze dropped to the tiny sweater between us. "I think I'm more leery of it after watching some of my close friends settle down and start families. Seeing the ways parenthood has changed them—and changed the whole fabric of their lives and their marriages—has given me pause. Not that the changes are bad, necessarily, but they're big. I'm not saying never, I'm just saying I want to pause and reflect, make sure I'll be a good parent rather than just assuming I will be. A whole human person is a big responsibility. I want to give the decision the consideration it deserves." She shrugged.

"Will Matt be okay with it if you don't change your mind?"

She smiled as her eyes drifted toward the kitchen where Matt was doing the dishes. "I know he comes across as pushy, but he's really not. He's just not shy about saying what he wants, which is one of the things I love about him. But he'd never try to pressure me into it. He simply enjoys reminding me where he stands on the subject."

My gaze went to Marie's knitting again. I couldn't seem to stop touching the neat rows of soft, perfect stitches.

"Maybe you should give knitting another try," she suggested. "I always find it therapeutic, especially when I'm stressed or have something on my mind. Keeping my hands busy with a repetitive task helps induce a state of calm reflection."

"Maybe I will." Calm reflection definitely sounded like something I could use in my life right now, what with everything else going on.

"There's this great yarn store called Mad About Ewe that's on East Randolph not far from the office."

"I've heard of it," I said. "I went to high school with the owner, actually."

"Speaking of high school…" Marie leaned closer, propping her arm on the back of the sofa. "What's going on with Erin's birth father? Spill."

"Um…well." An odd sensation formed in my stomach at the mention of Donal, and I gulped down a mouthful of wine. "We've gotten together a few times to talk. About Erin, but also about the past—about the way things ended with us. To find some closure, I guess. We're trying to put it behind us and be friends. For Erin's sake."

"That sounds very mature and sensible. How's it going so far? I seem to recall the word you used earlier was messy?"

"And complicated. And confusing. One minute we're both spoiling for a fight, and the next we're falling back into old habits."

Marie's eyebrows shot up. "When you say old habits, do you mean…?"

"Nearly." I took another large drink of wine. "He kissed me the other night."

"Interesting."

I snorted. "Interesting like an unexploded land mine. Have you ever been attracted to someone you find completely infuriating?"

A smile curved Marie's lips as her gaze jumped back to Matt in the kitchen. "I think I can relate."

"Except Donal and I aren't perfect for each other the way you and Matt are."

Marie laughed. "One day I'll tell you the story of how Matt and I met. Trust me, no one would have called us perfect for each other. And yet, somehow, we figured out a way to make it work." Her eyes lit up in delight and she smacked me on the leg. "Maybe it'll be like *The Parent Trap*, and Erin will bring you two back together!"

I smiled wryly as I shook my head. "Yeah, no. Somehow I don't think that's in the cards for us."

Her expression grew serious again. "Did you love him? Back in high school before everything else happened?"

"It doesn't matter. He didn't love me."

"It does matter, because hearts are bastards, always looking for a window." She shook her head, smiling when I stared at her in confusion. "It's just something my friend Dan once said. Answer my question. Did you love this guy?"

"I'm not even sure I'd know what love feels like now, and I definitely didn't when I was eighteen." I'd felt *something* for Donal back then. Something special that I hadn't felt since and was quite possibly starting to feel again. But was it love? Friendship? Or merely some kind of weird, uncontrollable chemistry?

"Maybe you need to find out," Marie said.

"What do you mean?"

"Give him a chance. See what happens." She smiled, her eyes drifting back to Matt again. "Don't close any doors or windows until you figure out what it is you want."

CHAPTER FOURTEEN

DONAL

One of the changes I'd made since the divorce was a commitment to keeping my phone silenced and in my pocket on the rare occasions I got to spend time with Maddy and Jack. It was hard enough holding their attention without having to compete with texts from their friends, social media notifications, and the whole of the internet, but I couldn't very well ask them to put their phones away if I was constantly checking mine.

Which was why I didn't see Tess's text until nearly midnight.

It was only as I was heading to bed—two hours after I'd gotten home from dropping the kids back at Wendy's, sat down at my laptop, and gotten sucked into responding to work emails—that I belatedly remembered to turn my phone off Do Not Disturb.

My heart gave a kick of…something at the sight of the text from Tess.

How did it go with Maddy and Jack tonight?

So we were pretending the other night hadn't happened, I guess? Was that really how she wanted to play it?

I reached up to unbutton my shirt as I stared at the text, trying to decide how to respond. Tess was probably asleep by now, but I figured I should text her back anyway so she wouldn't think I was ignoring her.

I think it went okay? Jack seemed mostly happy about it, but Maddy was harder to read.

I tossed my phone onto the bed and went to change out of my work clothes. When I came back into the bedroom after brushing my teeth, I was surprised to see Tess had responded.

I'm glad to hear it. Hopefully Maddy just needs time.

Apparently Tess was still up. I cradled my phone in my hands as I sank down on the foot of the bed.

On impulse, I hit the call button.

"Hi," Tess said, picking up immediately.

Did my ears deceive me, or did she actually sound pleased to hear from me?

"I thought you'd be asleep by now." I scooted back on the bed so I could lean against the headboard.

"I'm working, actually."

"This time of night? That boss of yours must be a real hard-ass."

"I couldn't sleep."

"Any particular reason?" Like that mind-blowing kiss we'd shared, perhaps? It had certainly left me tossing and turning the last two nights.

"Chronic insomnia," she said, dashing my hopes. "I've had it for years."

Right. I should have known better than to expect Tess to lose any sleep over me. "I'm sorry to hear that."

"Eh. I'm used to it," she said, brushing off my concern. "What's your excuse for being up this late on a school night?"

"I'm a workaholic, remember? Got caught up answering emails and lost track of time."

"Of course." She paused, and when she spoke again her voice was softer. "It really went all right with your kids tonight?"

Had she actually been worried about me? Or only worried how the kids' reactions would affect Erin? Probably the latter. Hadn't I learned by now not to get my hopes up where Tess was concerned?

Fuck no, I hadn't. And I probably never would.

Slouching down in the pillows, I leaned my head back and closed my eyes. "They were pretty shocked—and a little scandalized, I think. Jack had a million questions, which I tried to field as best I could. But Maddy barely said a word the whole night." I sighed and scrubbed a tired hand over my face, remembering her tight-lipped expression. "I honestly have no idea what she's thinking. I only hope she doesn't take her problems with me out on Erin."

"She'll come around."

"Will she?"

"I don't know," Tess admitted. "I was trying to be comforting. But I hope she does, for your sake."

I swallowed, my chest feeling tight. Even though I knew it was foolish, I wanted Tess here with me right now. I wanted to see her so badly I had to clench my jaw to keep from straight-out asking her to come over. My arms itched to hold her, and my heart…my heart was a useless piece of shit that was aching for a woman who'd only break it all over again.

"Donal?"

"Yes." I cleared my throat. "I'm here."

"Are you okay?"

No. Definitely not.

"I'm fine," was what I said. "I should let you get back to work."

Before I say something really stupid…

"I'm sorry about the way I left Saturday night."

Her words surprised me into silence. I wasn't expecting to hear Tess apologize, and after she'd spent the last few minutes acting like Saturday night never happened, the sudden subject change gave me whiplash.

"I got scared," she admitted, surprising me still further. "And I had to get out of there. I know you wanted to talk about it, but I couldn't. I was afraid if I stayed…"

I sat up, desperate to hear her finish that sentence.

But she left me hanging—again. "Anyway, I regret the way I ran off. I know it was hurtful, and I'm sorry."

The vulnerability I heard in her voice softened the bite of my disappointment. She'd confessed to being scared *and* apologized, both of which were huge for Tess. The least I could do was meet her halfway. "I shouldn't have said it was just a kiss."

"It's fine." Her clipped tone told me otherwise.

I probably should have left it there, but I didn't. Maybe it was because I was exhausted, or maybe it was the same reckless impulses I'd never been able to control around Tess. "It wasn't just a kiss to me. It wasn't *just* anything. You matter to me. I want you to know that. Whatever happens, you're important to me."

I heard her draw in an unsteady breath. "You're important to me too."

My heart leaped, hearing her say those words. But then she took a breath, and my heart came crashing back down to earth. I could tell there was a *but* coming.

"That's why I think it's best if we keep things strictly nonphysical."

I rubbed my forehead while my hopes rearranged themselves yet again. "Right."

"What you said before, about us being friends—I'd like us to be able to do that. I think it's important, for Erin's sake."

For Erin's sake, of course. Tess wasn't thinking of me, or of her own feelings. She was only thinking of Erin. That was the only reason she was willing to put up with me and make an effort to get along.

"Sure. Whatever you want." It was what I'd asked for, wasn't it? I ought to be content with that, instead of yearning for something I was never going to get.

But then she shocked me all over again by saying, "I don't want to lose you."

My mouth opened, but before I could find the words to respond she went on in a rush.

"I lost you before, and now that I've finally gotten you back I don't want to mess this up. Which is why I think we should avoid a repeat of what happened Saturday night. I'm afraid if we let ourselves go down that road, it'll complicate an already complicated situation and potentially ruin any chance we might have of building a lasting friendship."

I seemed to be having a little trouble breathing, because it was dangerously close to what I'd always wanted to hear from Tess—that she actually cared about me enough to like having me around. That I wasn't just some meaningless fling who was only useful for sex.

She actually wanted my friendship. But there was a downside, of course. If we were going to stand a chance of making it stick, we needed to not make the same mistakes we'd made before.

"Okay," I said, finally finding my voice. "I agree."

"Really?"

"You're right," I admitted reluctantly. "It's an additional complication we probably don't need right now, and..." I took a breath. "I don't want to lose you either."

"Oh." She sounded surprised and relieved. "Good. I was afraid you'd be disappointed."

"I'm a *little* disappointed, not gonna lie."

"It's not that I didn't like it. Just so you know."

I felt myself grin. As much as I wanted her to want me for more than sex, I liked knowing she wanted me for sex. "Well I'm glad to hear that, considering how enthusiastically you climbed into my lap."

"You *put* me in your lap."

"I didn't hear you complaining, but it was probably a little hard to talk when you were shoving your tongue down my throat."

"I, uh—may have gotten a little carried away." I could practically hear her blush through the phone. "It was a hell of a kiss."

"I'm sorry. Could you repeat that? Because it sounded like you just paid me a compliment."

"I suppose I did."

"Hang on, I need to go to the window and check for locusts or falling frogs or some other sign the End Times are upon us."

"Very funny." Beneath the sarcasm, I could hear a smile in her voice.

"I liked it too." *Way too much.* I squeezed the phone, forcing levity back into my tone. "I can't seem to control my fucking mouth around you."

"That makes two of us," she returned, her tone wry and teasing. "Apparently."

I stared up at the ceiling, smiling as I remembered the feel of her lips on mine. "Say what you will about us, but we never lacked for chemistry."

"No," she said, and I could swear she sounded wistful. "We sure didn't."

"But I can also see the sense in what you're saying. It's better if we focus on being friends." I paused before adding. "For now."

Nothing but silence on her end.

An uncomfortable sensation burned behind my breastbone. It could have been heartburn from the pizza I'd had for dinner, but it felt more like heartache. I rubbed my chest, flailing for something to say next. "So...uh, I told my mom about Erin yesterday."

"How'd that go?"

"Scary as shit. But she took it in stride, all things considered. And she's thrilled about Erin and the baby, of course." I sighed and raked a hand through my hair. "She also helpfully reminded me that I'd better tell my ex-wife before I broke the news to our kids, so I got to come clean to Wendy yesterday as well."

"So what you're telling me is that you've gone over your quota of emotional conversations in the last forty-eight hours."

"Yeah, I have." I tried and failed to stifle a yawn. "No wonder I'm so exhausted."

"You should get some sleep."

The thought of hanging up left me desolate, but she was right. I had work in the morning. "You too. It's late."

"Fine." She sounded vaguely disgruntled. "I'll try if you do."

"Deal," I said. "Good night, Tess."

"Go to sleep, Donal."

I didn't know if Tess kept up her end of the bargain, but I fell into a deep, peaceful sleep two minutes after getting off the phone. It was my first good night's sleep in days.

CHAPTER FIFTEEN

TESS

Deciphering knitting patterns was like trying to decode a spy cipher. I'd always considered myself an intelligent person, but apparently you needed a PhD in cryptography to understand the damn things.

I'd decided to finish the baby blanket I'd started for Erin when I was pregnant. What with her being pregnant now, there was a nice sort of symmetry to it. Although I wasn't sure if I'd actually have the courage to give it to her. I'd cross that bridge when I came to it.

Assuming I could figure out how to recreate the pattern.

The first thing I'd done was watch a bunch of knitting how-to videos. I'd even practiced the basic stitches with a pair of chopsticks and a shoelace. I planned to make a trip to Dawn's knitting store for proper supplies soon, but in the meantime, I wanted to see if I could still remember how to do it, and I'd had to improvise with what I could find in my apartment.

Bizarrely, my hands seemed to remember the motions even if my head didn't. The video tutorial hadn't made any sense the first time I'd watched it, but as soon as I held the chopsticks in my hands like knitting needles something clicked into place. My fingers started moving through the steps automatically—albeit a little clumsily—as if they still knew what to do. Muscle memory was the real deal.

Obviously, I couldn't actually knit anything with a shoelace, but I'd been able to at least review the basics of casting on, knitting, and purling. And the more I practiced, the more familiar it had started to feel. Amazing how much information our brains kept stored just out of reach.

Now I was on an internet quest to see if I could find the pattern I'd been using—or at least something similar enough to help me reverse engineer it. I'd already identified one of the two repeating stripes as a basic garter stitch, which was easy enough. The other section, however, was proving more of a challenge. It was some kind of lace eyelet pattern, but I hadn't been able to find an exact match.

I was starting to go cross-eyed from staring at stitch patterns when my phone chirped beside me, offering a welcome distraction. When I saw it was a text from Donal, my stomach performed an ill-considered skydiving maneuver.

Donal: You up?

The fact that those two particular words were the standard booty call opening gambit wasn't lost on me—or my racing pulse. Suddenly, my thoughts were dominated by a single image: Donal naked in my bed.

Or his bed—either would do fine. Although I'd never seen his bed, so it was difficult to imagine him in it. It was much easier to imagine him naked in *my* bed.

What in the Bad Idea Jeans am I doing? Hadn't we just agreed not twenty-four hours ago to keep our relationship firmly in the Friend Zone? Naked fantasies were off-limits in the Friend Zone, as were booty calls.

Forcing the image of Donal's naked body out of my mind, I tapped out a neutral reply to his text.

Tess: I am.

Donal: Still working?

Tess: Not exactly.

Donal: What does not exactly mean?

Tess: Just surfing the internet.

Instead of texting me back, he sent a request for a video call.

I accepted without thinking about the fact that I was wearing pajamas and no makeup, with my hair piled up on my head in a disheveled bun. And not one of those cute messy buns like twentysomethings on Instagram wore, but a truly disastrous rat's nest that had canted neglectfully to one side.

But I didn't have a chance to worry about that, because Donal's face filled my screen, and my stomach started doing a weird fluttering thing when he broke into a grin that showed off both of his devastating dimples.

"Is that code for watching porn? Please tell me I interrupted you watching porn."

I tried not to smile and utterly failed. "Sorry to disappoint, but I was researching knitting patterns."

"That's not nearly as much fun as watching porn." His hair looked damp, and I wondered if he'd just taken a shower. He also appeared to be shirtless, which did nothing to help me avoid thinking about him naked. Nor did the fact that we were talking about porn.

"No, it definitely isn't," I agreed, feeling my face flush with heat—along with other assorted parts of me.

The way his eyes seemed to darken as they swept over my image on his screen made me desperately want to know what he was thinking. "I never knew you were a knitter," he said anticlimactically.

I exhaled, simultaneously relieved and disappointed he'd steered the conversation away from sex and into safer territory. "I'm thinking of taking it up again."

His pensive silence reminded me he'd seen the half-finished baby blanket at my apartment, which meant he'd probably figured out what had prompted my newfound interest in knitting.

Feeling uncomfortably exposed, I attempted to cover the awkward conversational lull. "Did you know that in World Wars I and II, spies sometimes used encrypted knitting to smuggle military intelligence? The US and UK even banned the printing of knitting patterns during WWII because they were afraid the Germans might hide code in them."

"Like the old woman in *A Tale of Two Cities*," Donal said, surprising me.

"I can't believe you remember that."

"We read it freshman year in Mrs. Whatshername's class."

"Mrs. Vassallo. And I'm shocked you actually read the book." I used to get so mad at him because he almost never did the reading for English. He'd skim the Cliff's Notes instead, and half the time he'd end up getting a better grade than me. He'd even scored higher than me on the AP English exam, which was *so* unfair, but Donal had always been lucky like that. He had a knack for performing well on tests, which had allowed him to skate by without putting in as much work. It was how he'd nearly beat me out for valedictorian despite his sloppy study habits.

Back when school was my whole life—and the only thing I was any good at—things like that had seemed so important. Now it felt like a silly, pointless thing to care about. Being good at studying didn't make me any smarter than being good at taking tests made Donal. They were two different skills, each useful in different applications.

"It was one of the few books I actually bothered to read," he said, reaching up to run a hand through his damp hair. "I thought it sounded like a cool wartime thriller, but then it actually turned out to be this tragic love story. Kind of like *Casablanca*."

For some reason, talking about tragic love stories made me almost as uncomfortable as talking about porn. "What are you doing up, anyway? Were you working late again?"

"I just got back from the gym. I needed to work off some tension."

Well. That explained the shirtless dampness.

"Bad day?" I asked, trying very hard not to picture him naked *and* sweaty.

"*Long* day." He was walking across his apartment holding his phone. The image on my screen bounced around, making me vaguely seasick. "I was stuck in back-to-back meetings almost the whole day, which meant I didn't get any actual work done. So tomorrow I get to play catch-up—in between even more meetings. I need to clone myself so I can send one of me to meetings while the other one stays in my office reviewing SEC filings and redlining contracts." When the camera finally stopped moving, there was a headboard behind him.

Oh great, now he was in bed.

Shirtless.

And *damp*.

I bit the inside of my cheek to distract myself from my inappropriate thoughts. "Too bad there are no Cliff's Notes for lawyering."

"Oh there are—we call them summer associates." His lips curved in a slow, easy smile before the wry humor in his expression was replaced by something softer. "What about you? How was your day?"

"My day was fine." In an attempt to keep the conversation in safe territory, I told him about the pitch I'd spent the day preparing for a new client I was hoping to get in the door with.

"I have a confession to make," he said. "I don't actually know exactly what product marketing is."

I laughed. "That's okay. I don't really know what a corporate attorney does either."

"Nothing interesting, that's for sure. I'd much rather hear about what you do."

"The short answer is that I help bring products—in my case mostly software products—to market."

"Software like Microsoft Word?"

"It could be. My focus is business-to-business software as a service, which is a cloud-based distribution model that includes things like office management, customer support, or communication software used within a business—as opposed to business-to-consumer products like Microsoft Office."

"Things like Slack or Salesforce, then?"

"Yes, exactly," I said.

"So what's the difference between product marketing and other kinds of marketing?"

"There's a lot of overlap, but basically my role is to be the connective tissue between the technical product manager and the different marketing channels. I build the go-to-market strategy, including product positioning, messaging, pricing, managing the launch, collecting customer feedback, and making sure the sales team understands the product well enough to talk about it."

"Do you mostly work from home?" he asked.

"Only in the evenings. During the day I go to an office I rented in a co-op nearby. But most of my work is virtual, and my clients are located all over the world."

"Sounds like heaven. I'd love to be able to work from home."

"That was what I thought until I started doing it, but it wasn't all it was cracked up to be."

"How so?"

"It wasn't great for my mood and mental health. I realized I function better when I have a reason to get dressed and leave my house every day."

It felt weird to be talking to Donal like this—like we were regular friends getting to know each other, instead of two people with a complicated and painful history between us. Weird but good, like something I might be able to get used to.

He ran his hand through his hair again, rumpling the damp layers. "So there's actually a reason I called you."

"You mean other than to find out if I was watching porn?" As soon as the quip slipped out, I realized my mistake. Rather than deflecting from my discomfort, I'd reintroduced the source of it—sex—into the conversation.

"Yeah," he said slowly, an odd expression on his face. "Anyway." He cleared his throat. "I was wondering if you were free on Saturday."

I blinked at him, taken off guard by the question. "Why?"

"My mom's hosting a get-together at her house to welcome Erin to the family. My kids will be there, and my dad and his wife—and I was hoping you could come too."

"Me?"

The corner of his mouth twitched in amusement. "Yes, you. Are you free? It starts at four."

"Um…" I didn't need to check my calendar to know I'd be free. Other than working and going to the gym, my Saturdays were empty, stretching out forever. "Are you sure you want me there?"

"I wouldn't have asked if I didn't want you there."

"But if it's a family thing—"

"It's Erin's family, and that includes you." His smile was as warm as his words. "Please tell me you can come. Having you there will help me stay sane."

My heart pounded thickly at the back of my throat as I nodded. "Of course I'll come."

His answering smile made my chest feel tingly. It was almost enough to drive away the heavy lump of dread in my stomach.

A get-together with Donal's parents and teenaged children. Splendid. Delightful.

This didn't promise to be uncomfortable at all.

CHAPTER SIXTEEN

TESS

I hadn't been back to the old neighborhood since I'd sold my parents' house a few months ago. And now here I was again, in my old, familiar haunt, much sooner than I'd ever expected.

Currently, I was parked on the street in front of Donal's childhood home. From the outside, it looked exactly the same as it had thirty years ago, the last time I'd darkened the Larkins' door. I sat in my car, staring at the familiar brick house and trying to shake off the memories and uneasiness the sight of it brought up.

There was still time to back out. I could invent an excuse—some sort of work emergency maybe.

No. I couldn't do that. Donal had said he wanted me here, and that meant something. Besides, Erin was here. This was an opportunity to get to know her better, and I wasn't going to pass that up. I had to go in there and face Donal's family.

I could handle this.

Straightening my spine, I got out of the car and made my way down the sidewalk and up the concrete steps to Mrs. Larkin's front door. The familiar gong of the doorbell took me back to all the times I'd come here to work on a school project or hang out with friends in the Larkins' basement rec room—not to mention those three months during our senior year when Donal and I had been messing around in secret. I shuffled my feet on the stoop, feeling like an awkward teenager again.

To my intense relief, it was Donal who answered the door. "You made it."

"Sorry I'm late." I forced a smile as I stepped past him into the small foyer. The house smelled like my childhood: Pine-Sol, polished wood, and fresh-baked cookies.

The sound of voices coming from the next room set my heart pounding in my ears. Usually, in difficult social situations, I cloaked myself in an armor of detached indifference. But I didn't want to come off detached or indifferent today. Not with Donal's family, and especially not in front of Erin. Which left me floundering, unable to adequately hide my apprehension.

Donal's eyes swept over my face, and he surprised me by slipping an arm around my waist and kissing my cheek.

Oh.

Okay. I could deal with this. I wasn't the least bit thrown by the feel of Donal's soft, warm lips on my skin. It definitely didn't make me think of the kiss we'd shared a week ago. That was my story, and I was sticking to it.

While I was still recovering from the cheek kiss, he surprised me further by pulling me into a hug.

Oh, jeez. Now we were doing this.

It was too much. Donal's muscles, his skin, his smell, it was all too good. I couldn't help but lean into him, enjoying the feel of his body against mine. Something tightened in my stomach, a tingling warmth that suffused all my limbs.

When he let go of me I wavered a little, feeling like I'd lost my equilibrium. But he hadn't let go all the way. His arm was still around my waist, anchoring me, holding me upright, and it stayed there as he drew back and smiled at me. "I'm really glad to see you."

I swallowed, attempting to pull myself together. "Is Erin here yet?"

"She got here about ten minutes ago."

"How's it going?" I searched his face for evidence of tension, but if there was any, he was hiding it well.

"Great. You know my mom—she could make friends with a Bengal tiger. She and Erin hit it off right away. And Jack seems taken with Erin as well. Between him and my mom talking her ear off, no one else has had much chance to get a word in edgewise." His smile grew wider, showing off his dimples. "You look gorgeous, by the way."

I felt his words—and his smile—all the way down to my toes. I'd agonized over what to wear, and in the end had settled on a floral dress paired with a light-weight mint green sweater that seemed appropriate for the pleasant late April weather we were having.

Before I could form a reply, Donal started to guide me out of the foyer. "Come on, I want to introduce you to my kids, and my mom will want to see you."

"Wait." My steps faltered, and I put a hand on his stomach to stop him—before realizing what I'd done and quickly drawing it back. "Is your mother—" I swallowed, my eyes drifting to the large crucifix hanging on the wall. "Does she think badly of me?" I remembered Mrs. Larkin as a kind but slightly intimidating figure. Apparently, I still wasn't too old to quake at the prospect of facing her now that she knew about my sinful transgressions with her son.

Donal blinked and his arm slipped away from me. "Of course not."

"She doesn't think I'm an immoral tramp who seduced her son and gave her grandchild away?"

He burst out laughing. "First of all, she'd put the fear of God into anybody she heard calling any woman a tramp. Second of all, my mom doesn't go around judging people like that. I promise you, she doesn't blame you or resent you or anything else you might be worried about, okay? She always really liked you."

"She did?"

"Yeah, she did." His mouth twisted wryly, but his eyes were still crinkling with amusement. "She always used to ask me why I didn't date a nice, smart girl like you."

I barked out a wry laugh. "Little did she know."

"It was her idea to invite you today."

"Oh." I was torn between being relieved his mother didn't hate me and feeling disappointed it hadn't been Donal's idea to include me.

"Come on." His arm slipped around me again, herding me out of the foyer. "It's going to be fine."

Conversation in the living room came to a stop as everyone turned to look at us. My spine stiffened, and Donal's hand squeezed my hip.

"Tess is here," he announced unnecessarily as he guided me into the center of the room where everyone was seated on matching floral sofas. The upholstery had been updated since the last time I was here, but otherwise the furniture looked exactly the same. "You remember my dad," he said to me as he gestured at an older, silver-haired gentleman I only vaguely recognized as Donal's father. "And this is his wife, Diane."

They stood up, and I exchanged handshakes with the pair of them. Next, Donal introduced me to Jack and Maddy, who each lifted a shy hand in greeting, keeping their seats on the couch as they surveyed me with undisguised curiosity.

Erin was seated next to them. Her husband was working on a job out of the country until the end of the summer, so she'd come alone. She smiled warmly as she got up to greet me. We'd shaken hands the last time I'd seen her, but this time she opened her arms to hug me.

Our very first hug. A lump formed in my throat as I clutched her. I had to force myself to let her go before it went on so long it became weird.

Donal's mother had been sitting on a dining chair she'd pulled up on Erin's other side, and she pushed herself to her feet as we separated. Mrs. Larkin looked much the same as I remembered. Her eyes, so much like Donal's, were surrounded by more wrinkles these days and her hair was silver instead of light brown, but she still wore it in the exact same chin-length bob with feathered bangs.

"You remember my mom, of course." Donal's hand touched the small of my back in reassurance.

Mrs. Larkin's eyes crinkled with warmth as she broke into a smile every bit as radiant as her son's. "Teresa McGregor, what a beautiful woman you've grown into!"

The tension that had bunched in my shoulders eased as I returned her smile. "It's nice to see you again, Mrs. Larkin. Thank you for inviting me today."

"None of that, now. You're to call me Kathleen, do you hear?" Her smile dimmed as her expression softened with compassion. "I'm so sorry about Sherry, sweetheart. She was a good, kind woman. And your poor father." She tutted softly. "What a terrible thing."

The next thing I knew, she'd enveloped me in a hug, and I felt my chin wobble as I clutched her soft middle.

"There now," she murmured, holding me as tight as I'd wanted to hold Erin. "I know how much you must miss her. And your father too, I'll bet."

When she finally let go of me, my eyes were burning traitorously. As I blinked away the tears that threatened, Donal's knuckles stroked down my back.

"Let's get you fixed up with a drink." Kathleen hooked her arm through mine and led me away toward the kitchen. "I've got beer and pop—or would you prefer a cup of tea? I'll even put a shot of whiskey in it if you like," she added with a wink.

I accepted her offer of a beer, as well as one of the homemade butterscotch cookies she pressed on me.

"Don't tell the others I let you have that," she whispered. "I told them they weren't allowed to spoil their appetites."

While I ate my contraband cookie, we lingered in the kitchen chatting about my job, her volunteer work, and some of my old friends from high school who she'd seen more recently than I had. By the time we returned to the living room a few minutes later, I was feeling considerably less anxious. Kathleen insisted I take the chair she'd vacated next to Erin, and directed Donal to fetch another from the dining room.

I sat quietly, sipping my beer while Erin talked to Jack and Maddy. Jack was clearly the outgoing one, offering a gushing, longwinded monologue about his favorite video game in answer to Erin's question about his hobbies. Whereas Maddy was much quieter, keeping her answers more succinct. Despite her reserve, I didn't detect any unfriendliness in her manner, and she seemed to be as curious about Erin as Erin was about her.

Erin's skill as an educator showed in the easy, confident way she engaged with both her adolescent half-siblings, listening with interest to Jack's enthusiastic ramblings before drawing Maddy into a conversation about her upcoming graduation and summer plans before she left for Purdue in the fall.

Donal's father and his wife didn't talk much, but Kathleen piped up frequently to tell funny family stories or ask Erin questions about her own family. I listened to Erin's answers with interest, learning a great deal more about her parents and childhood than she'd volunteered previously.

Occasionally I'd glance over at Donal, sitting on the other side of his mother. When he wasn't wincing at an embarrassing anecdote his mother had shared about him, his expression settled into a fond half-smile as he watched his three children interact.

After about an hour, Kathleen excused herself to put the finishing touches on dinner, and I volunteered to assist her. A mouthwatering smell had filled up the house, which I discovered was the pot roast cooking in the oven. While Kathleen heated up the mashed potatoes she'd made earlier, I was put to work slicing vegetables for the salad. When Donal wandered in for another beer a short time later, he was conscripted to open a bottle of wine and call everyone to the table.

I couldn't even remember the last time I'd sat down to eat a home-cooked meal with so many people. As an only child without much in the way of local extended family, holiday dinners had been quiet affairs in my house. In more recent years, as my father's condition had declined, Sherry and I had abandoned them altogether. Last year I'd spent Christmas alone, eating Chinese takeout on my couch and watching *Die Hard*.

We were crammed in three to a side at the table, and once grace had been said, a noisy free-for-all of plate-passing and dish-serving commenced. As before, I remained mostly quiet, listening to the conversation around me more than participating in it.

Apparently, Maddy had recently become a vegan, and Kathleen had made vegan mac and cheese just for her. Jack turned his nose up at it, ranting about the blasphemy of fake cheese until Donal gently chided him to leave his sister's dietary choices alone.

When Maddy started talking about the boyfriend who'd inspired her lifestyle change, I sensed Donal tense beside me. I glanced at him, but his attention was completely absorbed by Maddy as she chattered about Tyler, who it sounded like she'd been dating for quite some time.

"What are Tyler's college plans?" Kathleen asked her granddaughter.

"He doesn't have any," Maddy answered breezily as she helped herself to more mac and cheese. "He says college is a waste of money."

"Does he now?" Kathleen's eyebrows lifted slightly as she exchanged a glance with Donal. "What does he plan to do after high school?"

Maddy shrugged. "He'll probably keep working at Jewel-Osco while he builds up his art portfolio."

"What kind of art does he do?" Erin asked.

"Mostly pencil and ink, although he's starting to practice more with watercolors. But what he really wants to do is become a tattoo artist."

Kathleen's smile didn't slip, but it did freeze in place a little. Meanwhile, a vein was now visibly throbbing at Donal's temple.

"Now I understand why he thinks college is a waste of time," Donal's father mumbled, reaching for his wine.

"He thinks it's a waste of *money*," Maddy corrected. "The days when a college education guaranteed a better job are long gone, Grandpa. Now all it buys you is crushing debt for the rest of your life while you're stuck working minimum wage jobs that you could have gotten without a degree."

I glanced at Donal and saw a muscle tighten in his jaw. When he opened his mouth—to argue, presumably—I laid my hand on his leg beneath the table. His gaze jumped to mine, and I gave a tiny shake of my head. Attacking Maddy and her boyfriend's opinions would only drive her farther away, and might very well drive her closer to Tyler just to spite her father.

"Isn't it nice you don't have to pay for college yourself?" Kathleen said cheerfully, filling the awkward silence. "Not everyone's lucky enough to have parents who can afford to pay for their education outright."

Erin gave Maddy a thoughtful look. "I remember when I was eighteen and I'd just gotten accepted to UIUC, one of my mom's friends asked me what I wanted to major in. I started complaining about how hard it was to get a job after college and telling her how I was still trying to figure out which major would give me the best chance in the job market after I graduated. And do you know what she said?"

"What?" Maddy asked, listening with interest.

"She said 'You don't go to college in order to get a job. You go to college to learn how to think.' I'd never thought of it like that before, but it's always stuck with me."

Maddy gave her a skeptical look. "Do you think that's really true? Did college teach you to think?"

Erin's brow furrowed as she gave the question serious consideration. "I feel like it did, yeah. I'm not saying every single class was a golden font of knowledge, but enough of them were that it opened my eyes to things I might not have appreciated otherwise. Going to college changed my understanding of the world and the people around me, but more than that it helped me figure out who and what I wanted to be."

"So you didn't always know you wanted to be a teacher?" I asked her.

She smiled and shook her head. "No, definitely not. In fact, I was dead set against it, determined to walk my own path instead of following in my mom's footsteps. But because of what her friend said, I signed up for a few classes I might not otherwise have taken, just because they sounded like something I wanted to know more about. After trying a few different things on for size, what I figured out was that I really liked science—but more than that, I liked helping other people understand it. So I decided to become a science teacher, not because it was my mom's path, but because it was mine too."

"That's cool," Maddy said, smiling at Erin, and I heard Donal exhale a long breath.

After dinner, there were cookies and blueberry pie for dessert. Once everyone had stuffed themselves, the party migrated back to the living room and Kathleen brought out a stack of family photo albums.

As everyone was poring over them and swapping family stories, I gathered up the last of the dessert plates and carried them into the kitchen. While I was loading them into the dishwasher, Maddy came in to get another soda pop from the fridge.

"Grandma likes to have the fork tines pointing up," Maddy commented, glancing my way. "She's really particular about it."

I tossed her a smile as I set about correcting my mistake. "Thanks for the tip."

She set her pop on the counter and came over to help me rearrange the errant silverware.

"Are you excited about being an aunt?" I asked her.

"I guess." She shrugged, straightening again when all the forks had been righted.

"I imagine this all must be pretty strange for you."

She shrugged again and reached for her pop. "It's fine or whatever."

"Is this where your grandmother likes these?" I asked, cautiously slotting a pie plate in the lower rack.

"Yeah." Maddy lingered by the fridge, silently watching me load the rest of the plates into the dishwasher. When I moved on to hand-washing the wineglasses, she got a clean dish towel out of a drawer and began drying the glasses as I rinsed them. "So you and my dad dated in high school, huh?"

"That's right." Technically, Donal and I had never gone on a single date, but that seemed like an unnecessary hair to split with his daughter.

"He's never mentioned you before." Her tone held a note of challenge that made me think she might have come to some conclusions of her own about the nature of our relationship.

I glanced at her, my expression carefully neutral. "Does he talk about his other high school girlfriends a lot?"

"No, not really." Her brow creased in a thoughtful frown that reminded me of Donal. The similarities between them were subtle, but became more noticeable the longer I spent around her. "Not at all unless Grandma brings them up."

I handed her another wineglass to dry. "I don't think your father's very nostalgic about the old days."

"Were you two together a long time?"

This conversation felt like tiptoeing through a minefield. I preferred not to lie to Maddy, but I also wasn't sure Donal would want me telling his daughter how casually we'd embarked on a sexual relationship as teenagers.

But then I reminded myself that she wasn't a child—she was an eighteen-year-old woman with a boyfriend of her own and was about to go off to college in another state. Rather than learning about sex by sneaking Judy Blume books from the library, Maddy's generation had grown up with the internet at their fingertips and were considerably more jaded and worldly-wise than I'd been at her age—not that I'd been particularly innocent at eighteen either. Clearly.

"We were friends for a long time." I reached for a towel and dried my hands. "From elementary to high school. But we only dated for a few months."

"He said you two were together his senior year, but I know you weren't his prom date because grandma has his prom picture in a frame upstairs."

Crossing my arms, I leaned back against the counter, wondering where she was going with this. "I didn't go to prom, because it would have been too difficult to hide my pregnancy in a prom dress. But your father and I had already broken up months before that."

"Because he found out you were pregnant?" The challenging tone was back, but it wasn't me she was challenging. I finally understood what she wanted to know —if her dad had been a good guy or a bad guy.

"He didn't dump me. I broke up with him."

Her confounded expression told me my hunch was right. "Why?"

"It was complicated." There was no way to explain my reasoning without giving Maddy more ammunition to use against Donal. So instead I told her the *real* truth—the truth I'd only recently begun to admit to myself. "What it really comes down to is that I got scared and pushed him away. I think I needed to believe I was still in control of my own life, that I was strong enough to handle what was happening to me without showing any weakness. I was so afraid of letting anyone see how terrified I really was that I isolated myself from all my friends, including your father."

"He didn't abandon you?" Her reluctance to accept it made my heart ache for both of them.

"He wouldn't have done that." Despite what I'd convinced myself at the time, I'd come around to believing that Donal would indeed have stood by me if I'd let him. It was like he'd said: he might have been a dumbass, but he wasn't a complete dickhead. He would have tried to do the right thing. I gave Maddy a pointed look, hoping she'd see the parallel with her own relationship with her father. "He wanted to be there for me, and he would have if I'd given him a chance. But I shut him out, because I was too proud to admit that I needed him."

She lowered her gaze to the floor, shuffling her feet. "Sorry if I'm asking too many nosy questions."

"It's all right. I don't mind a bit." I offered her a smile as I pushed off the counter. "Show me where your grandmother keeps the dishwasher detergent, and I'll answer any questions you want to ask."

Maddy got the detergent out from under the sink and helped me start the machine. "What was my dad like in high school?"

I thought about it while I went to work on Kathleen's big roasting pan with a scrubbing brush. "He was a lot of fun."

"*My* dad?" Maddy said in disbelief.

"You don't think your dad's fun?"

She snorted. "No."

"He used to be. Everyone loved him. He was friendly and charming…" A smile curved my lips as I rinsed the soap off the roasting pan. "And kind. He was nice to everyone, no matter who they were, which is rare in high school, especially for someone as popular as your dad was."

"Huh," Maddy responded, taking the pan from me to dry it off.

"Your dad's a really good guy, is what I'm saying."

"Maybe in high school." She opened her mouth like she was going to say something else, then clamped her lips shut, seeming to think better of it.

"What are you guys up to in here?" Donal asked behind me. I turned and found him leaning against the kitchen doorway.

"Nothing," Maddy muttered, and I saw a flash of hurt in his expression at her cool response to him.

I offered him a consoling smile, keeping my tone cheerful. "Maddy's been helping me with the dishes."

Donal nodded, schooling his expression again. "Grandpa and Diane are leaving, Mads. You should go say good night to them."

I took the roasting pan from Maddy, thanking her for her help, and she left the kitchen without looking at her father.

"Is everything okay?" Donal asked, lowering his voice as he came closer. "She wasn't giving you a hard time, was she?"

"No, we were just chatting. She's lovely." I held the pan up to him. "Where does this go?"

He took it from me and squatted to put it away in one of the lower cabinets. The position, combined with the jeans he was wearing, did the most amazing things to his thighs and rear. I couldn't help admiring the view.

Friend Zone, I reminded myself sharply. *Friends don't leer at friends' butts.*

I considered asking Donal to pass me a saucepan so I could club myself unconscious with it. Instead, I said, "She wanted to know what you were like in high school."

"Oh God. I'm afraid to ask what you told her." He straightened and turned to face me, rubbing his palms on his jeans like a nervous teenager. Except Donal had never seemed nervous as a teenager. He'd oozed carefree self-confidence out of every pore. At least some of it must have been an act—no teenager could possibly be that confident—but I'd never thought to look beneath the surface before now.

I gave him a reassuring smile. "All good things, of course."

He drifted closer. "Really?"

"Promise."

"Like what?" His blue eyes twinkled as he leaned his hip against the counter in front of me. "I wouldn't mind hearing you say nice things about me."

"That's between me and Maddy." All that twinkling was way too much. My saucepan plan was sounding better and better. I lowered my eyes and cleared my throat. "She's a great kid."

"Yeah, I know." His voice was rough with the same pain that always crept into it when he talked about Maddy.

I angled my head to look into his eyes, and the sadness in them inspired me to forget how stupendously attractive he was and reach for his hand. "Don't let her push you away. She's testing you because she's afraid of being disappointed again. Keep showing up for her. That's all she wants—to know she matters to you."

His gaze dropped to our hands as he curled his fingers around mine. "I'm not going to give up on her, no matter how hard she pushes."

"She's doing the exact same thing I did to you."

The corners of his mouth pulled down as he rubbed his thumb over my wrist. "I failed that test pretty spectacularly. I never should have let you go so easily."

"What happened to us wasn't your fault." It was long past time I forgave Donal and took responsibility for my own part in it.

His eyes lifted to mine, but where I expected to see relief I saw only regret. "Wasn't it?"

"There you are, hiding in the kitchen! I wondered where Tess had snuck off to."

Donal dropped my hand at the sound of his mother's voice. I affixed a pleasant expression on my face as I turned toward Kathleen.

A canny smile crinkled her eyes as she marched into the kitchen. "What are you two up to in here, hmmm?"

"Nothing, Mom." Donal rolled his eyes like a surly teenager, and I smothered a smile.

"Looks like someone was doing the dishes, but I'm going to take a wild guess that it was Tess and not you." Shooting a reproving look at her son, Kathleen gave my arm an appreciative squeeze as she leaned between us to open a cabinet.

"I'm not about to waste the good stuff on your father, but now that they're gone" —her eyes twinkled as she drew out a bottle of Redbreast 12 Year Irish whiskey —"who wants a drink?"

My hand shot up at the same time as Donal's.

Kathleen's lips quirked as she uncorked the bottle. "That's what I thought."

Donal got down glasses, and his mother poured out three servings. After we'd each claimed one, she raised her glass. "May your troubles be less and your blessings be more and nothing but happiness come through your door."

"Sláinte." Donal's eyes locked onto mine as he lifted his glass to his lips.

"Now then," Kathleen said cheerfully, "who's up for a game of Boggle?"

CHAPTER SEVENTEEN

DONAL

"So these two guys are walking down the street," I said when Tess answered the phone.

She made a noise of irritation. "Don't do this."

Somehow or another, we'd gotten into the habit of talking on the phone almost every night. Don't ask me who started it. I couldn't remember.

(Me. It was me. I started it.)

Since we both tended to stay up late working, we usually started by texting each other in the evenings. Until eventually one of us would call the other and nag them about working too late and needing to get some sleep. At first, it was me doing the chastising, because Tess really didn't seem to sleep enough and it was genuinely a little concerning. But then she started doing it back to me and pointing out what a hypocrite I was, because I was usually up working as late as she was.

The funny thing was, when I'd originally suggested we should try to be friends, I hadn't actually expected it to work. Seriously, me and Tess? Getting along? Yeah, right. Maybe on a cold day in hell.

I'd simply figured if we aimed for friendly we might get lucky and land some-place shy of constantly wanting to murder each other. At least that would be an improvement, right?

Miraculously, we'd talked almost every day since the get-together at my mom's and hadn't fought once. That wasn't even the craziest part. The craziest part was that talking to Tess had become the best part of my day.

I flopped back on my bed, enjoying myself a little too much. "The two guys decide to go for a drink, and one of them says, 'Great idea. I heard about this new place that makes *the* best fruit punch you've ever had.'"

Tess let out a tortured sigh. "We've talked about this. You know how I feel about long-winded jokes."

"Shhh. Let me finish telling the story. So the first guy agrees to go to this new place, although he thinks it's a little weird—I mean, who goes to a bar to drink fruit punch, right? But the two guys head over to this bar anyway. They go up to the bartender, and the second guy says to him, 'We'll take two glasses of your best fruit punch, please.'"

"Why did I even answer the phone?" Tess muttered. "I should have known better."

I ignored her and carried on. "The bartender gives them this really long look. Just when they're starting to get nervous they've done something wrong, he finally says, 'If you want punch you'll have to go stand in line like everybody else.'"

"Why are you like this? What's wrong with you?"

"The two guys look around…" I paused for a breath, drawing out the suspense. "But *there's no punch line.*"

There was a protracted silence on Tess's end of the line. "I hate you."

I tapped the icon to request a video call. A second later, Tess's face appeared on my screen. "Ha! I knew you'd be smiling. You love my jokes."

"That was a terrible joke." She tried to glower at me and failed.

"Yeah, but it made you smile, so it fulfilled its purpose."

Her smile turned into a grimace as she glanced away from the phone. "Shit! Hang on. I've got to set the phone down."

"Tess?" I sat up, worried she'd hurt herself somehow. All I could see on my screen was a view of her ceiling. A weirdly hazy view of her ceiling. "Is that smoke?"

"No," she said from somewhere off camera. "Maybe."

"What's happening over there? Do I need to call 911?"

"I'm baking. Or trying to." She didn't sound panicked, so I figured she had it under control. Hopefully.

"Yeah? How's it going?"

"Not great, as you can probably tell from the smoke." There was a clattering sound, followed by, "Well, fuck."

"What were you baking?"

"It was supposed to be cookies, but instead I seem to have made a tray of carbonized hockey pucks."

"Sounds delicious. Can you send me the recipe?"

"Laugh it up, fuzzball. It was your mother's butterscotch cookie recipe."

"How'd you get my mother's cookie recipe?"

"I asked her for it when I called to thank her for dinner. And you better not tell her I messed them up this bad."

"Your secret's safe with me."

There was more clattering. "Fuck a duck. I think I figured out the problem. Somehow I accidentally put the oven into self-cleaning mode."

"Use your oven a lot, do you?" Since she couldn't see my face, I didn't bother hiding my smirk.

"When's the last time you used your oven, Paul Hollywood?"

"Where do you think I hide my dirty dishes when the kids come over?"

Tess picked up the phone again, and her face bobbed across the screen as she carried it through her apartment. The image stabilized as she sank down on the couch with a sigh. "Well, that was a total bust."

"What inspired you to bake cookies, anyway?"

Her eyes lowered. "I thought it'd be nice to take them to the caregivers at my father's facility tomorrow."

"You're going to see your dad tomorrow?"

"I go see him every Sunday." She chewed on her lip, still not looking at me.

"That must be hard."

She shrugged as if it was nothing, but the way she avoided meeting my eyes said otherwise. "I'm fairly certain he doesn't know I'm there most of the time."

"But you still go anyway."

"He's my dad." Her eyes lifted to the phone finally, and her mouth pulled tight. "He's the only family I've got."

I hated how sad she looked. I wished we were having this conversation in person so I could pull her into my arms and hold her. "No he's not. Erin's your family. And I'm Erin's family, which means I'm your family too."

She pinched her lower lip between her thumb and forefinger without saying anything.

Not gonna lie, I'd been hoping for a little better reaction than that.

My hands squeezed the phone as I rubbed my chest. "Tell me what you're thinking."

The side of her mouth kicked up, and just that faint hint of a smile made the world feel right again. "I'm wondering if your mom would be willing to adopt me."

"Are you kidding? Nothing would make her happier. She already likes you more than me."

"Does that mean I can come to Christmas?"

"You fucking better. Hundred bucks says my mom's already embroidering your name on a stocking."

Tess's smile grew wider, and my heart went thump in response. "Two men walked into a bar…"

I barked out a laugh. "Really? You're stealing my schtick now? I thought you hated my jokes."

"I do. I'm showing you how it's done. Now shut up."

Obediently, I pressed my lips together and gestured for her to continue.

"Two men walked into a bar," she said, totally deadpan. "The second one should have known better."

I laughed so hard I nearly dropped the phone. "Okay, that was pretty good."

"Better than yours."

"Yeah, you win."

"I know I did."

Fuck, I loved the sight of her smiling.

CHAPTER EIGHTEEN

TESS

It was time to admit I needed help. My solo effort to reverse-engineer the baby blanket pattern had been a bust. The only thing it had gotten me was eye strain and a series of tension headaches.

Clutching the strap of the WBEZ tote bag I'd tucked the unfinished blanket into, I pushed my way through the door of Mad About Ewe, the yarn store on East Randolph Street. I glanced around the shop, my gaze skimming past shelves of yarn in every possible color of the rainbow. There were several customers browsing the store, but no one behind the counter and no sign of my old high school friend Dawn, who'd opened the shop last year.

An older woman sat in a comfy-looking armchair by the front window with a pile of knitting in her lap. Her needles clicked together as her fingers worked with mind-boggling speed, and I wandered closer, mesmerized by her skill.

"Did you need help?" the woman asked without looking up from her knitting.

"I'm sorry," I said. "I didn't mean to stare."

"If I minded people looking at me, I'd stay home."

"You're really good at that."

"I ought to be. Been doing it long enough."

"Do you work here?"

"Nope. Just loitering." She inclined her head toward an open doorway off to one side of the shop. "There's someone in the back if you need something."

"I'm looking for Dawn. I don't suppose she's here today?"

"Dawn!" the woman shouted, loud enough to make my ears ring. "Someone's out here asking for you."

A moment later, Dawn appeared in the doorway, wearing a green apron with the shop's logo on it.

"Tess!" She broke into a smile as she came forward to hug me. "Wow. What a surprise!"

I'd known Dawn for as long as I'd known Donal. She'd been in most of the same classes as us and part of our extended friend group from elementary through high school. Dawn and I had both gone on to Northwestern, although I'd started a year later because of my deferment. We hadn't crossed paths all that much while we were there, but I'd attended her wedding shortly after college. Since then, we'd kept in touch on Facebook—which was how I knew she'd opened this shop after her divorce last year—but it had been ages since we'd seen each other in person.

Funny how that worked. Lives got busy, friends grew apart, and the next thing you knew, ten years had passed since you'd seen someone even though you both lived in the same city.

"The store looks fantastic," I told her. "It's so welcoming and cozy."

She looked pleased as her gaze wandered around the space. "I can't take all the credit. Angie helped with a lot of the decorating."

"That's great," I murmured, keeping my smile fixed firmly in place.

I'd served on our ten-year and twenty-year high school reunion committees with Angie, who'd been Dawn's bestie since sixth grade. Let's just say Angie and I didn't see eye to eye. We'd had diverging visions for the reunions and had clashed over every little decision. She was the main reason I'd resigned from the committee for our upcoming thirty-year reunion. Not to be petty, but I'd rather walk barefoot over a field of Legos than plan another reunion with Angie Ellis—and I didn't doubt the feeling was entirely mutual.

Dawn gave me a knowing look, no doubt aware of the friction between us. "So what brings you here? You didn't just come by to admire the store."

"I need some knitting help, actually." I pulled the tote bag off my shoulder and held it open for Dawn. "I found an old half-finished project I started back in high school, and I'd like to see if I can finish it. I've got all the yarn still, but I don't have the pattern anymore—or the needles."

Slipping on a pair of reading glasses, Dawn reached into the bag and pulled out a corner of the blanket for a better look. "This shouldn't be too tough to recreate. Let's take it over by the window and spread it out."

I followed her to the couch next to the older woman I'd spoken to. We sat down and Dawn removed the blanket from the bag, unfolding it across her lap.

She glanced over at me, her eyebrows drawing together. "It's a baby blanket?"

"Yes." I knew what she wanted to ask, so I saved her the trouble. "It's what you think it is."

Dawn was the only other person I'd told about my pregnancy back in high school. I hadn't planned on telling her, but she'd found me puking my guts out in the school bathroom one morning not long after I'd broken things off with Donal. When she'd tried to convince me to go to the nurse's office, I'd ended up confessing everything to her. She'd kept my secret for me and tried to be my friend during those dark, lonely months, but I'd been so ashamed of my predicament that I'd kept her at a distance—just like I'd pushed Donal away.

"I started knitting it when I was pregnant," I told her. "I planned to give it to the baby, so she'd have something to remember me by after she was adopted. But I never finished it."

The older woman was still knitting in the chair beside me, and I knew she could hear every word of our conversation, but the steady click of her needles never slowed or faltered.

"And you want to finish it now?" Dawn asked gently.

I nodded. And then I told her about Erin and how she'd found me. When I finished, Dawn reached out and squeezed my hand.

"Are you going to give her the blanket when it's done?"

"I haven't decided. For now, I just want to see if I can finish it."

"You should give it to her," the older woman said, speaking up for the first time since we'd sat down.

I looked down at the variegated pastel blanket. Both the colors and the pattern were extremely eighties, and not in a cool, retro way. It was a lot of dusty pinks and mint greens that struck me as ugly now. "It's a little dated, don't you think? I'm not sure she'd actually want to use it for the new baby."

"Doesn't matter. People always like to know that someone was thinking of them."

"Linda's right," Dawn said. "The real beauty of a handmade gift is the effort that went into making it. Every stitch represents a moment spent thinking about the person it was made for."

My hand smoothed over the old stitches I'd knit a lifetime ago, still not sure I wanted to give it to Erin. But I could figure that out later. "First I actually have to finish the thing."

"I think we can help you with that," Dawn said. "What do you think, Linda? Any chance you can figure out the pattern for Tess?"

"Give it here." The woman finally paused her knitting, laying her needles down as she gestured for us to pass her the baby blanket.

I handed it over and she peered at it, pulling the fabric taut between her wrinkled thumbs as she clucked her tongue. "This shouldn't be too hard."

Linda got up, leaving her own knitting behind, and carried the blanket over behind the counter.

"So," Dawn said, slipping her reading glasses off again. "How's Donal taking the recent developments? I assume he knows?"

"Oh yes, he knows all right."

"Don't tell me he was upset?" From the look on her face, she was all set to hunt him down and give him hell if that was the case.

I smiled. "No, not at all. He's been great, actually."

Dawn's eyebrows twitched toward her hairline. "Really? Does that mean you two are on speaking terms again?"

I shrugged, playing it casual. "Apparently."

"So you've seen him?"

"A few times, yeah." For some reason, I was reluctant to admit to our almost nightly phone calls, or exactly how close it felt like we'd gotten over the last few weeks.

Dawn's eyes narrowed as she studied me. "And?"

"And nothing," I replied, endeavoring to keep my expression neutral.

Her mouth fell open, and she pointed an accusing finger at me. "Oh my God, you're blushing, you dirty liar. Don't hold out on me!"

Curse this translucent complexion of mine!

Shaking my head, I pressed a palm to my heated cheek. "Relax, we're not getting back together or anything. We're just friends."

Dawn continued to scrutinize me, her sharp eyes missing nothing. "But you're thinking about getting back together with him, aren't you?"

"No. Maybe." Pressing my lips together, I shook my head again. "I don't know what I want, to be honest."

"Sure you do. Those cheeks don't lie. You want to do sexy things with him."

I couldn't help laughing. "Yes, fine, you've got me there. But who wouldn't? Have you seen what he looks like these days?"

"I've seen a few pictures." Dawn's eyebrows waggled appreciatively. "The man can still get it."

"I'll tell you what, he looks even better in person, which is completely unreasonable of him."

"*So* unreasonable," she agreed. "How dare he be so effortlessly attractive at our age? And you know he's not doing anything to deserve it. Probably just rolls out of bed and splashes water on his face. Meanwhile, I'm going through a ten-step skincare routine twice a day trying to stave off the ravages of time."

"Believe me, I'm right there with you." I smiled, remembering Donal's Rogaine confession, but kept it to myself. "Regardless, I'm not sure it'd be smart to get involved with him like that again."

"Why not? He's divorced now and you're single, right?" She frowned. "He's not still hung up on his ex-wife, is he? Hasn't it been over a year since they divorced?"

"It's not that." I chewed on the inside of my lip as I tried to articulate what was holding me back. "I just think our focus should be on Erin and trying to build a relationship with her. Things are complicated enough without me jumping into bed with Donal."

"From what you said, it sounds like things are going well between you and Erin."

"They are—or at least I think they are. But I've never been a parent before. I have no idea what I'm supposed to be doing or what she needs from me. I'm not equipped for any of this. I don't know how to be anyone's mother."

A hint of a smile touched Dawn's lips as she tilted her head. "I doubt she expects you to be. She's nearly thirty, right? A fully grown woman. You're off the hook with the parenting stuff."

"Yes, but she's having a baby, which means I'll be a grandmother, I guess? Sort of? Technically." It still weirded me out to think about it, but the weirdness came with a thrill of excitement. And with the excitement came a heaping dose of anxiety. "But aren't grandmothers supposed to be baby experts? I was never even a mother, and now I'm jumping over the beginner's bracket and advancing straight to the pro level. Only I don't know the first thing about babies. I haven't even changed a diaper since I used to babysit in high school."

Dawn laughed. "I know a lot has changed in the world since we were young, but I'm pretty sure babies and poop still work basically the same way."

"You know what I mean."

"I do, but I think you're worrying too much."

"Have you met me?" I mumbled. "Also, Donal's got two kids, so you know he's going to roll in like some kind of baby whisperer and wow everyone with his superior grandparent skills."

"It's not a competition," Dawn said, shaking her head at me. "I swear, you and Donal are like Alexander Hamilton and Aaron Burr, if Hamilton and Burr had secretly wanted to bang each other's brains out."

"Maybe they did and that was the problem. Are you suggesting we should settle this with pistols at dawn?"

"Or here's a thought…you could ask Donal for baby tips."

"Hmmm. Maybe." A month ago, the thought of admitting Donal was better at something and asking for his help would have made me break out in hives. But now I could almost imagine myself doing it. I supposed that counted as progress. "All of this is assuming Erin will even want us around after she has the baby."

"You don't think she will?"

"I don't know." I wanted to think so, but I had trouble letting myself believe it. "She's already got a mother she's close to. I'm not sure where that leaves me or what she wants from us long-term—if anything. Maybe she's only looking for answers to fill in the blanks, and once she's got them she'll be done with us."

"Or she could be hoping for some kind of deeper, lasting connection." Dawn studied me. "What about you? Do you know what you want from her?"

"I don't want anything from her." Everything I'd done so far had been about giving Erin whatever she needed. I didn't feel entitled to ask for anything from her in return.

"Sure you do. You want some kind of relationship, right? Or else you wouldn't have responded to her message in the first place."

"True."

"Do you know precisely what you want that relationship to look like?"

"No, not really." I didn't have any kind of template or model to work from. Erin was my daughter, but she was also a stranger. I was her mother, but that role had been filled by someone else all her life. It left me with no idea what we were supposed to mean to each other. All I knew for certain was that I wanted us to be part of each other's lives somehow.

"That's okay." Dawn's smile was understanding. "It's probably going to take you both some time to figure it out. In the meantime, try not to overthink it. Relationships are about the journey, not getting from point A to point B by the most efficient route."

My mouth twitched into a one-sided smile. "But the most efficient route is the only way I know how to get anywhere."

"I'm aware," she said with a knowing chuckle. "You're just going to have to suck it up and go with the flow."

"Blergh." I wrinkled my nose. "I hate going with the flow."

Dawn's smile lingered as she arched an eyebrow at me. "You know, the same goes for you and Donal."

"What do you mean?"

"Don't overthink it!" She rolled her eyes in exasperation. "Is the old spark still there?"

"Yes," I answered without hesitation. "Definitely."

"Then don't you owe it to yourself—to both of you—to give it a chance and see where it takes you? What are you afraid of?"

"That it won't work out, I guess." I didn't want to set myself up to fail. Or get hurt. Or lose Donal all over again. Not when we'd finally started to get our friendship back. The truth was I liked having him in my life. As much as I wanted to smush our naughty bits together, I'd rather not blow up all the progress we'd made.

"That's always a risk though, isn't it? It's not a good reason to let opportunities pass you by." Dawn's smile faded as she looked down at her hands. "You don't want to miss your window. It might be smaller than you think."

There was something in her tone—an odd sort of intensity—that caused me to take a closer look at her. For the first time, I noticed the subtle signs of tension in her expression and the dark circles under her eyes that she'd tried to hide with concealer.

"You know," I said, "we've been talking about me all this time, and I never asked how you were doing."

Dawn's smile quickly brightened. "Oh, I'm doing great! Couldn't be happier."

It was a good performance, but it rang hollow. Before I could say anything else, however, Linda came back with my baby blanket.

"Did you work it out?" Dawn asked, looking up at her.

"Yup." Linda dumped the baby blanket in my lap and handed me a piece of paper covered with handwritten code. "This'll do it."

"Thank you." I squinted at the pattern notes, attempting to translate them. I recognized most, but there were a few notations that stumped me.

"Don't worry," Dawn told me. "I'll walk you through it."

"I'd estimate size seven needles, but she'll want to check her gauge." Linda hooked a thumb over her shoulder. "I'm gonna go wet the lettuce."

Dawn smiled after her before turning her attention back to the blanket pattern. "This doesn't look too tricky. I'll go grab some needles for you. Do you have a preference between wood and metal, or do you want me to choose for you?"

"Dawn." I reached out to touch her arm as she started to walk away. "I know we haven't exactly stayed close, but if you ever need anything or want to talk, you know I'm here for you, right?"

She grasped my hand and squeezed it, her smile growing a little more genuine. "I appreciate that. I do. But everything's fine."

I didn't believe her, but I wasn't going to force the issue. If anyone could under-stand not wanting to show weakness, it was me. "We should go out for drinks sometime and catch up. What do you say?"

"I'd love that. Really." Her smile slipped a bit. "I'm going to be busy for the next few weeks, but maybe after that?"

"Sure," I said. "Sounds great."

⸻

My conversation with Dawn haunted me for the rest of the day. Something was definitely going on with her, but we weren't close enough friends that I felt enti-tled to pry. She'd rebuffed my gentle inquiries, which meant she didn't want to share whatever was troubling her. I had no choice but to respect her boundaries.

Nevertheless, I planned to follow up on my drinks invitation in a few weeks. I was determined to put more effort into cultivating friendships, and Dawn was the perfect candidate for a friendship date. We'd drifted away from each other in part because she'd gotten busy with married life and having kids, but she was recently divorced and her kids were grown now. She could probably use a single friend her own age.

God knew I could. For pity's sake, it was Friday night and what was I doing? Sitting at home by myself knitting.

Or trying to, anyway. Dawn's explanation of Linda's instructions had made sense in the store, but now that I was on my own, I kept getting mixed up and losing my place in the pattern.

"Fucknuts," I muttered after realizing I'd screwed up yet another yarn over. I backtracked painstakingly, undoing the last few stitches. If nothing else, I'd gotten a lot of practice at fixing my mistakes.

Either I totally sucked at this, or I was too distracted tonight. My money was on the latter. I kept thinking about what Dawn had said about missed opportunities and how I owed it to myself to give things with Donal a chance. Hadn't Marie said almost the same thing? Something about not closing any doors prematurely.

And yet that was exactly what I'd done. Instead of acting on the attraction between us, I'd frozen up and shut down all possibility of physical intimacy.

Did I really want to make choices based on fear?

Fuck no, I didn't. I was a badass boss bitch who wasn't afraid to go for what I wanted.

And what I wanted was Donal.

Trying to ignore my attraction to him hadn't magically made it go away. If anything it had grown even stronger. Being friends was great and everything, but all this repressed lust was seriously starting to get in the way. I was horny all the time. I couldn't even think about Donal without getting hot and bothered. My pulse raced whenever I got a new text from him, and just the sound of his voice over the phone made my panties wet.

What would it be like the next time we were in the same room together? My overeager vagina might actually explode.

It was requiring way too much energy to hide my carnal impulses and maintain a platonic facade. Maybe it'd be better to just give in to our urges. Go with the flow, like Dawn had said.

As if fate was sending me a sign, Donal chose that very moment to call. My heart skipped a beat as I set my knitting aside and answered the phone.

"Hey." The husky rumble of his voice sent the situation between my legs into meltdown, as per usual. "What're you up to? You working?"

"No, not tonight. I'm knitting, actually. What about you?"

"I was trying to work, but my head's not cooperating. Figured I'd call you instead."

"You probably need a night off. You work too much."

He grunted in wry amusement. "Okay, kettle. Thanks for the advice, but it's not like you're any better than me."

"Excuse you, I just said I'm not working tonight, didn't I? You know why? Because I understand the importance of work-life balance."

"Sure," he scoffed. "So this is how you spend your precious night off? Knitting?"

"It's supposed to be relaxing and meditative."

"Is it?"

"No, it's stressing me the fuck out."

Donal laughed. "I thought you might have gone out tonight."

"Nope. Just enjoying a quiet evening at home."

"We're a couple of real party animals, aren't we? Home alone on a Friday night."

This was my opening. A chance to climb through that window of opportunity Dawn had talked about. I took a breath and edged a toe over the sill. "The really sad part is that I forgot to go to the store, so I don't even have any alcohol in the apartment to celebrate my night off."

"That is sad." A pause. "I happen to be fully stocked up over here."

"Oh yeah?" I asked trying to sound casual. "Lucky you."

SUSANNAH NIX

"Mmm hmmm. Beer, wine, a few kinds of whiskey..." I leaned forward as I heard him draw in a breath. "Did you know I make a mean Manhattan?"

"I did not know that about you."

"It's true." We were both working hard at the casual act. I wasn't sure which one of us was winning.

"You know, I'm not sure I've ever had a Manhattan," I said, breezy as a stroll on the Lake Shore path.

"I could make you one if you want to come over."

"Okay." I might have forgotten to play it cool and accidentally answered too quickly. *Oops.*

"Really?" Donal asked after a beat.

"Sure." My throat felt like it was lined with cotton. "If it's a serious offer."

"It's a serious offer."

I exhaled. "In that case, I'll be right over."

CHAPTER NINETEEN

DONAL

Standing on my doorstep in an ankle-length dress that clung to her curves and showed off enough cleavage to obliterate my composure, Tess looked like she'd stepped straight out of a fantasy.

Inviting her over here tonight was asking for trouble. Big time. The last time we'd been alone in my apartment I'd completely lost my head. The chances of me doing something similarly stupid were astronomically high.

I couldn't afford a repeat of that mistake. She'd made it clear where her boundaries were, and I'd agreed to abide by them. Hell, I was even pretty sure she was right. Us plus sex almost definitely equaled a Very Bad Idea.

I'd have to keep myself in check tonight. If we were going to be friends, this would only be the first of many tests to come. I needed to get used to being around her without crossing any lines.

Starting now.

"I feel underdressed," I said as I stepped back to let her in. I'd changed into a pair of jeans and a T-shirt, but I'd purposely avoided dressing to impress. Friends didn't dress up for each other. Sure, I'd brushed my teeth and applied some fresh deodorant, but only out of politeness. Proper hygiene was just basic good manners.

Tess's gaze slid down my body in a way that felt a lot like a taunt. "You look good to me."

"Yes, but you look beautiful. Then again, you'd look beautiful in a paper bag." Friends were allowed to compliment each other, okay? It was called being supportive.

I bent to kiss her cheek, and if my lips lingered on her for a second longer than strictly necessary, who could blame me?

She smiled as she turned away, slipping out of her shoes and leaving them by the door. Her toes were painted a dark ruby red, and I couldn't take my eyes off them. "You always were good at flattery."

My compliment had been entirely genuine, but it was probably for the best if she wrote it off as insincere bullshit.

I watched her set her purse down and shrug out of her denim jacket, exposing thin straps that bared her shoulders. She was all swaying hips and breasts in that thin fucking dress. And she definitely wasn't wearing a bra. *Jesus Murphy.*

I needed to get myself in hand. Literally, once she was gone, or else my dick was going to explode. But for now, I needed to cool the hell off and stop ogling her like a horny teenager.

Slow and purposeful, I inhaled a breath through my nose and blew it out through my mouth. We were friends. F-R-I-E-N-D-S. That meant no messing around. She was like a work colleague. Totally off-limits.

"So…" Her eyebrows raised as she turned to face me again. "I was promised a Manhattan?"

"Right. Yeah. Coming right up."

Tess trailed me into the kitchen, and I got to work making our drinks. It was a relief to have something to focus on besides her, but I was acutely conscious of her eyes on me as I got out the ingredients.

"You really do have a lot of alcohol," she observed.

I nodded as I measured shots of rye whiskey into the shaker. "I get a lot for Christmas every year from clients and coworkers. More than I can drink. Or more than I should drink, anyway."

Her hip rested against the counter as her fingernails tapped on the granite surface. They were painted the same dark red as her toes. Not that I was looking. I was way too busy paying attention to the drinks I was making. I definitely had not just accidentally added too much vermouth. *Shit.*

"Would you mind grabbing an orange from the fridge?" I asked.

"Sure thing."

I was proud of myself for not glancing around to watch her bend over to open the produce drawer. Even though I could imagine what an incredible sight it must be in that dress, with the soft T-shirt fabric clinging to her backside.

"Here." An orange appeared on the counter beside me with Tess's red fingernails curled around it.

"Thanks." I capped the shaker and pushed it toward her. "Like to do the honors?"

Because I was a good boy, I did not let my eyes slide over to watch her breasts jiggle while she shook the Manhattans. Instead, I grabbed a paring knife and concentrated on cutting two twists off the orange. No leering or gawking here. *Look at me, doing this friends thing right. Someone should give me a fucking gold star.*

"Impressive," she murmured when I'd produced two perfect strips of orange peel. "Where'd you learn to do that so well?"

"Worked as a barback one summer in college." I poured the Manhattans into two cocktail glasses. For the finishing touch, I expressed the citrus oil from the peels before dropping them into the drinks. "Picked up all kinds of handy skills."

"Oh yeah? Such as?"

"Making the perfect Manhattan, for one—as well as pretty much anything else you might want to drink." I slid one of the glasses toward her and picked up the other. "But also, washing glasses, mopping floors, and cleaning toilets."

A flash of amusement in her eyes made my stomach tighten. "Those are handy skills."

"Cheers." I tapped the rim of my glass against hers. Instead of taking a sip of my drink, I watched Tess taste hers, unable to drag my gaze from her lips. "Pretty fucking good, right?"

"It's excellent." She smiled at me over the rim of her glass. "You swear an awful lot for a fancy corporate lawyer."

I grimaced. "Yeah, I know. I've always had a dirty mouth."

"I remember."

She probably hadn't meant it as a double entendre, but that was where my mind went anyway. Because of course, it did. And now I could feel my ears getting hot, which meant I was blushing.

Tess's lips twitched into a smirk as she watched me knock back an imprudently large gulp of my drink. Okay, so maybe she had meant it that way. *Damn.*

Lifting her glass, she took a leisurely sip, her eyes never leaving mine. "So is this your signature move? Do you invite a lot of women up here and woo them with your Manhattan-making skills?"

"You're assuming I have moves."

"I know from firsthand experience you have moves."

My mouth went dry as dust, and I set my drink down a little too hard, the base of the stem clattering against the countertop. Lucky I hadn't broken the damn thing.

Much more gracefully, Tess echoed my movement, setting her own glass next to mine. But her eyes never left my face. What I saw in them threatened to dismantle my hard-won self-control.

"Tess." My tone held a note of warning.

"Hmmm?" She was staring at my mouth now. Very obviously. With a focus that sent all the blood in my body straight to my crotch.

My hands twitched, aching to reach for her. "You need to stop looking at me like that."

Her eyelashes fluttered, but her gaze didn't waver from my mouth. If anything, it grew even more intent. "Like what?"

She had to know what she was doing to me, right? Was this some kind of fucking test? Or was she playing with me for sport? Knowing Tess, it might be a little of both.

"Like you want me to kiss you."

The air seemed to crackle between us as her lips twisted in a slow, deliberate tease. "What if I do want you to kiss me?"

My cock jumped against the seam of my jeans, trying to answer for me, but somehow I managed to hold the rest of myself still. "I thought you just wanted to be friends. Strictly nonphysical, that's what you said."

"Friends are supposed to be honest with each other, right?" Her tongue flicked against her upper lip, and my dick gave another salute in response.

When I managed to speak, my voice was all gravel. "Yes."

"So I'm being honest." She shrugged lightly as she stepped closer. *Way* too damn close.

Automatically, my hands grabbed onto her hips. *To stop her*, I told myself. To keep her from coming any closer.

"Now it's your turn," she said, maddeningly calm. "Tell me what you're thinking. And you have to be honest."

This was almost certainly a giant mistake. What were the odds Tess would suddenly pull away from me again at some point? Pretty goddamn high, based on experience. But I couldn't help myself. Not when she was giving me those fuck-me eyes. She always made me too damn reckless—reckless enough to tell her exactly what was in my head.

"I'm thinking I want to know how wet you are right now."

Her breath caught, and I watched her pupils dilate like pools of spilled ink. "I'm thinking I want you to touch me and find out."

"Tess," I growled, my fingers tightening on her waist. My sense of self-preservation was telling me I should let go of her and step back, but I couldn't make myself do it. It was already taking every ounce of restraint I had not to push her up against the counter and kiss her. "I'm trying to follow the rules here, but you're not playing fair."

"I'm thinking I want to change the rules." She laid her palms on my chest, and I wondered if she could feel my heart pounding. "I'm thinking I want to get these clothes off you so I can feel your skin against mine."

"Fuck, Tess. If you don't stop, I'm going to lose it."

"Feel free."

I couldn't tell if the desire I saw in her eyes was purely sexual, or if she felt something deeper between us the way I did. Would she wake up tomorrow and see me as a mistake? Would she turn her back on me again and walk away? Would she break my heart like she'd broken it before?

Right this second, I was finding it hard to care.

"Are you giving me permission?" I was breathing heavy, every muscle in my body tense with the effort of holding myself back. "I need you to be absolutely fucking sure before you answer." If I let myself do this, there'd be no turning back. I'd be a goner for Tess McGregor all over again.

But as I watched the green in the depths of her eyes spark like emerald fire, I knew it was too late. I was already way past gone. Tess McGregor owned me, body and soul, and maybe she always had.

"Yes," she whispered, leaning even closer. "Kiss me."

I sank into her mouth like I'd been dreaming of doing ever since she'd broken off our last make-out session. She tasted lush and sweet, with a hint of citrus and bitters from the Manhattan she'd been sipping.

Her hands slid up my neck and into my hair, pulling me closer as her tongue twined with mine. When she pressed herself against me I pressed back, pushing her up against the counter.

Electric heat shot straight to my balls as her hips rocked into me. My hands shook as I slid them up her waist, stopping on her rib cage just below her breasts. I wanted to touch her so badly. Everywhere. I wanted to feel her muscles trembling under my hands, wanted to hear her breathless pants as I tasted her, wanted to feel her hot pussy clenching around me.

But she'd said "Kiss me," not "Fuck me up against your kitchen counter." If I pushed my luck too far she might change her mind again.

Only the way she was rubbing herself against me didn't feel like she was about to change her mind. One of her hands had dropped to my ass, which she was kneading shamelessly as she ground herself against my throbbing hard-on. It felt so good, I could hardly stand it. My body was going into overload, not enough oxygen in my lungs and too much blood shuddering through my veins.

Tess's other hand slipped under my shirt, dancing over the bare skin of my abdomen. Everywhere she touched me the muscles tensed and trembled. When I felt the sharp graze of her nails as her fingers dipped into my waistband, I realized I was on the brink of a serious calamity.

Wait," I grunted, pulling back to catch my breath. "Just—hang on."

Tess froze and let go of me, which was what I needed, but not at all what I wanted. "What's wrong?"

"Nothing's wrong." I screwed my eyes shut and shoved my hands through my hair. *Fuck. Fuck fuck fuck fuck FUCK.* "I just need a second."

"If nothing's wrong, why did you pull away?"

I opened my eyes, wincing at the wariness in her expression. Her walls were starting to go up again, and the only way to stop it was brutal candor. "Because I was afraid I was going to come, okay? That's why I needed a second."

She arched an eyebrow, her lips quirking in a smug smile. "Really?"

"Yes, really."

"Flattering." Her smile tugged wider. "For me, that is."

"Ha ha," I muttered, cutting a glare at her. "It's possible it's been a while since I've done this."

"How long's a while?"

I scrubbed a hand over my face, sagging back against the counter across from her. "I'd rather not say."

She frowned. "Why not?"

My gaze dropped to the floor as I forced myself to unclench my jaw and tell her the truth. Again. All my embarrassing secrets were coming out tonight. "Because I haven't slept with anyone since my divorce, and I don't want to admit how long it's been since my ex-wife and I last had sex."

Two years and change, for the record. One year since the divorce, and over a year before that since Wendy and I had been intimate. Amazing I hadn't seen the divorce coming. That was how far up my own asshole I'd been.

"Oh," Tess said softly. "Wow."

175

"Yeah." And now I'd killed the mood by oversharing. At least coming wasn't likely to be a problem anytime soon.

Silence sloshed awkwardly between us as a series of emotions flickered behind her eyes. The way she was looking at me made me feel like I was being evaluated and recategorized like a mis-shelved library book.

It must've seemed weird that I hadn't ventured into the dating pool since my marriage broke up. It wasn't as if I hadn't thought of it. I certainly hadn't been sitting around pining for my ex-wife or anything like that. I just hadn't had the time—or the energy, to be honest. All my focus had been on repairing my relationship with my kids. Between that and work, I hadn't had room in my life for anything else. Shit, I barely even remembered to eat half the time.

"It's okay," Tess said finally. "We don't have to do this if you're not ready."

"No way," I growled. "Fuck that. I'm ready. I'm *too* goddamn ready—that's the problem."

The corner of her mouth dimpled, and she hopped up onto the kitchen island. "In that case, I think you should come back over here."

I didn't need to be asked twice. Pushing off the opposite counter, I closed the distance between us in one long step. When my hips bumped against her knees, she spread them to welcome me between her legs.

I cradled her face in my hands, dragging my thumb over her kiss-swollen lips. Her fingers slid into my hair and tugged, urging me to kiss her. Instead, I gently bit her lower lip. Her eyes fluttered closed as she shuddered in my hands. I licked her next, sweeping my tongue across her lip. She squirmed, wriggling against me, and I bit her again, a little harder. This time she moaned, and I pulled back to drink in the sight of her.

"So beautiful," I whispered. "I love seeing you like this."

Her eyes blinked open, and her lips pressed together before curving at the corners. "Remember what you wanted to know earlier?" She captured one of my hands and placed it on her thigh. "Still want to find out?"

"Fuck yes." I grabbed a handful of her long skirt and hiked it up until my fingers flexed on soft, bare skin.

I watched her swallow, her body taut with anticipation as I slowly slid my hand up her leg and under the bunched hem of her dress. When I reached the apex of her thighs, I went still.

"Tess," I breathed. "You're not wearing underwear."

"I'm aware." Her eyes were overbright and slightly glassy.

"Is that…do you walk around like this all the time?" If she'd been going commando all along, I was going to lose my goddamn mind.

"No, I do not walk around without underwear all the time." Her mouth quirked. "Just tonight."

"Are you saying you came over here tonight planning to seduce me?" My fingertip drew teasing circles high up on her thigh. "Because that sounds a lot like premeditation."

She bit down on her lip. "Maybe."

"Goddammit. That is so hot."

Her eyes flashed in challenge. "Then hurry up and touch me."

So fucking impatient. Mother of God, how I loved it.

Bending my head, I moved my lips to her ear and murmured, "The payoff's sweeter when you have to wait for it."

Before she could reply, I pressed the heel of my hand against her pussy. She gasped and arched her back, exposing the column of her throat. My hand curled in her hair, dragging her head back farther. As I sucked at the skin below her jaw, I dragged a fingertip through her soaking wet folds.

"More." Her hips bucked against my hand, seeking more friction. "Harder."

"Say please," I murmured, holding my hand still between her legs as I licked a path along her collarbone.

"Donal, goddammit, if you don't—"

"Say the magic word, McGregor, and I'll give you what you want."

"Fucking please," she growled.

My thumb nudged her clit, and her whole body jerked. "There. See how easy that was?"

"I hate you," she panted, rocking against my hand.

I smiled as I stroked her, watching her dissolve with pleasure at my touch. "No you don't."

Her eyes opened and met mine, revealing something unexpectedly soft in their shiny depths. "No," she whispered. "I don't."

My heart caught in my throat as a burst of tenderness seared through my chest, threatening to crush me. I leaned in to brush my lips against hers, and she gasped into my mouth when I slipped a finger inside her.

Goddamn. I let out a groan at the feel of her slick, silken walls clenching around me.

"You feel so fucking good." I circled her clit with my thumb as I pumped my finger inside her. "Do you like that?"

"Yes." The word shuddered out of her, and *fuck*, the sight of her losing control like this, the way her face was open and unguarded for once, punched a hole straight through my chest.

So much for keeping my feelings in check. That ship had sailed. I'd never be able to look at her without thinking about her like this.

"Please," she whimpered, not even fighting it anymore. "Please I need more." Her hands were on my shoulders, her fingernails digging into my skin through my T-shirt, sending tiny pinpricks of pleasure-pain shooting down my spine.

I curled my finger inside her, and she let out a shaky moan when I found the sweet spot. "There," I murmured, licking my lips as I watched my hand fuck her. "There you go."

Her body bowed, and she threw her head back and cried out. I felt her walls pulse as her orgasm rocked through her, and I lifted my gaze to her face so I could watch her fall apart. For that one perfect moment, she was utterly exposed, uninhibited, and incandescent.

Dangerous, a warning voice whispered in my head.

But I didn't care. She was in my blood, and I needed to have her.

I'd already fallen headfirst over the cliff. There was no going back now.

CHAPTER TWENTY

TESS

"You've gotten a lot better at that," I murmured as I came down from my orgasm high. And *whew*, what a high it was. It'd been a minute since a man's touch had made the earth move like that.

Donal laughed, smoothing his hands down my back as I sagged limply against his chest. "Shit, I hope so. I didn't even know what a G-spot was the last time we did that."

"You certainly know what it is now." I lifted my head, and a smile curved his lips as he reached up to brush my hair off my face.

There was something so incredibly tender about the gesture—not to mention the way he was looking at me. It caused something to burst in my chest, warming me from the inside out. The feeling was so strong it left me unsettled.

I'd given myself permission to have sex with Donal, but that didn't mean I'd sanctioned losing my head over the man—especially not this quickly. Sex was one thing, but feelings this intense could lead to trouble if I wasn't careful.

I couldn't let myself get into a position where I *needed* him. That way lay disappointment and heartbreak. I'd have to be careful not to get too carried away.

He kissed my temple, my forehead, and my cheek, lingering gently at each spot with more of that disorienting tenderness. When he finally touched his lips to the corner of my mouth, it was more than I could bear. We needed to get this train back on the proper tracks.

Turning my head, I captured his mouth roughly and stroked my tongue deep inside until I felt his breaths grow staccato with hunger. Only then did I pull back to look at him, my lips curving in a seductive taunt. "I can't wait to find out what else you've gotten better at."

"Bedroom?" he proposed, and I eagerly nodded my agreement.

As much as I'd enjoyed that incredible orgasm he'd given me, his kitchen counter wasn't the most comfortable place to conduct the rest of our sexual explorations. Once upon a time I might not have minded prolonged periods of sitting on hard surfaces, but these days I had a deeper appreciation for comfortable furniture and proper back support.

Donal plucked me from the counter and set me on my feet, kissing me once more before taking me by the hand and leading me into his bedroom.

"You're a slob," I said as I took in his unmade bed and the clothes strewn on the floor. "How shocking."

Aside from the mess, it featured the same sad sparseness as the rest of the apartment. The main difference was that it smelled like him in here, like his shampoo and the laundry detergent he used, mixed with the unmistakable scent of his skin.

"A single man's bedroom is his sanctuary that should be a place free from judgment and why are you still wearing clothes?" He pulled me into his arms with arousing possessiveness and lowered his mouth to mine, lavishing me with deep, devouring kisses.

My lashes fluttered as his lips traveled down my throat, and he tugged the thin strap of my dress aside to mouth a wet trail across the top of my shoulder. His other hand palmed my breast, and I moaned as his fingers dipped inside the low neckline and found their way to my nipple.

"Off," he growled, extracting his hand to grab a fistful of my skirt and yank it up.

I helped him ease the maxi dress over my head, tossing it to the floor behind me.

Donal's eyes widened in appreciation at the sight of me standing naked before him, and he made a rough noise in the back of his throat as he bent to lavish my breasts with kisses.

"Your turn." Impatiently, I shoved his T-shirt up, and we parted long enough for him to drag it over his head.

Confronted with the sight of his bare torso for the first time, I sucked in a breath and literally licked my lips.

"How?" My fingers skimmed over the taut skin of his shoulders and down through the scattering of hair on his firm chest to his unreasonably flat stomach. "How do you still look this good? Do you have an enchanted portrait hidden in your closet?"

He grunted, yanking me flush against him, and dipped his mouth to my breasts again. "I spend a lot of time working off stress in the gym."

I didn't like the idea of him dealing with that much stress, but I certainly couldn't complain about the resultant state of his physique. My hands continued their appreciative wanderings as his breath heated my already feverish skin.

He guided me to the bed, and I lay back as he knelt over me. Our mouths fused in a greedy kiss, and his forearm depressed the mattress next to my head as his knee pushed between my legs.

Pulling his head back, he aimed his heated gaze at my body, intensifying the ache between my legs as his thumb circled my hard nipple. "I love the way your flush goes all the way down."

It was too much, the way he was looking at me. When his fingertips skimmed worshipfully over my stomach, I shuddered beneath him, overwhelmed by an unexpected surge of emotion. This pull between us was stronger than anything I'd experienced before—a force beyond my control, wild and unremitting.

I'd always prided myself on my ability to keep my feelings in check and make rational decisions, but the passion coursing through my body was a force too powerful to resist.

When I'd made the decision to come over here tonight and basically throw myself at him, I'd done it in full knowledge I might be making a huge mistake. I knew it would irrevocably change the friendship we'd tentatively forged.

What I hadn't predicted was that *I'd* be irrevocably changed along with it.

Once we turned this corner, there'd be no going back. I wasn't just inviting Donal into my body tonight. I was inviting him into my heart. Because lurking beneath all this sexual attraction was something deeper and far scarier. Something I wouldn't easily be able to shake off.

"Tess." The whisper of his fingertips along my jaw was as gentle as the sound of my name on his lips. His eyes were clear and knowing as they looked into mine, making me feel naked inside as well as out. But they were also soft, and I saw his own struggle to balance his doubts and desires reflected in his expression.

He bent his head, and my eyes closed when his nose brushed my cheek. For a moment we lay still, breathing in tandem as he nuzzled into my hair.

"We don't have to do anything else," he murmured. "If you want to stop here, it's okay."

That wasn't what I wanted. Now that we'd started this, I was desperate to have him. We'd already come too far to turn back.

I tipped my face toward him, and our noses bumped as my lips drifted over his. "I don't want to stop. Do you?"

"No." His weight pressed down on me, his erection offering extremely hard evidence to back up his assertion.

Our mouths tangled in a slow, exploring kiss that quickly grew more heated as I greedily stroked my hands over the hard muscles of his back. I loved the feel of them, the way they flexed as he braced himself above me. Even more than that, I loved the warm, solid weight of him on me.

My heart thumped harder as his lips traveled down my body, and I sucked in a sharp breath when his teeth grazed my nipple. As good as it felt, I'd had enough foreplay. If we didn't get to the main attraction soon, I was going to combust.

Hooking my fingers in his waistband, I yanked him closer so I could stroke him through his jeans.

A groan shuddered through him, and he trapped my hand with his, holding it still. "There's just one small problem. I don't have any condoms."

I stared at him. "Are you serious?"

"Why are you so surprised? I told you I haven't done any dating since my divorce."

"I don't think I've ever encountered a single adult male who didn't have an ample supply of condoms on hand at all times." I pressed my hand against his erection, and he dropped his forehead to my chest with another groan.

"Sorry I'm not more of a player." He slipped a finger inside me, smiling when I squirmed. "We'll just have to find other ways to enjoy each other."

Appealing as that was—and it was very appealing—what I really wanted right now was Donal's dick in me. "Go get my purse."

Instead of moving, he arched an eyebrow and circled my clit with his thumb. "Why?"

"Just do it," I gritted out as my whole body clenched with pleasure.

Smiling, he pushed off the bed and left the room. A moment later, he came back and dropped my purse beside me. I sat up and reached inside a zippered inner pocket, removing a short strip of condoms.

He broke into a grin, catching them on his chest when I flicked them at him. "You packed condoms."

I rolled my eyes as I deposited my purse on his bedside table. "I'm a single woman on multiple dating apps. I always carry condoms with me."

"I'm taking it as further evidence of premeditation." The cocky bastard was still standing at the foot of the bed, and still not nearly naked enough.

"Lose the pants and bring that dirty mouth of yours over here."

Donal wasted no time shoving his jeans down, along with his underwear. As soon as his cock sprang free, I felt an unmistakable tug in the pit of my stomach. The sight of his dick triggered some sort of involuntary, animal reaction that shot through my body like an electric current. A goddamn Pavlovian response.

If I'd been wearing panties, they definitely would have blown right off. Apparently, my brain still had access to archived data on Donal's penis, and the summary of that data was a resounding *YES, PLEASE.*

I didn't even remember moving across the bed, but the next thing I knew I was kneeling on the mattress in front of him, compelled by an arcane force or some sort of supersensory dick mating call.

Holy shit, Marie was right.

That was the last coherent thought I had before I reached out to fondle Donal's magnificent member. After that, I couldn't think about anything except the feel of his thick heat in my hand and the way his hips jerked with every stroke.

"You have to stop that," he growled, seizing both my wrists when I ran my thumb over the slit in the swollen head. "I'm seriously hanging on by a thread here."

I liked the idea of that. I also liked the feel of his large hands holding my wrists, and the rough, slightly frantic way he was squeezing a little too hard, as if he wasn't quite in control of himself. I wanted to drive him all the way over that edge. But first I needed him to put that pretty penis inside me.

Backing up, I pulled him onto the bed by the hold he kept on my wrists. When I lay back, he came with me, pressing my arms into the mattress on either side of my head. His body caged mine, his weight bearing down on me, bare skin on bare skin. My legs reflexively parted, my body aching for him as his eyes seared into me, dark with the same animal desire coursing through my veins.

I thought he would kiss me, but instead he dipped his head, his ten o'clock shadow dragging over my skin as his tongue traced the swell of my breast. While I squirmed restlessly beneath him, he painted hot, teasing circles around my nipple.

"You sure you don't want to take it slow?" he asked between tortuous flicks of his tongue.

"Fuck slow. I want you inside me."

In response, I felt him smile against my skin. His grip on my wrists tightened as he rubbed his rough stubble over my nipple before sucking on it hard enough to make me gasp.

I strained against him, the anticipation nearly unbearable. "Your dick's not in me yet. Do you need a map?"

Donal huffed an amused breath as he switched his attentions to my other breast. "You're so fucking bossy."

"I'm not bossy, I'm authoritative. And you like it."

"I do." His voice was deep, husky, and deadly serious. "I really do."

The way he said it made my chest warm with pleasure that was more than just sexual. But then his stubble was back as his lips dragged a path between my breasts and down to my stomach.

He released my wrists to run his hands up my thighs, spreading them even wider before he parted me with his thumbs. "Is this where you want me? Did I find the right place?"

My back arched as his hot breath whispered over my sensitive, aching sex, and I fisted my hands in his hair. "Not like this."

We'd never done this in high school, but as much as I wanted to feel his mouth on me for the first time, I wanted his cock inside me even more. I wanted to feel his body moving against mine as he filled me up. I wanted to see his face as the pleasure became too much, hear his groans and grunts as he lost that control he'd been fighting to keep, feel his muscles tense, quiver, and release.

Donal's gaze lifted to meet mine, the connection sparking a *zing* in my chest. "Please just let me taste you first. I want to make you feel good. Will you let me do that?"

All I could manage was a garbled sound that roughly translated to *goddammitye-spleasejustfuckingdoit* as my resolve melted to goo along with the rest of my body.

The self-satisfied look on his face would have made me want to smack him if I wasn't too busy losing my damn mind. He nuzzled lightly against me, and my hips lifted of their own accord, straining toward his taunting mouth as my fingers tightened in his hair.

When he licked me, my whole body contracted with a breathy gasp. With a low groan of appreciation, Donal pushed his face between my legs and got down to business. His tongue was bold and deft as he worked me into a frenzy, alternately flicking, stroking, and sucking with exactly the right amount of pressure.

I was a trembling, whimpering mess, completely at his mercy. My heels dug into the mattress as I arched against him. I was *so close*, my vision already starting to white out as the tension inside me built to an unbearable level.

Then he stopped.

Fuck.

I groaned in misery and frustration as my eyes flew open. Donal was kneeling over me, tearing open a condom, and he winced as he hurriedly rolled it down his hard length. When he'd finished, he lowered himself onto me again, settling between my thighs. The head of his cock lined up with my entrance, and with no hesitation or holding back he plunged inside me with one powerful thrust.

His face dropped to my neck with a tortured groan, every muscle in his body tense and quivering as he hissed a string of expletives. I tilted my pelvis, taking him even deeper, and shuddered at the incredible sensation—exactly the perfect amount of too much—as I stretched around him.

"You good?" he asked, his voice low and shaky.

My hands smoothed up his back and sank into his hair as I nodded. "So good."

He eased out of me, and we let out twin moans as he slid back in, setting a pace that was slow and exquisitely deep. His lips brushed over mine in a clumsy kiss, the muscles in his neck taut as steel cables, like he was fighting to hold himself back. "God, Tess. You feel amazing."

I could still feel the orgasm that had been interrupted building at the base of my spine. Chasing the itch, I rocked against him, seeking more friction. "More," I panted desperately. "Oh my God."

"Come on, baby," he rasped, giving me what I needed. "I want to feel you come around my dick." His eyes were dark and intent, consuming me with the force of his gaze.

The intimacy was overwhelming. I couldn't look away, but I'd never felt so exposed as I did under his potent, hungry gaze. My body bowed, every muscle tensing as I splintered beneath him, the surge of ecstasy leaving me a shaking, mindless wreck.

Donal's lips ghosted over mine, murmuring something I was too far gone to hear. I felt him shift, and his hands cupped my ass as he lifted it higher. A whimper clogged my throat when I felt him slide out, but it quickly turned to a cry of pleasure as he grasped my hips and slammed back into me.

He thrust again, harder and deeper, his fingers digging into my flesh as he leveraged his grip on my hips. A sheen of sweat covered his face, which was caught in an expression of tortured bliss as he pistoned into me. Skin slapped against skin, rough and raw, the force of every thrust tearing sharp, breathy cries from me.

Right when I thought I couldn't take it anymore, his thrusts stuttered and grew erratic. A tremor racked his body, and he folded forward with an agonized groan, burying his face in my neck.

I ran my fingers through his hair and over his back as he lay limp and panting on top of me. Once his breathing eased, he nuzzled at my neck with a growly, contented hum. Bracing himself up on one arm, he deposited a line of soft kisses up my throat, along my jaw, and across my cheek. Before he reached my lips, he drew back and gazed into my eyes.

Neither of us spoke, as if we were both afraid of breaking the spell. An unfamiliar emotion twisted in my stomach. It spread through my body and filled up my chest before getting caught in my throat.

Ever so slowly, Donal lowered his mouth to mine. My lips parted as I reached for him, afraid to let myself think about what any of this meant.

I felt him withdraw, and he pressed one last kiss to my lips before rolling off the mattress to dispose of the condom. A chill shivered over the surface of my skin as I watched him walk into the bathroom.

The reality of what we'd done started to sink in, and with it came a huge dose of uncertainty and apprehension. Up until now, I'd had a clear goal in mind. But this part—the after part—was a big, precarious blank.

I didn't deal well with ambiguity. What I needed to do was come up with a game plan. Figure out what the next steps were and how to navigate them. I needed time to process and strategize my next move.

Sitting up and scooting to the foot of the bed, I bent to retrieve my dress from the floor.

"What are you doing?" Donal asked, coming back into the room. "You're not leaving."

"It's late, and I don't really do"—I waved my hand at the rumpled bed, the sheets damp and smelling of sex—"this."

"What? Sleep in a bed?" He broke into a grin as he came closer. "Are you trying to tell me you sleep hanging upside down like a bat?"

I couldn't help laughing. "No. It's just that I can't sleep next to another person. It's nothing personal. It's just insomnia."

"Too bad." He flopped onto the bed and stretched an arm out toward me. "I require at least ten minutes of naked cuddling after sex before you're allowed to desert me. House rules."

My eyebrows arched. "I thought I was the first woman you'd had here?"

"It's a new rule. I just made it up. Now put the dress down and get up here." He patted the mattress beside him. There was a smile on his lips, but his gaze was serious and challenging, daring me not to leave.

"Ten minutes, huh?" I bit my lip, my urge to flee warring with my desire not to hurt him by leaving precipitously.

"At a minimum. Longer is encouraged, but if you really want to leave after ten minutes, I'll let you go with only a little bit of pouting."

He was too damn appealing, that was the problem. How was I supposed to say no to him when he was all naked and charming?

"Fine." I crawled up the bed and lay down beside him.

His arms came around me, pulling me against him. He curled his body around mine, his bare chest warming my back. One arm slipped under my pillow as the other wrapped around my waist, holding me close.

"There." He brushed my hair aside and nestled his face against the back of my neck. "This isn't so bad, is it?"

"No. Not bad at all." More like divine. Not that I was going to admit that to him.

"Why would you want to leave all this to go back to your cold, empty bed?" His deep voice rumbled through his chest and into mine.

"Because I won't be able to fall asleep." Years of experience had taught me this was true, although the warm, fizzy feeling spreading through my limbs seemed to be saying otherwise.

His lips touched the back of my neck. "We'll see about that."

"Please tell me you don't think the magic healing properties of your dick have suddenly cured my lifelong insomnia."

"Shhhh," he murmured. "It's quiet time now."

His hand smoothed up my side and down my arm before retracing its path, stroking over my hip and down my thigh. Touching me everywhere he could reach. Caressing, soothing, claiming. Whatever he was doing, it felt amazing.

I'd only stay a little while longer. No reason to hurry off. There was still plenty of time to go back to my place and try to get some sleep.

My breathing slowed to match Donal's as his chest moved against my back, expanding and contracting. The steady, slowing rhythm lulling me into a deeper state of relaxation.

Any minute now, I'd get up and go.

Any minute…

CHAPTER TWENTY-ONE

DONAL

For someone with insomnia, Tess slept like the dead.

Not only had she fallen asleep before me last night, she was still out like a light when I woke this morning. Her head was resting on my chest, using me as a pillow while her arm clutched me like a cuddle toy.

I didn't mind one single bit.

It'd been a long time since I'd woken up with another person in my arms, and even longer since I'd actually appreciated the feeling. Wendy and I had long ago fallen into the habit of retreating to opposite sides of our king-size bed. Most nights, we hadn't touched at all. Even when we were still having sex, we'd only cuddle for a few minutes afterward before rolling apart to fall asleep in our own separate spaces.

This was a lot better. Yeah, my arm was sort of numb and I couldn't change position. Tess's hair was tickling my chest, and I was pretty sure that wetness I could feel meant she was drooling on me. But I didn't care. All those minor discomforts were nothing compared to the feeling of waking up with Tess's body pressed against mine and the scent of her on my skin.

I lifted my free hand and trailed my fingers over her arm, unable to resist touching the acres of soft, beautiful skin on display. Gently, I stroked my fingertips along the curve of her shoulder blade and down her spine. She slept on as I traced each of her ribs. Only when I followed them around to the swell of her breast did she stir, making rumbly, sleepy noises as she came awake.

"What happened?" she muttered, rubbing her eyes.

"As far as I can tell, you had two fantastic orgasms and promptly slipped into a coma in my arms, right after insisting you'd never be able to fall asleep here. And then at some point in the middle of the night you climbed on top of me and started drooling."

"I'm not drooling." She swiped at her mouth and frowned when her fingers came away wet. Hastily, she wiped the drool off my chest. "Clearly you drugged me. What was in those Manhattans?"

A laugh rumbled through my chest. "You mean the Manhattans we barely touched before you seduced me?"

"I did not seduce you."

"What else do you call showing up without any underwear on and ordering me to kiss you?"

"It wasn't an order. It was more like a suggestion."

"It was a good suggestion. I don't mind you giving me orders like that." I cupped her jaw, urging her face toward mine for a kiss, but she turned away at the last second so I ended up kissing her cheek instead.

"Morning breath," she mumbled, covering her mouth with her hand. She started to roll away, but I caught her with my arms.

I wasn't ready to let her get away yet. Once she got out of bed, things might change. I didn't know what would happen with us after this, and I was a little afraid to find out. For now, I just wanted to stay right here in this moment with her for as long as I could.

"Tess." I nudged her cheek with my nose as I plucked at the hand blocking my access to her lips. "I don't give a fuck about your morning breath. Please kiss me."

She let me pull her hand away, her softening gaze belying her argumentative words. "What if I care about *your* morning breath?"

"I'll make it worth your while. I promise."

Her eyes fluttered closed as my lips ghosted over hers in a closed-mouth kiss. The little half moan, half sigh she let out and the way her hand curled around the nape of my neck told me she wanted me to keep going. So I did.

Taking my time, I pressed a soft, firm kiss to each corner of her mouth. When I moved on to her top lip, she strained toward me and our noses bumped as she tilted her head for more. But I wasn't going to give it to her. Not yet. She was going to have to wait for it. Instead, I flirted with her bottom lip, sucking at it gently before grazing it with my teeth.

She was full-on squirming now, and when my tongue darted out to lick her lower lip, she made an impatient noise in the back of her throat. Smiling, I angled my head to cover her mouth with mine, giving her the pressure she wanted. Her lips parted for me, and I slipped my tongue past her teeth.

The kiss grew harder as our tongues twined together, delving deeper. It went on and on, Tess meeting me stroke for stroke as we battled for dominance. When we finally parted, her eyes were hazy and we were both breathing hard.

I pressed my thumb against a reddening spot at the edge of her lips where my stubble had abraded her skin. "Acceptable?"

Her mouth quirked as she failed to suppress a smile. "Barely."

"Barely, huh? Next time I'll bring my A game." Rolling her onto her back, I pressed my lips to her breastbone. "If it'll make you happy, I'll get a pack of Listerine strips to keep by the bed."

Of course, that implied there'd be a next time, which we hadn't exactly established yet. It might be wishful thinking on my part. *I want to sleep with you* didn't necessarily translate to *I want to be with you*.

"Make it Altoids," she said, threading her fingers through my hair.

I hid my smile by kissing her stomach. "Anything you want."

Her fingernails stroked over my scalp, and I hummed in blissful contentment as I lay my cheek on her stomach.

"Please feel free to keep doing that forever." Pretty sure I was glowing. Having her here, being close like this, was the next best thing to heaven. I couldn't remember the last time I'd felt this content.

She fidgeted a little at the prickle of my stubble, but didn't stop her exquisite scalp massage. "I can't believe I actually fell asleep last night."

"What was it you said about the magic healing properties of my dick?"

"This has nothing to do with your dick."

"Really?" In retribution for the insult to my manhood, I rubbed my scratchy face on her stomach, making her wriggle beneath me. "I'm pretty sure I read something once about orgasms releasing an endorphin that induces sleep."

"It's never worked that well before."

I propped my chin on her stomach, gazing at her as I stroked my hand up the inside of her thigh. "Clearly I deliver a higher quality of orgasms. Other orgasms pale in comparison. On account of my magic healing dick."

"Sorry. Nope. Not buying it." So she said, but the way her eyelids fluttered when my fingers traced her entrance told a different story.

Rising up on my forearms, I nuzzled the spot on her neck where I knew she was most sensitive. I'd politely been trying to keep my hard-on to myself, but now I pressed it shamelessly against her leg. Purely for illustrative purposes, of course. "I think we owe it to ourselves to test it out again. It's the only way to know the truth. We have to have sex again. For science."

"For science, hmm?"

"It's a moral imperative." I cupped her breast, rolling her nipple between my thumb and forefinger until she gasped.

"I do like science an awful lot." Her hand wrapped around the base of my cock, and my eyes rolled back in my head as pleasure shot down my spine.

"Me too. I like it so fucking much."

"Something's different about you," my secretary said when I walked into the office Monday morning.

I attempted to school my expression, but my mouth twitched without my permission. I deposited the coffee I'd picked up for her on the desk next to her keyboard. "Good morning, Debra."

Her eagle-eyed gaze narrowed as she scrutinized me even more closely. "Something happened."

"I had a relaxing weekend," I said with a shrug, avoiding further eye contact by heading for my office. "Got enough sleep for once."

While that was all technically true, the extra spring in my step this morning wasn't because of sleep. It had more to do with what I'd done when I wasn't sleeping. Namely, having a lot of sex with Tess.

Somehow we'd ended up spending most of the weekend together. After a leisurely morning in bed on Saturday, we'd gone to a coffee shop where both of us spent a few hours doing work. After that, we went back to her place, fooled around, ordered dinner, and made an attempt to watch a movie that quickly turned into more fooling around.

Much to my delight, Tess had let me sleep over without much protest. We'd parted for a couple of hours Sunday morning while she went to visit her dad, then met back up for a run along the lakefront, followed by a late brunch, followed by more catching up on work, this time sitting side by side on her couch.

It was kind of great how well our lifestyles meshed. We were both workaholics who used exercise to work off stress—although all the sex we were having almost made the exercise superfluous. Turned out I could do work as well on Tess's couch as my own, with the added bonus of sex during breaks.

Debra pushed her chair back and followed me to the doorway of my office. She stood with one hand on her hip and the other holding her tablet as she watched me hang up my suit jacket. "You met someone. That's it, isn't it? That smile on your face was put there by a woman."

And now I wanted to die. Debra might only be ten years older than me, but I'd always thought of her as a maternal figure. Definitely not someone I talked about my sex life with.

"That's an interesting shade of red you're turning," she observed wryly.

"Seriously, are you telepathic? How do you do that?"

She shrugged. "It's written all over your face."

"Great," I muttered, sitting down at my desk and plugging in my laptop.

"So who was it?" Furrows sprouted across her brow. "It wasn't your ex-wife, was it?"

"No! God, no." And that was as much as I'd be telling Debra for now. I didn't want to go jinxing anything by getting ahead of myself. If things kept going well, she'd know soon enough. The woman managed pretty much my whole life for me and had dossiers on my kids, mother, and ex-wife that included their birthdays, food sensitivities, and favorite flowers. It was only a matter of time before she started collecting information on Tess as well. Hopefully. Assuming I didn't fuck this up.

"Good." Debra gave me a proud nod. "In that case, I'm happy for you. It's about time you put yourself back out there."

I shot her a warning look. "It's not a big deal. Don't go making too much of it."

Except it felt like a big deal. The biggest. But I needed to keep a wrap on those kinds of feelings. At least for now.

In all the time Tess and I had spent together this weekend, not once had we ventured near the subject of our relationship. We'd both skirted carefully around any discussion of the future beyond what we wanted to order for our next meal. I wasn't sure if I should be grateful for that or not. This whole situation felt like walking on a tightrope. If I leaned too far out, my precarious balance would fail and the ground would come flying up to meet me.

We hadn't even decided to spend the whole weekend together. It had just sort of happened. A series of seemingly spur-of-the-moment decisions that had never ended up with us going our separate ways.

Until this morning, when my alarm had gone off and I'd scrambled around for my clothes before bidding Tess a hurried goodbye on my way back to my place to get ready for work.

We hadn't made any plans to see each other again. Something I was seriously regretting now.

Unlocking the physical intimacy achievement had changed things between us, but the big unanswered question was how, exactly. I didn't have a clear idea where we stood. Were we serious? Exclusive? Friends with benefits? Had this weekend been some kind of one-time-only extended booty call? Or the start of something more?

I knew what I wanted—serious, exclusive, and definitely a lot more. My heart had gone all soppy and squishy where Tess was concerned. But I was trying to take a wait and see approach. Not add any unnecessary pressure into the mix.

Which was all well and good in theory, but I needed to know when I'd see Tess again. I needed to know that I *could* see her again. On the one hand, I didn't want to seem too clingy and scare her off. On the other, I didn't want her to think I wasn't interested in seeing more of her. A *lot* more.

Dammit, this dating shit was complicated—assuming that was even what we were doing—and I was seriously rusty. It'd been over twenty years since I'd had to navigate this kind of stuff. All the rules had probably changed.

We hadn't had smartphones the last time I'd done any dating. We'd only barely had texting or social media. I'd spent a lot of late nights chatting with Wendy on AOL Instant Messenger. It had taken me forever to ask her out. I'd had my head stuck pretty far up my own ass, and somehow hadn't realized the girl who stayed up past midnight almost every night talking to me was actually interested in going out on a date.

I liked to think I was a little more self-aware these days. I also wasn't inclined to sit back on my heels and do nothing. If I wanted something, I went for it. Nothing ventured, nothing gained.

After Debra finished going over my calendar and to-do list with me and retreated back to her desk, I typed out a text to Tess.

Are you free for dinner tonight? I was thinking I could take you out.

I stared at it, trying to decide if it was a good idea to send it.

Fuck it. I wanted to see her. What was the point of pretending otherwise? She could always say no if she wasn't up for it. But one of us had to put ourself out there. It'd be ridiculous not to ask when there was a chance she might be into it.

I hit send and set my phone down.

What I wasn't going to do was sit here staring at it while I waited for her to reply. I had a full day ahead of me and needed to get my head in the game.

Except no matter how hard I tried to concentrate on my laptop screen, my eyes kept sliding over to my phone, checking for a new notification.

Over.

And over.

And over again.

Annoyed, I flipped the phone facedown and pushed it beyond my peripheral vision.

Tess was probably working, like I should be doing. That was why she hadn't responded right away. She might be on a conference call. Or trying to concentrate. She'd reply when she had time.

I was worried now though. Was I coming on too strong? Maybe Tess needed some time apart after our weekend-long sex marathon.

The buzz of my phone on the desk startled the shit out of me. I scrambled for it, grinning when I saw Tess's reply.

Tess: What time?

Donal: 7:00?

Tess: That works.

Tess: I like sushi.

I tried to wipe the grin off my face as I wandered out to Debra's desk. "Would you block off my calendar tonight starting at six thirty?"

Her eyebrows lifted slightly as she turned her attention to her computer. "Block it off for what?"

"Personal business."

"Done."

"Also, do you know of a good sushi restaurant around here where I can get a table on short notice?"

Debra's mouth curved in a knowing smile. "I'm sure I can find something. Would you like me to make you a reservation?"

"That'd be great. Tonight at seven."

She reached for her mouse, bringing up her browser menu. "How many people?"

"Two."

Her smile got even wider. "Two people. Got it."

"Don't look so smug."

"Who, me?" Her smile didn't waver. "Never."

CHAPTER TWENTY-TWO

TESS

Everything was a lot, and it was only Tuesday.

Things with Donal had progressed way more quickly than I was used to. Like light speed fast. And yet I couldn't bring myself to suggest putting the brakes on.

We'd spent the last four nights in a row together. The whole night. Which wasn't something I usually did. The last time I'd slept over at a man's house, we'd already been dating for a month. And I'd spent most of that night wide-awake and staring at the wall while he snored beside me. It had taken weeks for me to get comfortable enough with him to fall asleep in the same bed.

Not with Donal. Nope. I'd dropped right off to sleep every single night. What the hell was that about?

Maybe it was all the great sex we were having—not that I'd ever in a million years admit that to Donal. The last thing he needed was a reason to get even cockier. But there might be something to that orgasm theory of his. Either that or our vigorous bedroom activities had tired me out enough to overcome my insomnia.

But it felt like something more than that.

Being with Donal felt different. There was something about having his arms around me. His warm skin pressed against mine. The soft, steady murmur of his breathing in my ear. It lulled me into a state of contentment. Sure, the post-orgasm haze didn't hurt either. But there was something in Donal's presence that calmed me. Instead of feeling trapped or claustrophobic, the way I usually did when a man draped himself over me, I felt comfortable in Donal's arms. Safe. Like I was where I was supposed to be.

When I was with him, I didn't feel like I was all alone in the world.

That was the most terrifying part. Because everyone was alone in the world. It was a fact of life. Letting myself be fooled into thinking otherwise was dangerous.

People left, or lost interest, or stopped liking you altogether. The same traits they'd once found endearing about you eventually became the annoying habits that drove them away. Either that or they got so caught up in their own lives they stopped having time for you.

You couldn't expect someone else to make your comfort a priority over theirs. The only person you could rely on in this world was yourself. Dependency was a trap that inevitably led to disappointment and weakness.

I wasn't going to fall into that quicksand. Not me. I knew better, and I was stronger than that. No way was I sitting here in my apartment longing for Donal after a mere fourteen hours apart. That would be irrational and pathetic.

I didn't need to see him every day. We didn't even need to talk every day. We weren't tied at the hip. We both had our own busy and fulfilling lives to live independent of each other.

It didn't matter that I hadn't heard from him all day. We could spend a night apart, for fuck's sake. We could spend *every* night apart and I'd be just fine. I definitely wasn't worrying that he'd already gotten tired of me. Four nights in a row should be enough for anyone. It made perfect sense that he needed a break.

The question was, why didn't *I* need a break?

You'd think after screwing like bunnies all weekend we'd have taken care of all that excess sexual tension. So why was I sitting here aching for him, my desire an incessant buzz under my skin? Why couldn't I stop thinking about him? And why did the thought of him fill my chest with an odd warmth that hummed through my whole body and threatened to turn my muscles to jelly? I was way too old and cynical to be acting like the main character in a sappy rom-com, for Christ's sake.

When my phone rang, I was ashamed to say I dove for it like a teenager. Only it wasn't Donal calling me. It was Erin. Hard to be disappointed about that.

"Hi!" I answered, a little too bubbly and loud.

"Hey. It's not too late to call, is it?"

"No, not at all. I'm just surprised. I was led to believe your generation didn't like to talk on the phone."

She laughed softly. "Most of us don't, but I've never minded it. Sometimes it's easier to talk out loud than trying to type long sentences with your thumbs, you know?"

"I do know, and I completely agree."

"I guess that's something else we have in common."

"I guess so," I said as my lips pulled into a smile.

"So the reason I'm calling is that I got to thinking after looking through those photo albums at Kathleen's house. Seeing all those pictures of Donal and his sister and the rest of their family—actually recognizing the physical resemblances between myself and other people I was related to—I've never been able to experience that before."

I rubbed my chest, trying to chase away the hollow sensation there. I was glad Erin was finally getting to make those kinds of connections. Feeling guilty she'd missed out on them for so long didn't do anyone any good.

"Anyway," she went on, "I was wondering if you had any family photo albums I could look at some time."

"I do." A small frog seemed to have lodged itself in my throat. "My mother wasn't quite as organized about it as Kathleen, but I've got everything she had. You're welcome to look at them if you like."

"I'd love that," she said. "Whenever's convenient."

"What about this weekend? I could make dinner."

Despite my baking fiasco the other night, I was a halfway decent cook. I'd taken a cooking class last year after Sherry's death in an attempt to keep busy and distract myself from my grief. Unfortunately, I'd ended up being the only single woman in a class full of couples, which had only made me feel even more alone in the world. But at least I'd learned how to make a serviceable chicken piccata.

"Does Saturday work?" she asked.

"Saturday's perfect."

"I can't wait," she said, sounding excited enough to mean it. "If you want, I could borrow my old baby album from my mom—unless that would be weird for you? I don't know, maybe you'd rather not—"

"I'd love to see it."

"Okay." I heard her let out a breath. "In that case, I'll bring it with me."

I squeezed the phone. "Would it be all right if I invited Donal to join us? I'm sure he'd love to see your baby pictures too."

"Of course! As long as…" She hesitated. "You don't have to spend time together for my benefit if it's uncomfortable for you."

"Why would it be uncomfortable?" She'd only seen us together once, at Donal's mom's, and I thought we'd done a good job of acting friendly toward one another.

"I was under the impression you two didn't get along."

Since I'd never hinted at anything of the sort, there was only one place Erin could have gotten that impression. "Is that what Donal told you?"

"All he said was that things had ended badly between you. And I know you hadn't spoken in years before I forced you to talk to each other again."

I couldn't exactly fault Donal for telling the truth. "Well, that's true, but it's all ancient history. We've put it behind us."

"Really?" Her tone was hopeful rather than dubious.

"You saw us at Kathleen's. Didn't we look like we were getting along fine?" Maybe a little too fine when Kathleen interrupted us. We'd need to be more careful unless we wanted Erin guessing what was going on. Which didn't seem like a good idea.

"You did. I was just worried it might have been an act and secretly you were both miserable having to be around each other for my sake."

I couldn't help my laugh. "We're not that good at acting, trust me. You don't need to worry about us. We're fine." Hopefully. Maybe. It still felt too early to tell.

"Oh good. That's a huge load off my mind. I was feeling a little guilty, to tell you the truth."

"About us? You definitely shouldn't feel guilty. If anything, you did us a favor by putting us back in touch."

"In that case, yay! I'm so glad to hear you've patched things up. It's really cool, actually, that I was the one who brought you back together."

"We're not together," I felt compelled to clarify. Perhaps too strongly. *The lady doth protest too much, methinks.*

Were we together? I honestly had no idea at this point. But whatever Donal and I were doing, it was best to leave Erin out of it for now. I could sense from her enthusiasm that she was rooting for some sort of happy ending to our story, and I was afraid she'd get her hopes up only to be disappointed.

"We're back to being friends," I said. "That's all."

"Right," Erin said slowly. "No, of course. Still, it's nice that the two of you are getting along again."

"It is nice," I ventured as an uneasy feeling settled in the pit of my stomach. If the situation between Donal and me got messy, it would make things awkward for Erin. I didn't want her to be affected by our mistakes any more than she already had been.

"You should definitely ask Donal to come on Saturday," she said. "I'd love for the three of us to spend time together."

Like a family, a voice whispered in the back of my head.

I liked the idea of that. A little too much. I had to remind myself that whatever we were, the three of us would never be a regular family.

Erin and I chatted for a few more minutes before we said good night. After we hung up, I texted Donal to ask if he was free to have dinner with Erin and me on Saturday. I'd been avoiding reaching out to him in case he needed a breather. But I figured this was a legitimate reason to text.

He didn't respond. I waited five minutes. Ten minutes. Twenty. *He must be busy tonight.*

It shouldn't have bothered me, but his silence left me feeling even more uneasy. And annoyingly made me miss him even more.

It was an hour later when my phone rang again. This time it was Donal.

"Hi," I said, absurdly happy to hear from him.

"Hey." His voice was low and warm, like tea with honey and whiskey. "I saw your text. Dinner on Saturday sounds great."

"Erin wants to come over and see my family photos. She offered to bring her baby album for us to look at."

"I can't wait." His response was more subdued than I'd expected.

"You okay? You sound tired."

"I had a client dinner tonight that felt like it was going to go on forever. I just now got home."

"Ah. Right." That explained why he hadn't answered my text. See? He had been busy—with work.

"Don't tell me you've been missing me." There was a smile in his voice that made me feel all wobbly inside.

"You'd like to think so, wouldn't you?"

"I would. It'd be nice to think you missed me."

I swallowed, brushing a bit of yarn fluff off my couch. "You don't think we've been spending too much time together?"

"Too much for who?"

"Whom."

"Christ almighty." His laugh was deep and rumbly. "Tell you what," he said, growing serious again. "Instead of overanalyzing everything, how about we try being straight with each other?"

"Okay," I agreed. Even though the odds of me being able to do anything of the sort were vanishingly small. Overanalyzing was my specialty.

"So if I say I want to see you, and you don't feel like it that night, all you have to do is tell me that. And it goes both ways. If you ever want to see me, all you have to do is say so. And I promise to tell you if I'm not up for it. But the important part is that neither of us reads too much into anything or gets our feelings hurt without talking about it first."

It was like he knew exactly how much time I'd spent reading too much into the fact that I hadn't heard from him all day. He probably did, damn him.

"What do you say?" he asked. "Do we have a deal?"

"Sure, I can do that." Why not? I could try, anyway. Although it seemed like the kind of thing that sounded great in theory but was a lot harder to implement in practice.

"Great. So if, for example, you'd spent the whole day fantasizing about my sexual prowess, you could tell me that." His voice was smug and lightly teasing. "Because this is a judgment-free zone. A safe space, if you will."

I laughed even though he wasn't all that far off the mark. "You caught me. That's exactly what I've been doing. Because I have nothing better to do than sit around thinking about your penis all day."

"It does have magical healing properties. That's been scientifically proven."

"I'm pretty sure the jury's still out on that. We haven't collected enough data to reach a valid conclusion."

"So what you're saying is we need to repeat the experiment?"

"Exactly." Somehow I managed to keep my voice steady despite the giddy fluttering in my stomach. "If we want the science to be solid, we'll need to replicate the same results in a series of independent experiments."

"How many, exactly?" There was a roughness to his voice that had nothing to do with exhaustion, and it made my insides go all melty.

"Hard to say. But I imagine it'd have to be a lot."

"So like an ongoing thing? The sort of experiment that doesn't have an end date."

I bit my lip, both nervous and excited. "I suppose so."

"I like the sound of that."

"Me too," I admitted, my voice high and faint.

"In that case, maybe I should come over?"

"I think you should." *Yes, please. Hurry. Before I expire.*

"I'm already on my way."

.

210

CHAPTER TWENTY-THREE

DONAL

"Are you really sure you want to cook for Erin tomorrow night?"

Tess rolled over in the bed and glared at me. "Are you doubting my cooking skills?" She might have been more intimidating if she hadn't been naked, her skin still flushed and dewy from our latest round of wild monkey sex.

The woman had me feeling like an oversexed teenager again. Before she came back into my life, I'd actually started to worry my libido was on the decline. But nope. Still working just fine. All it needed was the right inspiration.

I tangled my fingers with hers and brought her hand to my lips. "Do I need to remind you that the last time you tried to cook something you nearly burned the building down?"

"I did no such thing. It was only a little smoke. And that was baking, which I haven't done in a long time. It's not my fault my oven controls are overly complex and anti-intuitive."

"Yes, it's all the big bad oven's fault." It was too much fun messing with her. I loved the way her eyes flashed and her cheeks turned red.

"Don't patronize me. I can cook." She reached out and tweaked my nipple. If it was meant to discourage me, it had the exact opposite effect.

Pushing her onto her back, I pinned her under my weight as I buried my face in her neck. "Can you though? Can you really?"

"Yes! I'm not saying I'm Julia Child, but I can manage chicken piccata."

"There's no shame in ordering takeout." My hand smoothed down her side as I nuzzled between her breasts. "You don't have to risk all our lives just to impress Erin. She likes you even if you can't cook."

Tess's fingers tangled in my hair and gave it a retaliatory tug. "I'm a perfectly good cook. No one's lives are at risk. You'll see."

"Food poisoning is no one's friend, Tess."

"I'm going to make you eat those words."

I lifted my head and grinned at her. "As long as you don't make me eat under-cooked chicken."

"Fuck you," she muttered, failing to hide her smile.

I dropped my mouth to her breasts again. "Give me another five minutes and I'll be ready again."

"You're insufferable."

"Sorry, what's that?" I mumbled into her cleavage. "I'm adorable? It's hard to hear while I'm busy kissing your glorious tits. Did you say I'm lovable? Or delectable maybe?" My fingers danced over the ticklish spots on her ribs, making her wriggle enjoyably beneath me.

"I don't know why I put up with you," she complained, swatting my hands away.

"Pretty sure it has something to do with how adorable, lovable, and delectable I am, in addition to being a god of sex."

Her laughter washed over me like sunshine. "It's definitely not your modesty, that's for sure."

"It's a good thing I've got you to keep me humble."

I felt her still beneath me, a subtle ripple of tension displacing the ease of a moment before. Propping myself up on one elbow, I studied her face.

Her eyes tried to slide away under my perusal, but I cupped her jaw in my hand, drawing her attention back to me. "I have you, don't I?"

The way she hesitated just about stopped my heart in my chest.

"Do I have *you*?" she countered quietly.

A swell of tenderness chased away the flicker of panic as my heart squeezed with the need to reassure her. "Fuck yes. Don't you know that by now?" I brushed my lips against hers. "You have me as much as you want me."

She let out a long, slow breath. "Okay. Good."

I arched an expectant eyebrow at her. Fair was fair, and I needed some reassurances too. "Now it's your turn."

Her eyes softened as they looked into mine. "You have me too."

I could have jumped over the fucking moon, but I managed to keep my reaction limited to a small smile. "Good."

Tess smiled back at me, and affection flared in my chest like a forest fire, wild, bright, and powerful. I slanted my mouth over hers, kissing her slowly and thoroughly. Glowy, warm happiness spread through my limbs, and I rolled onto my back, dragging her with me.

She shifted to make herself more comfortable on top of me and laid her cheek on my chest, using me as her pillow. I let out a contented sigh. This right here? This was as close to heaven as I could imagine.

I stroked my hand down her back and cupped her ass. "So you're not going to date anyone else, right?"

Her soft laughter vibrated through my body. "Honestly, where would I find the energy? How much sex do you think I need?"

"For the avoidance of doubt, I think we should amend our existing contract to include an exclusivity clause."

She lifted her head and gave me an amused look with accompanying raised brows. "I wasn't aware we had a contract."

"Verbal agreements are legally enforceable."

"Hmmm." Her cheek rested against my chest again. "In that case, maybe I should consult an attorney."

"Lucky for you, you happen to be sleeping with one."

"Isn't that a conflict of interest, counselor?" Her fingers sifted through my chest hair.

"Not at all. As your lawyer, I advise you to agree to everything I say."

She snorted. "Oh, well in that case…"

"Tess," I said softly, squeezing her hip to let her know I was serious. "I just need to hear you say I'm the only man invited into your bed."

She wasn't the only one in this relationship with insecurities. My feelings had run away with me, and I needed to know I wasn't all alone standing on this cliff. Getting her to talk about mushy stuff like feelings and commitment was about as easy as catching a fish with your bare hands. It was hard not to notice how her gaze shifted away uneasily whenever things started to get too emotional.

I had to wonder how a woman as extraordinary and exquisite as Tess had become so afraid of expressing her feelings. She behaved like someone who'd been taught to expect rejection, using snark and sarcasm as a shield to avoid saying anything too real. It was almost as if, underneath all her defense mechanisms, she didn't believe she deserved to be loved. It was a troubling thought, considering how crazy hard I'd fallen for her.

She tipped her head up and rested her chin on my chest, pinning me in place with her eyes. For once, she didn't make a joke or shy away. "You're the only man invited into my bed," she said quietly.

I let my smile break free. "Thank you."

One of her eyebrows twitched upward. "I assume it goes both ways?"

"Obviously."

"Good," she said and laid her head down on me again.

My hand smoothed up her back, and she made a happy noise. Silence fell between us as a siren passed by on the street outside. Her condo was lower than mine and got a lot more city noise. I kind of liked it though. It felt less isolated than my place higher up in the sky. Although maybe it felt that way because Tess was here.

"Can I ask you something?"

She sighed. "I assume it's going to be uncomfortable if you feel the need to ask permission."

"I'm just being nosy. You don't have to answer if you don't feel like it."

"Fine."

"You've never been married, right?" I was pretty sure she hadn't—I'd never heard anything about it through the alumni grapevine—but it seemed worth clarifying.

"Correct."

I stared at the ceiling as I tried to figure out how to phrase my question without sounding like an asshole.

When I didn't say anything else, she lifted her head and gave me a curious look. "Was that it? That seems too easy."

"I wanted to ask you something else, but now I'm reconsidering the wisdom of it."

She rolled her eyes. "Let me guess—you want to know why I never got myself a husband and settled down, right?"

"I was trying to say it in a less shitty way, but yeah—not that everyone has to want that, but…did you ever want that?"

She laid her head back down on me. "It wasn't like a life goal or anything. Not that I was opposed to it either. If a situation that felt right had ever presented itself, I like to think I would have been game. But maybe the fact that I never felt that strongly about anyone means it wasn't something I wanted after all. I don't know."

I wished I could see her eyes, to get some sense of what she was thinking and feeling behind the casual indifference of her tone. "You never even came close?"

She snorted. "The longest relationship of my life is with Microsoft Excel, and it's love-hate at best.

My fingers toyed with her hair. "There's really never been anyone serious?"

"There was someone I was with for two years. For a while I thought maybe we'd get there…but we never did—or at least I never did."

I frowned. "Is that the asshole who called you passionless?"

"Yes."

"I hate that guy. If I ever meet him, I'm going to kick his ass for saying that to you."

"Really?"

"He's not an athlete or a bouncer or anything, is he?"

"No, he's an environmental engineer," she said on a yawn.

"Does he do CrossFit?"

She shifted, making herself more comfortable on me. "His idea of exercise was walking to the coffee shop."

"Okay, then yeah," I said. "I'll totally kick his ass for you."

"That's very sweet, but unnecessary."

I cuddled her closer and kissed the top of her head. "I don't think you're passionless," I whispered. "In case there was any question about that."

"Good to know," she murmured sleepily.

After a while, her breathing slowed the way it always did when she fell asleep. Her limbs had grown heavy and limp on top of mine, her skin giving off warmth like a sunlamp.

I always tried to stay awake until she fell asleep because I loved seeing her relaxed like this. Knowing she felt safe and comfortable sleeping in my arms. But tonight I didn't need to fight off sleep. My brain was too twitchy to rest.

Something inside me felt brittle. Uneasy. I was ninety-nine percent sure I'd already fallen in love with Tess. Hard. And a thousand percent sure she wasn't there yet. Which was fine. It hadn't been that long. Not like I'd expected her to lose her head and fall head over heels this fast. The fact that I had was my problem, not hers.

It was just…it felt like I'd been living in a fog the last few years. Barely living at all, really. And then Tess had come along like a flare of sunlight and burned all the haze away. She'd reminded me what it felt like to be truly alive. To want something so bad it was all I could think about. To need someone as much as I needed to breathe.

But what if she never got there? Never felt the same way I felt? The woman had built up a hell of a lot of walls. Would she ever really let me past the barriers?

I wanted to think so. She just needed time, right?

CHAPTER TWENTY-FOUR

DONAL

"I think she looks exactly like you in this one," I said, elbowing Tess.

We'd been flipping through photo albums with Erin for the last hour. Tess and I were currently on our second pass through Erin's baby book while she flipped through Tess's old family photos, snapping occasional pics with her phone.

Tess shot a sour glance at me. "You mean because she's frowning?"

"Look at her. She's definitely got your frown."

Erin leaned across Tess for a peek at the baby picture in question. "I kind of do, don't I?"

"Maybe," Tess said, staring at the photo with a frown almost identical to toddler Erin's. "I still think she mostly looks like you."

"That's what I thought at first," Erin said. "But the more I look at photos from your side of the family, the more I see resemblances."

My chest tightened at Erin's use of the word *family*. Tess's eyes met mine, and I knew she was thinking the same thing. That Erin had just casually spoken as if the three of us were part of the same family. Maybe it shouldn't be a big deal, but it felt like one. It felt huge.

I started to reach for Tess's hand, but she pulled it away as Erin plopped a photo album on her lap and tapped one of the photos.

"Look at this baby picture of your father, and then look at that picture of me," Erin said. "Don't you think we look alike?"

Tess peered at the two photos. "I suppose you do, a little. Around the eyes."

"And the shape of the face," Erin added excitedly. "I look like my grandfather!"

I leaned in for a better view. When my shoulder bumped Tess's, she leaned back to give me more space.

"Erin's right. She's definitely got some of your dad in her." I glanced up at Tess, comparing her face to the photo of her father. "You look a lot like your dad. I've never noticed how much."

"Everyone always said that," she mumbled, staring down at her lap.

"I've been wondering," Erin said. "You know how you go visit your father every Sunday? Do you think I could come with you sometime and meet him?"

Tess seemed to flounder, partly from surprise and partly something else. "He's not…he can't really meet anyone."

"He's not allowed visitors?"

"No, he is. It's just that he won't understand who you are. He doesn't even recognize me anymore."

Erin touched Tess's arm. A small, comforting gesture, offered so easily. I watched Tess's eyes fixate on Erin's hand and wondered if Erin knew how much importance a small touch like that held for both of us.

"That's okay," Erin said gently. "My grandmother had Alzheimer's too, so I know what it's like. And I'd really like to meet him in person at least once, even if he doesn't respond to me. Unless you think it would be too upsetting for him?"

Tess covered Erin's hand with hers. "No, I don't think it will upset him. It's more likely to be upsetting for you."

"I can take it," Erin said. "If you're okay with it."

"Of course I am." Tess produced an admirable approximation of a smile. Only someone who knew her as well as I did would guess that it was forced. "When I go tomorrow, I'll talk to his caregivers about it. You can come with me next weekend if they give the okay."

My insides knotted at the brittleness of Tess's expression. It was always like this when the subject of her parents came up. She didn't talk about it much, but I knew her stepmom's death was still a raw wound, and the situation with her father was an ongoing source of grief.

She'd been putting on such a good act until now that it hadn't even occurred to me how difficult it must be for her, looking through all these old photo albums and answering Erin's questions. Being confronted by photos of the mother who'd walked away from her, the father who'd slowly disappeared piece by piece, and the stepmother she'd lost last year.

Erin looked down at Tess's photo album again and flipped the page to a photo of Tess and her father. In it, Tess looked to be three or four, her tiny hands wound around her father's neck. They both wore huge smiles on their faces as if they'd been laughing. Erin's fingers smoothed down a bubble under the clear plastic photo protector. "It seems like you two were really close."

Tess swallowed and tipped her chin down. "We were. But we had a lot of happy years together before he got sick. He had a good, long life, so it's…" She trailed off with a small shrug.

If we'd been alone I would have pulled Tess into my arms and held her until she smiled again. Instead, I settled for running my knuckles over the small of her back.

She pushed Erin's baby album at me and picked up her wineglass as she stood up from the couch. "I'd better go finish putting dinner together if we want to eat anytime tonight."

My mouth settled into a frown as I watched her walk away. She'd been doing that a lot tonight—moving away when I got too close. It seemed she wasn't comfortable with PDA in front of Erin. At least I hoped that was all it was.

Erin gave me a questioning look, and I dredged up a smile for her.

"You want some more water?" I asked, nodding at her empty glass on the coffee table. "Got to keep you hydrated."

She rolled her eyes. "Sure, so I can pee even *more* often. As if every five minutes isn't enough."

Laughing, I snagged Erin's glass and my own off the table.

"Need any help with dinner?" Erin asked Tess, following me to the kitchen.

"Nope. I've got it under control." She was melting butter in a large skillet, a plate of thin chicken breasts on the counter beside her. She didn't turn around when I passed behind her on my way to the fridge.

After I'd refilled Erin's water, I got out another bottle of white wine and grabbed the corkscrew from the drawer by the refrigerator.

Erin slid onto a barstool at the island as she watched me open the wine. "You do that like a pro."

"That's because he is one." Tess threw a sidelong glance at me. Our eyes met, and her lips crooked before she turned her attention back to the stove. "He used to work in a bar."

"I was just a barback." I shrugged as I refilled Tess's wineglass. "But I learned a few tricks from the bartenders while I was there."

"He makes a mean Manhattan," Tess said over the sizzling of the skillet as the kitchen filled with the scent of sautéing onions and garlic. "It's a shame I don't have any vermouth or bitters."

My lips automatically twitched into a smile at the memory of the night I'd made us Manhattans. "You don't have the right kind of whiskey either. You need bourbon or rye, and all you have is Irish whiskey."

"I don't see why you couldn't make a Manhattan with Irish whiskey." Tess cocked her head as she stirred angel hair pasta into boiling water. "I'll bet it'd be damned good."

"I've never had a Manhattan." Erin's nose wrinkled. "I'm not really a fan of whiskey, to be honest."

"That's probably just as well," I said as I topped up my own wineglass. "There are more than a few poor souls in the Larkin family tree who fell down a bottle of Jemmy and never came out."

Erin frowned in confusion. "Jemmy?"

"Jameson," I explained. "The most common Irish whiskey brand."

"Emphasis on the common," Tess piped up from the stove.

"You're such a whiskey snob." I smiled, liking the way this felt. The three of us standing around Tess's kitchen talking, getting ready to sit down and have a meal together. Funny how something this mundane and simple could feel so special.

"Can you pass me the wine?" Tess asked. "I need some for the chicken."

As I handed her the bottle, I moved her glass where she could reach it more easily.

"Thanks." She threw me a small smile as she poured wine into the hot pan, sending up a giant cloud of steam.

"Sure you know what you're doing?" I asked, leaning my hip against the counter next to her. "You're aware alcohol is flammable, right?"

"Fuck off," she muttered, directing a glare in my direction. "I told you I've got this."

I met her glare with a smirk. "When's the last time you changed the batteries in your smoke detector?"

"It was one minor baking mishap." The corner of her mouth quirked as she shook her head. "You're never going to let me live it down, are you?"

"I thought she was going to burn the building down," I explained to Erin, who was watching our banter with interest.

"He doesn't believe I can cook." Tess picked up her wineglass, taking a sip as she gently stirred the sauce. "Because I burned one batch of cookies."

I had to admit, she seemed to know what she was doing at the stove. Color me impressed. I'd be more surprised if this wasn't Tess we were talking about. I'd never known her to be bad at any task she set her mind to, which was why the cookie incident was so much fun to tease her about. "It was a lot of smoke, Tess. I thought I was going to have to run over here and save you from a raging inferno."

"That's right," Erin said. "Tess mentioned you guys live near each other."

I nodded as I sipped my wine. "I'm only six blocks away. Funny that we never knew it until a few weeks ago. I'll bet we used to pass by each other all the time without even noticing."

Erin's smile grew wider. "It's like fate or something."

I saw the corners of Tess's mouth turn down slightly before she turned away.

"You sure I can't help?" I asked, watching her closely. "For real. I'm not just busting your balls."

She fiddled with the neck of her floral blouse as she whisked flour into the sauce. Her gaze darted around before sliding past me, not quite meeting mine. "I suppose you could drain the pasta for me, if you think you can handle it."

"I can probably manage that," I said, moving around her to get down the colander I'd seen the other night when I'd helped Tess unload her dishwasher.

"I could set the table," Erin volunteered. "If you point me toward your silverware."

"It's here." I leaned over to open the silverware drawer for her before grabbing the pot holders off the counter.

Erin gave me an odd look as she picked up a handful of utensils. "Plates?"

"Above the dishwasher," I told her as I poured boiling water and hot pasta into the colander.

When I'd finished, Tess had me toss the angel hair with butter while she got down serving dishes and threw together the salad. "Grate some of this over it," she said, setting a hunk of parmesan on the counter next to me.

I caught Erin giving me another peculiar look as I fished the cheese grater out of a drawer.

"Okay, I have to ask," she said, her gaze moving from me to Tess. "I know you told me you were just friends, but are you *sure* there's nothing going on between the two of you? Because I'm definitely picking up a vibe."

I looked at Tess, wondering when she'd told Erin we were just friends. It must have been last week, before we'd started sleeping together.

A muscle clenched in Tess's jaw as she looked away.

I opened my mouth, all set to tell Erin the truth, but Tess got there first.

"Of course, there isn't anything going on," she said, and the happy feeling I'd had a moment ago fell away like sand slipping through my fingers. "What a ridiculous idea." And then she laughed.

I fucking hated the sound of that laugh. It twisted through me like a shard of ice, cold and razor-sharp. Dismissing me. Dismissing *us* and everything I thought we'd started to mean to each other.

"It's just that you guys seem awfully comfortable around each other." Erin narrowed her eyes at me. "And you sure seem to know your way around Tess's kitchen. Almost like you've been spending a lot of time here recently."

I swallowed down the taste of bile in the back of my throat. Was I expected to play along with Tess's fiction and pretend the last few days hadn't happened?

Tess spoke again when I didn't, her tone light and careless. "It's like I told you, we've gotten together a few times to talk things out and put the past behind us. That's all." She turned to look at me, her gaze silently imploring. "Isn't that right?"

She really expected me to agree. To lie right to Erin's face like it was no big deal.

Except maybe Tess wasn't lying to Erin. Maybe she really didn't think what was going on between us was important enough to acknowledge.

Of course. Of fucking course that was it. Just because we'd agreed to be exclusive didn't mean we'd agreed to be serious. It didn't mean she considered us anything real or lasting. So why tell anyone about it?

It was like high school all over again. Here I was, falling head over heels, and meanwhile, she didn't even like me enough to want people to know we were together.

Why had I thought things would be any different now? That Tess would actually welcome me into her life? I shouldn't be surprised. Hadn't I always been dispensable to her? Good for a fuck and not much else? I'd been stupid to believe otherwise.

It was just that I'd wanted her so much. She'd felt so right and familiar, I'd tricked myself into thinking we could have this. Worse, I'd goaded her into playing along with it when she'd never really wanted it in the first place. I'd brought this on myself. On both of us.

I realized Erin and Tess were looking at me. Still waiting for me to say something.

I had to make a choice. Either contradict Tess and have it out with her in front of Erin, or swallow my wounded pride and pretend to go along with Tess's story.

It wasn't much of a choice.

My heart was pounding and my stomach roiling, but I produced the smile I'd perfected to ingratiate myself with clients and judges and senior partners over the years. It stretched painfully over my face as I looked Erin right in the eye and lied.

"It's true," I agreed, keeping my voice pleasant and light, carefully pitching it to sound believable. "It's exactly like she said. We're only friends." My smile didn't falter as I swiveled my head to meet Tess's gaze. "Nothing more."

Fuck it. Fuck it all.

CHAPTER TWENTY-FIVE

TESS

Donal was upset with me. He was doing a damned good job of hiding it in front of Erin, but I could tell. His posture was a little too rigid, his smile a touch too wide, and his eyes oddly glassy. I could feel him withdrawing from me and putting up defenses. Hiding his feelings behind that damned smile.

I desperately wanted to tell him I hadn't meant what I'd said, to explain that I'd only done it to protect Erin. But I couldn't very well say any of that in front of her.

At least she didn't seem to have noticed anything wrong. She'd bought our story. Or she'd chosen to pretend she had, anyway.

The conversation moved on from that uncomfortable, emotionally fraught moment, and the three of us sat down to dinner like everything was fine. Donal and Erin generously complimented the food, but all I could taste was acid. Donal was back to making jokes as usual, laughing and generally being the life of the party, but it all rang hollow. I couldn't help noticing the way he avoided even inadvertent physical contact and that he never looked directly at me.

A terrible, doomed feeling lodged itself in my chest. The more Donal smiled that too-wide smile, the one that made me feel cold instead of warm, the bigger the bad feeling grew, until my chest hurt so much I could barely breathe around it.

I'd done the right thing, hadn't I? Enforcing boundaries in front of Erin. Keeping this thing happening between Donal and me separate from the relationship we were trying to build with her.

This was all getting too messy and complicated. I didn't like mess or complications. I preferred to keep things compartmentalized. Everything in its proper place.

Whatever was going on with me and Donal was too new—too fragile and volatile—to risk bringing Erin into it yet.

Not until we were on firmer ground and there was less risk of disappointing her. Not when my feelings for Donal were too chaotic to make any sort of sense.

He made an impressive show of keeping up the charade for the rest of the evening. If I hadn't known better, I would have called the whole night a sparkling success. But he left before Erin, making an excuse about some work he needed to do. On a Saturday night. It was so obviously a lie. He wanted to get away from me. He was making sure he wouldn't have to be alone with me after Erin went home.

He held himself stiffly away from me as I walked him to the door. Thanked me for dinner without meeting my eye.

"You don't have to go," I whispered desperately.

His mouth tightened into a thin line. "Yes I do."

When he leaned in to kiss my cheek, it was brisk and offhand, and I knew he was only doing it because Erin was watching. My hand curled possessively in the front of his shirt as the familiar, warm smell of him engulfed me for a too-brief moment before he stepped back. My hand fell uselessly away, unable to hold on to him.

"I'll call you in a little bit, okay?" My eyes burned with an unspoken apology.

"Don't bother," he said in a low, flat voice. Then, in a tone pitched loud enough for Erin to overhear, he bid me a fake, cheerful good night.

When he turned his back and walked out the door, I felt like I'd been punched in the stomach.

Only it was Donal who'd been punched in the stomach tonight.

By me.

I needed to fix this. If I could just explain, then he'd understand why I'd done it.

Only Donal wasn't answering his phone. Or returning my calls. It was impossible to explain anything when he wouldn't talk to me.

My stomach churned with guilt. Even though I'd thought I was doing the right thing, I felt as if I'd betrayed him. When I looked at it from his perspective, I guess I had. By denying our relationship, I'd made him think I was ashamed of him. I remembered the way I felt when he'd done the same to me in high school, and it killed me to think I'd made him feel like that tonight.

I'd only been trying to protect Erin, but by doing so I'd ended up hurting Donal. The irony was, I was pretty sure I'd given the game away with Erin anyway. After Donal had left, she'd given me a shrewd look and asked if everything was okay. I doubted she'd believed my empty reassurances. She'd left soon after, giving me a tight hug on her way out the door and telling me to call her if I wanted to talk.

So yeah. She definitely knew something was off. Which meant I'd hurt Donal for nothing.

I tried calling him again, but it went straight to voicemail once more. Guess I'd have to do this over text.

I'm sorry, I typed out and hit send.

A minute passed. Then two.

I tried again.

Erin's gone home. Please can we talk?

Still nothing. I waited and waited, staring at my phone, but those three little dots never appeared.

Maybe he needed space. Or more time to cool off before he was ready to talk.

I should give it to him, right? Wait for him to tell me when he was ready.

But how long should I wait? An hour? A day? What if he still hadn't responded by tomorrow?

The feeling of doom sitting on my chest had gotten almost unbearable. It felt like I'd lost something precious by being too careless with it.

Thirty minutes later, I was in the middle of putting on my shoes, about to walk my ass over to Donal's and confront him, when I was interrupted by a knock on my door. I hobbled over to see who it was, one running shoe on and one still in my hand.

Donal's face filled up the fish-eye lens of the peephole, and I nearly cried with relief. But when I flung open the door, his grim expression made my stomach twist with even more dread.

"Hi," I whispered.

He didn't say anything. Just stared at me, his eyes guarded and glacial.

"Do you want to come in?" I asked uncertainly.

He nodded, and I stepped back to admit him. As I closed the door, I took a deep breath before turning around to face him.

He'd only walked a few paces into the apartment, as if he wasn't planning to stay. His brow furrowed as his gaze caught on my feet. "Why are you only wearing one shoe?"

"I was about to go to your apartment to see if you were okay." Bracing a hand against the wall, I toed off my running shoe and dropped the other one next to it. "You weren't answering any of my calls or texts."

"That's because I'm pissed off at you. So no, I'm not okay."

It wasn't like I hadn't guessed as much, but it felt even worse to hear him say it in that cold, resentful voice. I nodded slowly, absorbing the discomfort. When I spoke, my voice sounded scratchy like I was going hoarse. "What happened to 'no one gets upset until we've had a chance to talk about it'?"

He ran a hand through his hair and sighed. "Why do you think I'm here?"

"I'm sorry," I said, wishing I could go back in time and do tonight over.

"Do you know what you're sorry for?"

"I hurt you when I told Erin there was nothing between us."

"You did, yeah. It made me feel like shit."

My stomach clenched, and I sucked in an unsteady breath. "I really am sorry."

A little of his anger seemed to drain away. Enough that instead of furious he looked tired and sad, which was even worse somehow. "We need to talk about why you said it. Because it feels like maybe we're not on the same page here."

"Okay." I swallowed and gestured at the living room. "Do you want to sit down?"

"Not really." He crossed his arms, pinning me in place with his gaze. "I'm listening."

Right. I'd asked if we could talk, and now he was here waiting for me to do exactly that. Talk.

"Well…" I'd had this conversation in my head a dozen times in the last hour, but now that he was here I couldn't think straight and all the words were slipping away. "I suppose I thought it wasn't a good idea to tell Erin about us yet, because she might get her hopes up and then be crushed if we—" My throat closed up, refusing to say the words *break up* out loud, so I skipped over that part. "It felt like we should wait and keep it to ourselves for now. Just to be safe."

"For *now*," Donal repeated, slightly disbelieving. "So I understand, what is it exactly that we're waiting for?"

I threw my hands up. "I don't know. This is all brand-new, and we're still figuring out how to navigate it—or at least I am. I figured we shouldn't out ourselves to Erin until we're on surer footing and know what it is we're doing, so she doesn't get dragged into our drama."

A muscle ticked in his jaw. "I know what I'm doing. I thought you did too." He gave me a long, hard look, and I dropped my gaze to his feet, which were much easier to focus on than his unhappy face. "If you're having regrets, I'd appreciate it if you'd just say that. Because I'm not interested in playing games with you."

"I'm not having regrets."

"Look at me and say it again."

Tipping my chin up to look him in the eye, I repeated myself slowly and firmly. "I'm not. Having. Regrets."

"All right," he said, slightly mollified. "Then tell me what you're so scared of."

"I'm not scared."

His lips pressed into a thin line. "Don't do that. We said we weren't going to lie to each other. Tell me what's going on so we can deal with it together."

"I wish I could, but it's not that simple." How was I supposed to admit to him that my instincts were telling me he wasn't safe? Nothing about any of this was safe. The more I let him in, the more he'd be able to hurt me. If I let him see my vulnerabilities, he could use them against me. I couldn't let myself *need* him, because then it would hurt too much if he left me and I'd be even more alone than before.

A scowl deepened the lines of his face. "I gotta tell you, Tess, this is starting to feel like high school again, with you not wanting any of our friends to know about us. And I'm not fucking doing that again."

Whoa whoa *whoa*. I was willing to admit I'd messed up tonight, but he had some serious nerve trying to gaslight me about the past. "I wasn't the one who didn't want anyone to know about us in high school," I countered, affronted.

"The hell you weren't!" His voice shook with enough anger to rock me back on my heels.

My mouth fell open in disbelief. "You're kidding, right? Craig Fontaine asked if you had a girlfriend and you said no, a girlfriend was the last thing you wanted. I overheard the whole conversation. You both had a big chuckle over how much more fun it was playing the field, and how you couldn't wait to get at all those college girls in the fall, and no way were you tying yourself down to anyone so close to graduation."

Donal stared at me like I'd started speaking in tongues. "I have no memory of that at all."

"*I* do. You think I made it up?" It was bad enough that I'd had to hear him say it the first time. I wasn't about to let him get away with pretending it had never happened.

His brow furrowed, his posture still stiff and defensive. "When even was this?"

"In the band hall before school, the first week we were sneaking around. We hadn't talked about what we were doing yet, but I got the message loud and clear."

He shook his head again and raked a hand through his hair. His anger had faded, leaving only confusion. "I swear to God, I don't remember saying *any* of that."

"Well, you did." I crossed my arms, standing my ground. I'd heard what I'd heard, whether he remembered it or not.

"It doesn't even sound like me."

I couldn't hold in my snort of derision and saw his expression harden again. "It sounds exactly like who you were back then. You were a serial scammer, in case you forgot. None of the girls you hooked up with could ever pin you down for more than a week or two."

His wintry blue eyes burned through me as he said, very quietly, "You did."

I opened my mouth. Then closed it again, realizing it was true. We'd been together for nearly three months. As far as I knew, that made me Donal's longest relationship in high school.

He turned on his heel and paced away from me, his movements tight and jerky. When he faced me again his expression was stark. "Is that why—" He broke off and swallowed thickly. "Is that why you were so gung ho to keep us a secret from everyone? Because you thought *I* was?"

"Yes." Foolishly, I'd thought I could protect myself by pretending to be as indifferent as he was. It might have protected my pride, but it hadn't done anything to safeguard my feelings.

"Fuck." Squeezing his eyes shut, he let out a laugh devoid of humor.

I stared down at the floor and took a deep breath, reaching for courage to admit the truth I'd kept hidden at the time. "It hurt to hear you say those things. But I didn't want you to know how much, and I didn't want to give you up, so…"

"So you acted like it was what you wanted."

"I thought it was the only way to hold on to you."

"Tess." The roughness of his voice made me look up. His expression was just as drawn and wretched as I felt. "It wasn't what I wanted. I swear. If I said those things—"

My chin jutted out. "You did."

"I'm sorry. I wish I could remember so I could tell you why I did it. My best guess is that I didn't want to kiss and tell. I was probably putting on an act because I wasn't sure where we stood, and telling Craig what he expected to hear was easier than telling the truth."

"Fine." It didn't matter anymore. What was the point of dwelling on something so far in the past that Donal didn't even remember doing it? It was one more example of how fucked-up our relationship had been back then. An absolute train wreck from start to finish, everything between us tainted by hurt and miscommunication.

Donal's eyes were sorrowful as they searched mine. "I'm sorry I hurt you like that. You must have felt the same way then that I felt tonight."

I pressed my lips together, feeling queasy. We really were cursed—doomed to keep repeating the same damaging patterns over and over again, carelessly wounding each other anew because of old scars that never seemed to heal. I was so tired of ending up right back in this same place with him. Whenever it felt like we were making progress, the past always reared up to drive us apart again.

"We still need to talk about tonight." Donal took a step closer. "What is it that's holding you back now, Tess? What are you so afraid of?"

I looked down at the floor with a sigh. "I'm afraid of this not working out and what happens after that."

"What happens after that?"

"It'll hurt." I hated how small and pitiful my voice sounded.

"Finally, we're getting somewhere." Donal rested his hands on my shoulders, kneading gently. My eyes closed as the warm pressure of his touch melted away some of the heaviness in my chest. "But allow me to offer a counterpoint: What if it does work out and we end up deliriously happy together? Isn't that worth taking a chance?"

I wanted to agree. I really did. But the words wouldn't come out.

"Ah," he said after a beat and dropped his hands from my shoulders. "I see now. You don't believe we can make it work. You don't think we have enough of a chance to be worth taking."

How could *he*? After everything? It felt like there were spike-filled Burmese tiger pits waiting for us around every corner. How could he honestly expect anything to come of us being together except eventual pain and misery? And now he wanted to make Erin a part of it, which meant she'd be caught in the blast radius when this relationship inevitably blew up in our faces.

"Tell me why," he said, staring me down. "Why are you convinced we won't make it?"

"Because it's too hard. There's too much painful history for us to overcome. You have to know that as well as I do." I shook my head, all out of words. If he wouldn't acknowledge the reality of the situation after everything that had already happened, I didn't see how I could convince him.

He crossed his arms, his lips pursing as he contemplated me. "Nope. Sorry, not buying it. The Tess McGregor I know would never back down from a challenge just because it's hard. Try again. For real this time, tell me why you're so certain we won't work out."

"Because nothing ever has," I muttered at the floor.

"Baby." The endearment tore out of him on an agonized breath, and I felt myself pulled into his arms.

I slumped against him, clinging a little as I inhaled the wonderful scent of him. My throat constricted at the thought that I might have lost this tonight—that I might still lose it—and I pressed my face into his chest. I couldn't stand how weak he made me feel. How much I already needed him. He'd sneaked through the cracks in my defenses and embedded himself in my life. I was stuck now. Addicted to the way he made me feel. How was I supposed to protect myself from that?

I'd sworn I'd never let myself become dependent on anyone or rely on some-body else to make me feel safe. Yet here I was, clutching at Donal for comfort and trying not to cry at the prospect of losing him.

"Hey." His hands smoothed up my back and into my hair. "I've got skin in this game too. You know it would hurt me as much as you, right?"

"Not if you're the one who does the leaving."

He pulled back, cradling my face in his hands as he searched it. "What makes you think I'm going to leave you?"

"I don't know." I hadn't, not until that very moment. But as I said the words, the vague misgivings that had been hovering at the back of my mind came into sharper focus.

His shoulders slumped as he continued to study me. "You do too know. I can see it in your eyes. Tell me."

Reluctantly, I looked into his eyes and asked the question I wasn't sure I wanted the answer to. "Are you with me because of Erin?"

"What? No." Donal let go of me, blinking as his brows pulled together. "Why would you think that?"

"Tell me you don't want a do-over. A second chance for us to be the family you couldn't give her when she was born."

A succession of emotions passed across his face. First shock. Then outrage. And finally sorrow. "That's not what this is. Is that what you really think?"

"I don't know what to think. Maybe you're working through old, unresolved feelings from high school. Or maybe you're using me to get over your divorce." The words felt like they were suffocating me, but now that I'd opened the door, my fears kept pouring through it and I couldn't make them stop. "But once you've gotten whatever it is you think you need from me, you'll realize I'm not actually what you want after all. You'll get tired of me and move on. Just like everyone does."

"Tess, no." He shook his head, aggrieved.

"Then tell me what you think this is. What do you want from me?"

"Everything." His hands grasped my arms as he stared into my eyes with an intensity that put the sun to shame. "I want everything you have to give me. I want you in my arms and in my bed, but more than that I want you in my life. Not just right now, but for as long as you're willing to put up with me." He paused, his mouth hitching slightly at one corner. "Which I'm hoping is going to be forever."

"Forever?" I repeated in a mix of surprise and disbelief.

His hands slid up to my shoulders, his thumbs settling into the hollow above my collarbone. "There are no guarantees in life—we're both old enough to know that. But I'm willing to work my ass off to make sure this sticks. I've already lost too much because I didn't fight hard enough to hold on to it. I'm not going to make that mistake anymore. But you have to want it too. Enough to take a risk and go all in with me."

I swallowed hard, frozen in place. "You know how risk averse I am."

"I know." His eyes crinkled fondly as his smile grew. "You've always got five different contingency plans in your pocket for every worst-case scenario. But Tess, if you don't take the big risks, you'll never get the big rewards. I'm asking you to have a little faith in me. Trust me when I tell you this risk is worth taking."

That was what it came down to. *Trust*. He was asking me to give him the power to hurt me. The thing I'd never wanted to do.

Only I already had. It had happened long before tonight, even if I hadn't consciously decided to do it. There was no use fighting it anymore. I was in too deep to turn back now. Donal had already stolen my heart. I had no choice but to trust him with it.

Shrugging out of his grasp, I took my phone from my pocket and composed a group text to Erin and Donal.

I lied tonight. Donal and I have been seeing each other. We're a lot more than just friends. I'm sorry I didn't tell you the truth when you asked. I should have.

When I looked up, Donal was watching me with a puzzled frown.

"Check your phone," I said.

He pulled it out and tapped the screen to unlock it. I watched his expression change as he read the message, his dimples peeking out as his lips curved upward. His eyes jumped to mine, and he broke into a grin. "Thank you."

"I really am sorry. I didn't consider how it might hurt you."

"You're forgiven."

"Really? Just like that."

"I'm done holding grudges, Tess. It's already kept us apart for too long."

My phone vibrated. I smiled as I read the text from Erin.

I KNEW IT!!!! (And I'm really happy for both of you)

Donal took my phone from me. He set it on the console table with his before winding his arms around my waist and pulling me against him. His fingers stroked over my cheek and into my hair. "I'm really happy for us too."

I released a shuddering breath as his lips lightly brushed over mine. My heart was flapping in my chest like a clumsy dove trying to take flight, and he was barely even kissing me at all. I strained toward him, needing more, and felt him smile against my mouth. His lips parted, and his tongue slid against mine in a deep, dreamy, savoring kiss.

Only when my lungs were crying out for oxygen did I finally break it off. "I have a question." I felt him tense, and my mouth twitched into a smile as I wound my hands around his neck to make sure he stayed nice and close. "Were you implying that you're the big reward in this big-risk scenario?"

He huffed out a laugh and dropped his forehead against mine. "Love is the reward, you doofus."

I froze, a heavy band pulling tight around my chest. *It's too soon*, a panicked voice screamed inside my head. We'd come so far to make it to a good place, I felt like I'd already climbed the Matterhorn tonight. I wasn't prepared to move on to Mount Everest yet.

"Eventually," Donal added, apparently sensing my panic. His hands squeezed my hips, tugging me against him as he murmured, "Stop thinking too hard and kiss me."

I did as asked. Gladly.

CHAPTER TWENTY-SIX

DONAL

I cut a worried glance at Tess as I put the car in park. Her face was turned to the window, as it had been for most of the drive to her father's nursing home. As I unbuckled my seat belt, I exchanged a silent look with Erin in the back seat.

We'd brought her here to meet Tess's father today. Tess had been stressed about it, so I'd offered to come along for moral support. Frankly, I'd been surprised she'd accepted my offer, but I was taking it as a good sign. It felt like she was starting to let me in more and more, instead of automatically putting up walls between us.

From the outside, the residential facility looked more like an apartment complex than a nursing home. There were gardens and fountains and a columned portico in front of the lobby. Some of the rooms even had balconies, although I doubted Tess's father's would. She'd told me he was in a special part of the facility designed exclusively for memory care patients, with round-the-clock care and tighter security to prevent them from wandering off the premises unsupervised.

I reached across the console and laid my hand on Tess's leg. She seemed to startle a little, as if she'd been so lost in her own thoughts she'd forgotten I was there. When she turned to look at me, my heart ached at her haunted expression. But as her eyes met mine, I was gratified to see some of the shadows recede.

The tense set of her shoulders loosened a little, and she covered my hand with hers. "Thank you for driving."

"Of course."

Erin had already gotten out of the back seat. The door slammed shut behind her, leaving us alone in the car.

My fingers twined with Tess's, and I lifted her hand to my lips. "It's going to be fine."

Her eyes closed briefly as she nodded. "I know."

Leaning across the console, I stroked her cheek before brushing a light kiss against her lips. "You ready?"

After inhaling a long breath through her nose, she gave me a tight nod.

We got out of the car, and Erin and I fell into step on either side of Tess. As we crossed the parking lot, I brushed my fingers against Tess's hand. She grasped onto them, interlacing them tightly with hers.

The lobby looked like a hotel but smelled more like a hospital. We all signed in, then followed Tess down a corridor lined with resident rooms to a nurse's station next to a security door. The nurse behind the window recognized Tess and buzzed us in with a smile.

"How is he today?" Tess asked as the nurse came out from behind the counter to meet us.

"He's been having a good morning so far." The nurse gave Tess's hand a squeeze as she turned a warm smile on me and then Erin. She was dark-skinned, nearly six feet tall, and wore pink scrubs with flowers on them. "It's the perfect day for visitors."

Tess let out a small, relieved breath. "This is Donal," she told the nurse. "And Erin." After a hesitation, she added, "My daughter."

"I can tell," the nurse said, beaming at Erin. "You and your mom have your grandfather's eyes." She looked me over, her eyes nearly level with mine. "And you must be Erin's father. I'm Sonja."

I swallowed thickly as I shook her hand. When she turned to greet Erin, I exchanged a look with Tess and we shared a small smile.

"He ate most of his breakfast today," Sonja said cheerfully as she led us down the hall past more resident rooms. "Then he let us get him dressed and up into his chair so he'd be ready to receive his guests."

"Has he been talking?" Tess asked, fiddling with the neck of her plain navy blouse.

"Not so much." Sonja stopped in front of a door that was partially ajar. The murmur of a radio announcer's voice drifted out of the room as she turned to smile at us. "He's listening to one of his ball games. God almighty, he loves those things. They always put him in a good mood."

She rapped loudly on the door as she pushed it open. "Joe? Your daughter Tess is here to see you. And she's brought some special visitors with her."

The only answer was the crack of a baseball bat and the tinny-sounding roar of a crowd.

Sonja held the door open and inclined her head for us to enter. Tess went first, followed by Erin, and I brought up the rear.

It was a small room, the decor landing somewhere on the coziness scale between a hospital and a budget-priced hotel chain. A few personal touches attempted to make it feel a little homier. Some framed photographs and mementos occupied pride of place on the dresser, and a collection of pictures that had been cut out of magazines were taped to the walls all around the room.

Joe McGregor sat in a wheelchair by the window. I remembered him as a stocky man with a flattop buzz cut and a friendly smile, but now he looked frail and stooped. His pale skin hung loosely from his once-thick forearms, what remained of his white hair stuck up in uneven wisps, and his face was slack and expressionless as he stared out the window, seemingly unaware of our presence.

Sonja gave me an encouraging smile before she slipped out of the room, pulling the door closed behind her.

Tess had knelt down in front of her father's wheelchair, and she took one of his hands in hers. "Hi, Dad. It's Tess. How are you doing today?"

He didn't react or look at her. His hand lay limp and unmoving in hers.

Tess looked up at Erin, offering a strained smile as she beckoned her closer. "Dad, I brought someone to meet you today. This is Erin. I told you about her before. She's the baby I gave up for adoption in high school. Look at her now, all beautiful and grown up."

My heart cracked in two as Joe continued to stare out the window as if he hadn't even heard.

Erin gamely knelt beside Tess and smiled up at Joe as she took his other hand. "It's nice to meet you, Joe. I'm Erin."

Tess stood up and swiped at her eyes. I moved to her side and rubbed the back of her neck as I pressed a kiss to her temple.

No wonder she got so upset whenever the subject of her dad came up. Seven years, she'd been watching him fade away like this. If that had been my mom slumped in a wheelchair like that, I'd be out of my fucking mind with grief.

Tess slipped her arm around my waist and leaned against me as Erin continued to talk to Joe, telling him about her job and where she grew up. She had a real knack for keeping up a conversation with someone who didn't give her anything back. I guessed it was a skill she'd picked up from being a teacher.

Turning my head to brush my nose against Tess's ear, I murmured, "He can hear us, right?"

She nodded. "His hearing is okay, but his language processing isn't great anymore, so he's not always able to follow what we're saying. I think he tunes out sounds that don't mean anything to him. It's like traffic noise—after a while you stop paying attention to it."

As far as I was concerned, Tess was a straight up superwoman for coming here by herself every week. It had to hurt so goddamn much to see her father like this. I was just glad she'd finally let someone else come with her.

No way was I letting her do this alone anymore. From now on, I was coming along every Sunday. I'd get my mom to come sometime too. I knew she'd be willing to do it for Tess, and Tess would probably like having her here. This kind of thing was right up my mom's alley.

"Is that Harry Caray?" I asked, noticing a familiar voice from my childhood coming from the small boom box on the table.

Tess nodded. "Dad's a huge Cubs fan. When I was growing up we always used to watch the Saturday and Sunday games together on WGN."

I looked at her sharply. "I didn't know that. Why didn't I know you were a base-ball fan?"

She shrugged. "It was only something I did with my dad. As his Alzheimer's advanced, I noticed that sometimes when there was a baseball game on he'd talk to the TV or stand up and mumble along with the seventh-inning stretch. So I tracked down a bunch of old Cubs radio broadcasts and burned them to an audio CD for him to listen to. It's about the only thing he seems interested in anymore. Sometimes he'll even smile or cheer when the Cubs get a run."

"Too bad that didn't happen more often," I said wryly, and Tess smiled.

When Erin finally stood up, brushing the wrinkles out of her pants, Tess tugged me over to Joe.

"Dad, this is my friend Donal Larkin from high school. He used to come over to our house sometimes." Her lips tugged into a small smile as she looked at me. "He's the one who almost beat me out for valedictorian. But I owned his ass in the end."

I squatted down so I was eye level with Tess's dad, ignoring the way my knees popped. "Hey, Mr. Larkin. It's good to see you again."

Nothing. Not even a blink.

I kept going anyway, figuring it was worth it if there was even a small chance anything was getting through to him. "Hey, I hear you and Tess are big Cubbies fans. Me too. You know, my dad used to take me to Wrigley in the summer sometimes when I was a kid. It was pretty much the only thing we ever did together. I'd always make him sit in the bleachers, even though he probably would have preferred nicer seats out of the sun. But nothing beats sitting out there above the ivy, heckling the other team's outfielders, am I right? We were actually in the bleachers for the Sandberg Game in eighty-four, if you can believe it. I just about peed my pants when Ryno clubbed that second homer off of Sutter."

Tess's dad turned and looked at me.

He was staring right at me, focused and present for the first time since we'd entered his room. I swore it almost felt like he recognized me, which was ridicu-lous. We couldn't have met more than a few times. No way he'd recognize me and not his own daughter.

His forehead wrinkled like he was trying to remember something, and Tess's hand squeezed my arm as she crouched down beside me.

"Keep going," she whispered.

So I did. I rambled on about the 1984 playoffs and then about a few of my favorite players from back then.

Joe's mouth moved, and he mumbled something that sounded like "Billy."

I looked at Tess. "Did he say Billy?"

"I think so." Her eyes were glued to her father's face.

"Who's Billy?"

"His younger brother. He died fifteen years ago."

"Billy," Joe said again.

Okay, so Tess's dad thought I was his brother. That was good, right? Him saying anything at all seemed like a pretty big win at this point.

"Do I look like him?"

Tess shifted her gaze to me. "A little, actually." A smile ghosted across her expression as she reached up and smoothed my hair down. "Just go with it."

All right. Whatever she wanted. I turned back to her father and smiled. "Hey, Joe. How's it going? Sorry it's been so long."

His hand twitched in his lap, and I reached for it. The bones in his hand felt fragile as glass, but he curled his fingers around mine with a surprisingly strong grip.

"Billy," he said again.

"That's right," I agreed. "I'm Billy. And you're Joe. My big brother."

It felt a little strange to be lying to him, but I supposed it couldn't hurt. If it gave him comfort to think his long-dead brother was here with him, then he could call me Billy all he wanted.

"Here," Erin murmured, sliding a chair up behind me and winning the undying gratitude of my poor fucking knees.

I reached between my legs and pulled the chair closer as I sat down. "I'll bet we used to go to a lot of Cubs games when we were kids. Sat in the bleachers, back when tickets were only a buck. We were a couple of bleacher bums, weren't we? Maybe we even hung out on Waveland with the ballhawks sometimes after school, hoping to catch a homer when we couldn't get into the game."

Joe's mouth pulled into a smile.

While I was still getting over the sight of that, he turned his head and looked at Tess. He didn't say anything, but he kept on smiling right at her.

It was impossible to know if he recognized her—or maybe thought she was someone else—but from the way Tess's breath hitched I could tell it was a big deal just for him to look at her.

"Hi," she said, her voice wobbling a little. "It's nice to see you."

I reached for her hand and brought it together with her father's, replacing my hand with hers. His fingers twined around hers, holding on tight this time.

Erin squeezed my shoulder when I leaned back in the chair.

"How about that?" I said, feeling a little choked up as I watched Tess and her father. "Go Cubbies, yeah?"

CHAPTER TWENTY-SEVEN

TESS

"You look like you're in a good mood," Marie commented as she popped her packed lunch into the break room microwave.

I realized I must have been smiling as I rinsed my coffee mug in the sink. "I suppose I am."

Marie edged closer as the microwave hummed behind her. "How'd it go yesterday with Erin and your dad?"

"Really, really great, actually."

As part of my new resolution to cultivate deeper friendships, I'd been keeping Marie up to date on the latest developments in my relationships with both Erin and Donal. I was still getting used to opening up voluntarily and sharing the personal details of my life, but it got a little easier every time.

I told Marie about Donal volunteering to come along and my father mistaking him for my uncle. It was the first time in weeks that my dad had made eye contact with me or spoken in my presence. And Erin had been there to see it. I'd been so afraid he'd be having one of his bad days. Sometimes he could be angry and violent—or worse, despondent and crying. But instead, she'd gotten to see a small glimpse of who he used to be.

"That's wonderful," Marie said when I finished the story. "I'm so happy for you and Erin." The microwave dinged, and she popped the door open to retrieve her lunch. "Are you eating here today?"

"No, actually, I'm meeting Donal for lunch in a few minutes. I need to get going."

"Well, have a good time. I'll be here eating my soggy stir-fry all alone."

"You want me to bring you something back?"

She smiled and shook her head. "No, I'm playing with you. Go. Enjoy lunch with your man."

I bid goodbye to Marie and stopped off at my office to grab my purse and jacket before heading out to lunch. As I was waiting for the elevators, I got a phone call from Donal.

"Hey, you." I couldn't contain my smile.

"Hey," he replied, sounding harried. "You haven't left yet, have you?"

I stepped onto the elevator. "I'm on my way out now."

"I'm so sorry to do this, but I'm not going to be able to make our lunch date today."

"That's okay," I said, trying to hide my disappointment. It wasn't as if I wouldn't see him tonight. Even when he worked late or had dinner with his kids, he always came over after he got home.

"There was a snafu with my clients' schedule and my two thirty got moved up an hour. I don't have enough time to make it out of here for lunch." He sighed, sounding stressed and aggravated.

"How about I pick something up and bring it to you?" I offered, wanting to cheer him up. And okay, yes, I selfishly wanted to see him, even if it was just for the time it took to hand him a sandwich. I'd been looking forward to our lunch all morning, and the thought of not seeing him at all made me unreasonably bummed out.

"You don't have to do that."

"You're not going to eat if I don't. Tell me I'm wrong."

He was always skipping meals when he got busy. The protein bars his secretary supplied him with were better than nothing, but hardly an adequate substitute for real food.

"I'll grab something from the cart downstairs," he said.

"No, you won't. You'll get caught up working and forget." The elevator doors opened, and I stepped off into the lobby of my building. "I've got to pick up something for myself anyway. I can get us sandwiches from Hannah's Bretzel."

"I do love their pretzel bread."

"I know."

"Temptress."

I smiled, knowing my plan had hooked him. "Let me do it. I could use the walk, and I've got extra time blocked off on my calendar thanks to my lunch date standing me up."

"It would be really great to see you," he said. "We could eat together in my office if you want."

I definitely wanted.

Thirty minutes later I pushed through the revolving glass door and into the shiny marble lobby of the building where Donal's law firm was located. I hadn't been here since the day I'd showed up unannounced and angry that he'd been ignoring my attempts to talk to him about Erin. Hard to believe how much had changed between us over the last six weeks. I could still remember how cold his expression had been and how much animosity I'd felt when he looked at me.

This time I was expected, and when I identified myself to the receptionist I received a guest badge and instructions to take the elevator to the thirtieth floor. Donal was waiting for me when the elevator doors opened on his floor, and his expression was the opposite of cold. As soon as he looked up from his phone and saw me, the deep furrows in his brow melted away, replaced by the same heart-stopping smile that had been dazzling me since I was fourteen years old.

"Hi," he murmured, leaning in to press a quick kiss to my cheek as I stepped off the elevator. "Thanks for doing this and for not being mad."

It had never even occurred to me to be angry. Obviously, work was more important than a casual lunch date.

But then I recalled the things he'd told me about his marriage and wondered how often he'd canceled plans with his wife at the last minute. How long had she weathered the disappointments like a good sport until she'd started to resent him? How long, I wondered uneasily, would I be able to do it?

Nope, now was not the time to indulge insidious thoughts like that. I was here to enjoy a lovely lunch with the gorgeous man standing before me.

Pushing my doubts away, I looked up into his blue eyes and smiled. "Honestly, my motives were entirely selfish. I really just wanted to see you."

His smile hitched wider, his dimples shining in all their glory. "You just made my shitty day a thousand percent better." Inclining his head, he shifted his arm behind me, his fingers barely grazing the small of my back as he ushered me down a long hallway. "My office is this way."

I let him shepherd me through a maze of offices, conference rooms, and bullpens full of cubicles. He tipped his chin at several lawyerly-looking suit-clad people on the way, and I noticed a few of the younger folks we passed giving him awed, deferential looks.

My estimation of his importance at the firm was reinforced by the office he led me to. Unlike the hive of tiny, glass-walled interior offices we'd passed, Donal's was located in a quieter, less-trafficked area. It was more private and set farther apart, with its own small waiting area and cubicle workstation located outside it.

When he gestured for me to precede him inside, I saw a slightly older woman standing behind the large desk shuffling stacks of papers around. She looked up at my appearance and smiled.

"You must be Tess," she said, coming around the desk and extending her hand. "I'm Donal's legal secretary, Debra."

"It's nice to meet you." I shook her hand and plucked a wrapped sandwich from the plastic bag I was holding. "I brought you a sandwich."

Her smile widened in surprise. "Aren't you thoughtful?"

"Donal said you'd like the veggie sandwich. I hope he was right."

"He was right. Thank you." Her eyebrows lifted slightly as her gaze shifted to Donal. "I'll get out of your hair now and let you two enjoy your lunch."

"You've made an ally for life," he said after she'd pulled the door closed behind her, leaving us alone.

"I imagine a sandwich is the least she deserves for putting up with you."

"Don't I know it. Here, let me take these." He relieved me of the plastic bag and my purse, setting them on a low table in front of a beige minimalist-style couch. All the furniture had a vaguely mid-century modern feel to it, as if the designer had been inspired by the sets on *Mad Men*.

"Very impressive office," I commented, gazing at the floor-to-ceiling windows behind his desk looking out on downtown. The two side walls were wood paneled, while the wall facing the interior hallway was made of frosted privacy glass. "You ever grab a little nap on that couch? Tell the truth."

"I wish I had time to nap during the day. Although I did catch a few hours on it once when I had to work through the night. Hey, come here." Grabbing my hand, he tugged me into his arms.

My hands slipped around his waist as our bodies came together. One of his hands pressed into the small of my back while the other curled around the nape of my neck. His nose gently brushed my forehead, then my cheek, before bumping against my nose. I wasn't sure if he'd actually kiss me here in his office until he did.

His lips pressed against mine, sweet and chaste and tender. A perfect kiss, followed by another, equally as sweet. But then the tip of his tongue touched my lower lip in a teasing invitation. My mouth opened as he angled his head, and I forgot where we were for a moment as his tongue swept into my mouth.

He made a growly noise and pulled back, gently pushing my hips away from his. "Yeah, we definitely need to stop before things get out of hand."

"Good idea," I agreed, running my fingertips over my tingling lips.

For a moment, he just stared at me. Then he smiled and dropped onto the couch, patting the cushion beside him. "Come on, sit. Let's eat so you don't get me in trouble."

SUSANNAH NIX

I joined him on the couch and doled out the sandwiches and drinks I'd brought. We ate leaning over the coffee table as we chatted about our days so far. I listened to him complain about one of the other attorneys at the firm who was a source of frequent frustration, then told him about a phone call I'd had with a prospective client I'd been trying to land. After that, we lapsed into a companionable silence as we finished our sandwiches.

"Hey," he said eventually, bumping his knee against mine. "You all right?"

"Yeah." I looked at him and smiled as I wadded up my sandwich wrapper. "Why?"

"You seemed lost in thought. Care to share with the class?"

Not particularly. I'd been turning over an idea I'd had last night. Something I'd planned to bring up with him at lunch today—but now I wasn't sure I wanted to.

"It's nothing," I said, gathering up all our trash.

"You're a terrible liar."

"No, I'm not." I shot him an indignant glare. "I'm an excellent liar."

His eyebrows twitched upward. "Then you must not be trying very hard, which means you want to tell me."

I sighed. "It's about my dad. I was considering trying to take him to a Cubs game sometime."

"Can you do that?"

"I'm allowed to take him out of the facility under my supervision. The question is whether it's a good idea."

Donal ran his knuckles over his lower lip as he thought about it. "Based on what I saw yesterday, it seems like a pretty great idea. If just hearing me talk about the Cubs can get through to him, imagine what actually being at Wrigley will do—seeing the sights, smelling the smells, hearing the sounds. That's gotta be a hell of a sense memory."

"That's exactly what I was thinking. It's something I've been wanting to do for him for a while. Wrigley has wheelchair-accessible seats, but I don't think I can manage him on my own. I'd need help getting him out of the car and into his wheelchair, and if he were to get upset while we were there—"

252

"I get it." Donal took my hand and squeezed it. "But you've got me now. You don't have to manage it alone. I can help you with all that."

I looked down at our hands. I'd never been any good at asking people for favors. And even though I trusted Donal…it was an awfully big ask. "Would you be willing to?"

"Of course, I would. I think it's a great idea. We should do it."

"It would need to be a day game." In addition to the sundowning effect that made evenings and nighttime much more challenging for Alzheimer's patients, they hadn't installed lights at Wrigley Field until 1988, so all the games my father had seen in his youth would have been played in the daytime.

"Definitely." Donal's thumb rubbed over my knuckles. "A night game at Wrigley would probably confuse him even more. Hell, they still confuse me."

I smiled faintly. And then I said the part that was probably going to be a deal-breaker. "A weekday would be better."

"Sure," he agreed absently. "Less of a crowd than on the weekend."

Hesitating, I slid a sideways look at him. "It means you'd have to take a whole afternoon off work."

"I know." He was staring across the room at his desk. Probably regretting his offer and trying to figure out how to back out of it gracefully.

"You really don't have to do it. I know it's a lot to ask."

He turned his head, his gaze locking on mine. "No it's not."

"I know how busy you are."

"This is important. I'll make the time." He looked like he meant it, and I really wanted to believe him.

"Are you sure?" I asked. "I hate to impose on you like this."

"It's not an imposition to be there for you." He brought my hand to his lips and kissed it. "The whole point of having a boyfriend is so you'll have someone to do stuff like this for you."

"And here I was thinking regular sex was the big draw."

He smiled against my fingers. "That's simply an added bonus."

"Are you really sure you don't mind?" I couldn't seem to shake the uneasiness in the pit of my stomach. "You really don't have to say yes."

"I've got your back," he answered with no hesitation. "Always."

CHAPTER TWENTY-EIGHT

DONAL

I watched Tess unpack a bag she'd just finished packing with the things she was bringing to the ballpark. Sunscreen. Antibacterial hand wipes. A light blanket. The three Cubs hats I'd picked up for us. A water bottle with a straw for her father.

It was the eve of the big day. We were taking her dad to Wrigley tomorrow. She'd gotten permission to check him out of the facility at noon, purchased special wheelchair-accessible tickets for the three of us in the field box behind home plate, and an usher was meeting us at the gate to help us get to our seats.

Now she stood at the dining table, muttering to herself as she surveyed the contents of the bag she'd just unpacked. Then she put everything right back into the bag where it had been a moment ago. It was the third time I'd watched her go through this ritual, and I decided it was time for an intervention.

"That's enough of that." I drew her away from the table before she could undo her work again. "You've got every contingency covered."

"But—"

I cut her off by pressing a finger to her lips as I gave her my most intimidating eyebrow raise. "No buts. You've done enough fussing for tonight."

She let out an irritated sigh in protest, but didn't argue the point further, which I considered a win.

My hands smoothed down her neck and over her shoulders. If her muscles got any tenser, they were going to snap her spine like chalk. "Turn around."

Reluctantly, she let me spin her. When my thumbs dug into her rhomboid muscles, she let out a low, satisfying moan.

"You need to relax, or you're going to give yourself a tension headache."

"Too late," she muttered.

"All right, come on." I continued kneading her shoulders as I steered her over to the couch. "We need to sit down if I'm going to do this properly."

Scooting back into the cushions, I positioned her between my legs. Her ass nestled against my crotch, but I ignored the happy signals from my cock as I focused on the knots in Tess's muscles. She was wound tighter than an industrial spring, but I could feel her starting to loosen up under my fingers.

"Fuck, you're good at that," she groaned as I worked on her traps. "Please don't ever stop."

"When's the last time you had a massage?" I asked. "Some of these knots feel like they're starting to fossilize."

"I don't like people touching me."

My mouth hitched as she let out another moan of pleasure. "Could have fooled me."

"I don't like people who aren't you touching me," she amended, letting her head fall forward limply.

"Tomorrow's going to be fine, you know."

She sighed again. "You don't know that. What if he's having one of his bad days and refuses to let them get him dressed? Or he doesn't want to get in the car?"

I brushed her hair aside as I worked my way up the back of her neck. "You can't control any of that. Stressing out about it in advance won't have any effect on the outcome."

"What if we get him to the ballpark and he gets agitated or aggressive?"

"That's what I'm there for," I intoned in a soothing voice. "If it happens, it happens, and we'll deal with it. Okay?"

She grunted as I massaged the base of her skull. "Are you sure you're going to be able to get away tomorrow?"

"I'm sure. I told you I've got it covered."

There weren't all that many daytime weekday home games to choose from. We'd decided on tomorrow's date a month ago, and I'd had Debra block off the whole afternoon on my calendar. Off-limits. Non-negotiable. No exceptions. As of tomorrow at noon, I was inaccessible.

She'd been telling people I was having a minor medical procedure and would be under anesthesia, because that was the only way they'd accept it without trying to wheedle their way onto my calendar. God only knew what everyone thought was wrong with me. There was probably a pool going around the office.

I didn't care as long as they left me the fuck alone. Nothing was going to prevent me from doing this for Tess.

"I can't do this without you," she said.

Bending my head, I brushed my lips over the shell of her ear. "I promise I'll be there. You don't have to worry."

A shiver rolled through her body, jumping into mine like an electric current, and her hand squeezed my knee.

My fingertips slid into her hair, and she let out a soft, whimpering sigh as I massaged her scalp. All her blissed-out sex-sounding noises were making it harder to ignore the way my cock was throbbing insistently between us.

I pressed a kiss to the back of her neck. "How's your tension headache?"

"What tension headache?" she murmured.

That was what I wanted to hear. Winding an arm around her, I pulled her to my chest and leaned us back. She exhaled as her weight settled against me, her body slack and compliant in my arms.

The increased pressure of her ass against my hard-on nearly made my eyes roll back, but my dick wasn't my priority right now. I had much more important things to do on my to-do list at the moment.

My lips traveled down her neck as I ran my hands over her body. She was wearing workout clothes, all stretchy and skintight. My palms stroked over her curves, under the swell of her breasts, down her stomach, and around her hips.

When I trailed my fingers up her inner thighs, I felt the hitch of her breath as her lungs expanded against my chest.

I licked around the rim of her ear. "You still seem a little tense to me. Whatever can I do to help you relax?"

Her hips jerked in response, letting me know what she wanted.

Pressing my hand against her stomach, I caught her earlobe between my teeth. "Hmmm. I wonder. It's a mystery."

She huffed impatiently, grinding her ass against my poor, tortured cock, and this time my eyes did roll back in my head.

"Maybe there's something under here that'll help." My fingers dived under her top and found the waistband of her leggings.

Her skin was satiny soft and warm, her stomach muscles trembling under my hand as I slid it inside her leggings. God bless spandex. The stretchy fabric allowed me plenty of room to maneuver. Even better, Tess didn't wear underwear with her workout leggings.

She gasped when my fingers made contact with the slickness between her thighs.

"Oh, hey," I whispered, cupping her sex as I sucked at the skin beneath her ear. "I think I found it. Is this where you want me?"

"Yes." Her legs splayed wider as her head lolled against my shoulder. *"God."*

"You sure?" I teased her entrance with my middle finger. "Here? Or maybe here?"

When my thumb rubbed across her clit she arched into my hand and whimpered.

"Hard to make up your mind, isn't it? I know the feeling." I couldn't help grinding my swollen cock against her ass as I slipped a finger inside her. "That's okay. There's no reason you can't have both."

She made the prettiest sounds when she was turned on. Soft little cries and fragmented moans. And the way her body was all lax and loose, completely at my mercy—God, I loved her like this.

I loved *her*. So fucking much. I was the one who was at her mercy. And I couldn't even tell her. I was too chicken. What if she wasn't ready to hear it yet? What if she didn't feel the same? I couldn't risk it. So I showed her instead, loving her body, giving her what she needed from me.

A moan shuddered out of her as I pumped inside her, keeping the pressure on her clit the way she liked it, driving her into a frenzy. Tangling my free hand in her hair, I tilted her head back so my mouth could reach her neck again. Her pulse jumped under my lips as I sucked at the skin under her jaw.

Our bodies rocked together as I stroked in and out of her, faster and harder, until I felt her muscles flutter and contract. I covered her mouth with mine when she cried out. Her body slumped against me, limp with pleasure, and I caressed her through the pulsing aftershocks.

When I took my hand out of her leggings, she curled into me, and I wrapped her up in my arms, cradling her against my chest.

The words *I love you* sat in a lump at the back of my throat, threatening to force their way out as I held her. I swallowed thickly, shoving them back down.

After a moment, she pushed out of my arms and stretched like a cat. Her head swiveled toward me, and she frowned as our eyes met. Shifting on my lap, she straddled my legs and smoothed her hands over my chest. "Tell me what you're thinking."

I couldn't. I doubted she wanted to know the real answer. So instead I told her a truth wrapped inside a lie of omission. "You're beautiful. It takes my breath away sometimes when I look at you."

She leaned down and brushed her lips against mine. "It's okay. You don't have to tell me if you don't want to."

I pulled her against me. She came willingly, nuzzling into my neck as I stroked my hands up her back.

"Before I forget," she said, her breath a soft tickle against my throat. "There's something I've been meaning to tell you."

"What's that?" I asked, staring up at the ceiling.

"I love you."

I stopped breathing. "What'd you say?"

"You heard me." She pushed off my chest, the corners of her lips tilting as she gazed down at me. Her eyes were clear and shining, and as warm as I'd ever seen them. "I love you."

For once in my life, I was at a loss for words.

"Look at that." Her smile grew wider as she stroked her fingers along my jaw. "I don't think I've ever seen you tongue-tied before."

I surged up, grabbing her face and pulling her mouth against mine. "Fuck," I mumbled in between kisses. "I can't believe you said it before me."

"You left me no choice. You were obviously never going to get around to it."

I pulled back to look at her. "You knew?"

"Of course I knew. I can always tell what you're thinking."

"Fuck." I pressed my forehead against hers. "I fucking love you so fucking much."

"Such a dirty mouth on you."

"You love it." It still hadn't quite sunk in. I kept waiting to wake up from the dream.

"I really do." Her fingers hooked in the waistband of my pants and she stood up, pulling me with her. "Now come on. It's time to put you to bed."

Debra appeared in the doorway of my office. "You need to get going."

"I know," I muttered, hurriedly scanning the email I'd just finished typing. "Let me just do…" I added a few more words. "One…" Fixed a typo. "More…" Gave it a final scan. "Thing." I hit send. *There. All done.*

She glared at me, tapping her wrist—not that she was wearing a watch. It was simply her way of saying *get a move on*. "You told me not to let you be late."

"I know. I'm leaving."

I shut my laptop and shoved it in my briefcase. Tapped my pockets, checking for my phone, and came up empty. *Shit.* It had to be around here somewhere. I shuffled papers and files around, looking for my damn phone.

"And yet somehow you're still here," Debra said.

"I can't find my phone." Of course it would go missing right now. *Fuck.*

Debra walked over to the desk and pulled my phone out from under my briefcase. "This phone?"

My entire body sagged with relief. "Thank you."

She passed the phone to me and pointed at the door. "Now get."

My phone started ringing as I shoved it in my pocket.

"Don't look at it," she warned.

"It might be Tess." I pulled my phone out again.

"Is it Tess?" Debra asked.

I blinked at the screen as my initial surprise shifted into an icy trickle of apprehension. "No."

"Then don't answer it. Let them leave a message."

I couldn't. Not this call. I had to take it.

Shooting Debra a regretful look, I accepted the call and lifted the phone to my ear.

CHAPTER TWENTY-NINE

TESS

Anxious and annoyed, I checked the time again. Donal was now officially thirty minutes late.

I was standing in the parking lot outside my dad's nursing home because the cell signal inside the building was spotty. It wasn't that great out here either, but it was at least good enough to send texts.

I'd already texted Donal five times in the last half hour and received a big fat nothing in response. At this point, I was pretty sure he wasn't coming.

Holding my phone up, as if those extra few inches of height were somehow going to make all the difference, I paced around the parking lot trying to find more bars.

I looked like a fool walking around with my phone in the air, and I felt like one too. I'd let myself trust Donal, and look what it had gotten me. Exactly what I'd always known it would: disappointment.

It was just like that basketball game when I was fifteen all over again, with me trying to find Donal to get the ride he'd promised only to realize he'd left without me. Forgotten about me. Abandoned me.

Shaking my head, I tried to stop the memory spiral from dragging me back there again. This was a completely different situation. There was no way Donal could have forgotten about today. Even if he'd lost track of time, Debra would have reminded him. Which meant something else had happened.

He knowingly stood you up, a voice whispered in my head.

Somehow that felt worse than being forgotten. He'd known exactly how much today meant to me and how anxious I was about it. We'd been planning this for weeks. He knew damn well I couldn't do it without him. And despite all that, he'd prioritized something else over keeping his commitment to me. Decided there was something more important, more deserving of his time and attention than I was.

Tears blurred my vision, and I stopped pacing and lowered the phone. Wiping my eyes, I stared at the screen, mentally willing some kind of message to come through. Something—anything—to explain why Donal had done this to me.

Just in case, I tried calling him again. The call actually managed to connect this time, but it went straight to voicemail and his outgoing recording kept cutting in and out. I left him a message anyway—or tried to. I wasn't sure it'd be intelligible on his end.

Damn phone reception. You'd think in this day and age we'd at least have decent coverage in the third-largest city in the U.S. I'd asked one of the nurses about it once, and she'd shrugged and said it just happened to be a dead spot for my particular carrier, but if I changed cell phone companies it'd be fine.

I dearly wished now I'd changed cell phone companies. Not that it necessarily would have made any difference. I didn't actually know that Donal had tried to call or get a message to me. Maybe he was ignoring his phone because he was sitting in some work meeting he'd decided he couldn't get out of, despite all his assurances to the contrary.

Well, shit. I certainly wasn't going to stand around crying in a parking lot because my boyfriend had stood me up.

It had turned out to be a beautiful afternoon, and I had the rest of the day off. As long as I was here, I might as well take advantage of it and spend the time with my dad. They'd gone to the trouble to get him dressed and ready to go out. I could at least take him for a walk around the grounds in his wheelchair, even if I couldn't take him to the ball game. Maybe I could even borrow a portable radio so we could listen to the game outside. It wouldn't be the same as being at Wrigley, but it was the best I could do under the circumstances.

Swiping the rest of my tears away, I typed out a final text to Donal.

Never mind. I guess we're not doing this after all.

CHAPTER THIRTY

DONAL

"I'm so sorry, Dad."

I looked over at Maddy's tearstained face and pulled her into my arms. "It's okay, baby. I'm just glad you're all right."

A slow trickle of cars cruised past us on the residential street, rubbernecking as they maneuvered around the accident scene still blocking part of the intersection.

Maddy clung to me, sniffling into my chest. "But the car…"

"I don't care about the car," I said, turning my head away from flashing emergency lights. The tow truck driver was cinching Maddy's crumpled Honda up onto the bed of his truck.

A woman had run a stop sign and T-boned Maddy. The driver's door and front fender were a crumpled mess. She'd had to crawl over the passenger seat to get out of the car. Thank God the woman who hit her hadn't been going that fast, or it could have been so much fucking worse.

The thought of it made me feel sick to my stomach, and I hugged Maddy even tighter.

"Mom's gonna care," she mumbled into my shirt. "As soon as she gets over the initial shock."

"No she won't. Your mom cares about you and your brother more than anything else in the world—definitely more than she cares about a car."

Maddy had tried to call Wendy first, but she'd been in a meeting with her phone silenced. I was just glad Maddy had called me next, and that I'd been able to race over to help her deal with the aftermath of the accident. She could have called her boyfriend, but instead, she'd called me. It felt good to know I'd been her second choice. Even if getting a tearful, semi-incoherent call from my teenage daughter had nearly given me a heart attack.

Not to mention that I'd had to bail on Tess after promising I wouldn't let her down. But I couldn't let myself think about that right now. One crisis at a time.

Maddy squirmed out of my hug and blinked up at me guiltily. "Thanks for coming to my rescue, Dad."

I used the cuff of my shirt to wipe the tears from her cheeks. "I'll always come to your rescue, kiddo."

"Mom would have had tissues in her purse."

"Yeah, she would. But you got me instead of your mom, so you'll have to suck it up and make do with my shirt."

Wendy had called in a panic five minutes after I'd arrived on the scene. Once I'd convinced her that Maddy was fine and I had everything under control, she'd told me she was heading home to meet us at the house when we were done here.

I brushed Maddy's dark bangs back, frowning as I inspected the red spot on her forehead. "Are you sure you don't want me to take you to the ER to have that looked at? Just in case."

The force of the impact when her car was hit had caused her head to bounce against the side window a little. Not hard enough to break either the glass or her skin, but still. She'd declined the police officer's offer to call the paramedics, but I couldn't help worrying.

"It's not that bad," she said, wrinkling her nose as she batted my hand away. "The airbags didn't even go off."

"Yeah, I don't know if that's a good thing or a bad thing." I had to admit she wasn't showing any signs of a concussion. It'd probably leave a small bruise, but it didn't seem to be forming much of a lump.

"I promise it's nothing. Trust me." She offered a watery smile. "I've gotten worse injuries hitting myself in the head with the hair dryer."

"Fine. You're the boss." As we watched the tow truck driver secure her car to the now-flat bed of his truck, I draped my arm around Maddy's shoulders. For once, she didn't pull away.

Christ, how I'd missed being able to hold her like this. It'd been years since she'd let me be this close to her. As I kissed the side of her head, I prayed to a higher power I no longer believed in that Maddy had finally started to forgive me for all the times I'd let her down.

"My poor car," she said, leaning against me. "Do you think they'll be able to fix it?"

"I don't know. Maybe."

"I loved that car. You let me pick it out for myself."

"Yeah." That day was one of the best family memories I had from the last few years. "You picked a good one."

Wendy had wanted to give Maddy a car for her sixteenth birthday so she could drive herself and her brother to and from school. I'd had some concerns about granting her that much freedom, but I'd gone along with it because I was tired of feeling like the bad guy all the time.

The four of us had gone to the used car lot together, and I'd talked Maddy through the pros and cons of all the cars that fit the budget we'd agreed on. But I'd let her make the final choice herself, and she'd picked the extremely sensible Honda sedan I'd secretly been pulling for. For a few wonderful hours that day, she hadn't seemed to mind being around me so much. It was the last time I could remember the four of us being all together and feeling like a happy, close-knit family. Six months later, Wendy asked me for a divorce and I moved out.

The police officer who'd showed up to the accident scene had finished talking to the other driver, and he made his way back toward us. "I've taken everyone's statements, so you're free to go. Here's the case number to give your insurance company."

I thanked him as I accepted the slip of paper he tore off his clipboard.

"He was kind of cute," Maddy said as we watched him stride back to his cruiser.

I grunted in response. If she was doing well enough to care what the cop looked like, she must be getting over the initial shock of the accident. My brilliant, resilient kid was going to be just fine.

"Come on, let's get you home," I said, leading her toward my car. "Your mom said she was going to pick up some of your favorite ice cream for you."

"Oh yay!" Maddy practically skipped the rest of the way to my car.

Yeah, she was definitely fine.

I fastened my seat belt and started the engine. While Maddy played with the stereo system, pulling up one of her playlists, I checked my phone to make sure I hadn't heard back from Tess yet.

Still nothing. Not a good sign.

I'd called her while I was racing to my car after getting off the phone with Maddy earlier and left a panicked message explaining the situation. But I knew from our weekly trips to visit her dad that Tess's cell reception was shit at the care home. I had no way of knowing if she'd even gotten my message. Based on the texts she'd sent while I was driving across town to get to Maddy, it sounded like not.

A painful lump settled in the pit of my stomach as I thumbed through them again.

Tess: I'm here. Waiting in the parking lot.

Tess: Are you running late?

Tess: You didn't forget, did you?

Tess: Please tell me you're on your way.

And then finally:

Tess: Never mind. I guess we're not doing this after all.

. . .

I felt like the biggest asshole of all time. Especially when I thought about Tess sitting outside the nursing home sending me all those texts with no idea why I'd stood her up on such an important day. She probably hated me, and I couldn't even blame her.

Hopefully, she'd forgive me once she understood what had happened, but I still felt like shit for putting her through that. And after all my grand promises too. So much for always having her back.

I'd texted her as soon as I'd made sure Maddy was okay, but she hadn't responded yet. I couldn't be sure she'd even seen it if she was still at the nursing home. Just for good measure, I fired off another groveling text telling her how truly sorry I was.

"Everything okay?" Maddy asked.

"Yeah, it's fine," I said as I finished typing my apology.

"Did I call you away from something important?"

I looked up from my phone. "There's nothing more important than you. I was supposed to meet someone is all."

"I'm sorry I messed up your day."

"Don't worry about it." Twisting in my seat, I pulled her into an awkward hug across the console. "I'm glad you called, okay? I always want you to call when you need me."

"Okay." She nodded against my chest before she pulled away, plucking at the seat belt that had been trying to strangle her.

I lifted my phone to my ear. "I need to make a quick call and then I'll drive you home."

Maddy nodded absently and went back to looking at her own phone.

The call went straight to Tess's voicemail again. I reached out to turn down the music Maddy had started playing. "Tess, it's me again. I hope you got my message earlier. Anyway, Maddy's fine. I've got her with me now and I'm about to drive her home. I'll try to catch up with you later."

It was the best I could do for the time being. Disconnecting the call, I dropped my phone into the cup holder.

"Your plans were with Tess?" Maddy asked as I pulled away from the curb.

"That's right."

"Were you supposed to have lunch or something?"

I glanced over at her quickly before turning my attention back to the road. "You remember how Tess's father is in a special nursing home for people with Alzheimer's? I was supposed to meet her there to help take him on a little field trip, is all."

"Oh." Maddy was quiet for a moment. "That sounds like it might have been important."

"It's fine. Tess will understand." I really hoped so, anyway.

There was a short silence before Maddy said, "Is Tess your girlfriend now?"

I shifted in my seat. I'd been planning to tell the kids about Tess, but I hadn't gotten around to it yet. Mostly because I'd been afraid of how Maddy would take it. Tess and I had talked about it and agreed telling the kids wasn't something we needed to rush into.

Today's circumstances weren't exactly how I'd planned to break the news, but here we were.

"Yeah, she is." I dared another glance at Maddy. "You okay with that?"

Her shoulder lifted in a shrug. "Sure."

It was impossible to tell if she actually meant it or not. My hands squeezed the steering wheel as I focused on the road. "I know it's probably weird for you that I'm dating. To be honest, it's kind of weird for me too, to be dating someone who isn't your mom."

"It's not that weird. Mom's got Patrick now, and he makes her happy." Maddy leaned forward and turned the music back up.

The unspoken implication—that I hadn't made her happy—hung uncomfortably in the air between us as a moody Taylor Swift song filled the silence.

"I like Tess," Maddy said after a while. "She seemed pretty cool."

"She is pretty cool," I agreed, relaxing a little. "I'm glad you like her."

"I like Erin too."

"Really?" I glanced at Maddy, but she had her face turned to the window.

"It is pretty weird to find out you had a kid before you had me."

"I'll bet. But I didn't have Erin the same way I had you. You'll always be my first daughter."

"Whatever. I don't mind having an older sister. And it's kind of cool that I'm going to be an aunt."

"I'm glad to hear it. I know Erin's pretty happy to have a younger sister—and a little brother."

Maddy snorted. "She's welcome to him."

A smile curved my lips as I shook my head at the familiar sibling rivalry.

Five minutes later, I pulled up in front of the house where Maddy had lived most of her life. Wendy had been five months pregnant with Jack when we bought it. We'd been so happy back then. I remember thinking on the day we moved in that we finally had everything we could ever want. Foolishly, I'd thought it would always be that way.

"Are you coming in?" Maddy asked as she unfastened her seat belt.

"For a minute, yeah." I dredged up a smile for her. "Just to make sure your mom's not too freaked out."

We got out of the car, and Maddy fell into step beside me as we headed up the front walk.

"You deserve to be with someone who makes you happy too," she said out of nowhere. "I hope I didn't mess things up with Tess."

My smile felt like it was going to burst through my chest, but I tried to play it cool so I didn't embarrass her by getting all emotional. "I appreciate it, kiddo, but you don't need to worry about that. Everything's going to be fine."

Unfortunately, everything was not fine.

CHAPTER THIRTY-ONE

DONAL

After I left Maddy at the house with her mom, I tried calling Tess again. Still no luck. She hadn't replied to any of my texts either. Total radio silence. I was starting to get scared.

Maybe it was just some snafu with her phone. Like she'd lost it or dropped it in a toilet or something. Sometimes that happened, right? It would explain why I hadn't heard from her.

I went to her place hoping we could straighten things out face-to-face, but she wasn't there. Or at least she didn't respond to my knocking and shouting her name through the door. I persisted until one of her neighbors stuck her head out into the hallway to give me the stink-eye.

Now I was back at my place, and I didn't know what to do. I'd gone from a little scared to seriously freaked out.

Where the fuck was Tess? It had been hours. Surely she'd gotten my messages by now.

Was she really that pissed off at me that she was giving me the silent treatment? Didn't she understand why I'd had to do it? I knew she had to be upset—it made me physically ill to imagine how much it must have hurt her when I didn't show up today—but she couldn't possibly expect me to pick her over my daughter?

Could she?

Fuck.

By six o'clock I was an utter nervous wreck. I'd been pacing around my apartment working myself into a panic for the last two hours. I must have tried calling her a dozen times and sent almost as many texts begging her to let me know she was okay.

It didn't help that this was my second scare of the day. The tearful call from Maddy earlier had already left my nerves a raw mess and my reserves of calm were running on fumes.

I was at a complete loss for what to do with myself until I heard back from her. The last thing I wanted to think about was work. I was too distracted to focus on TV or reading. I couldn't even have a drink to calm my nerves in case Tess was in trouble and needed me to come get her or something.

When my phone finally rang and I saw Tess's name on the screen, I just about fainted with relief.

"Tess. Thank fuck. Are you okay?"

"I'm fine." Her voice sounded breathy and tight. "How's Maddy? Is she all right?" There was traffic noise behind her, like she was out in public somewhere or in a car with the window rolled down.

"Maddy's fine. A little shaken up, is all. I'm so fucking sorry I didn't make it today. I've been trying to get a hold of you for hours."

I heard her take a long breath before she said, "I just saw all your messages and texts."

"Just now?" Jesus Christ on a cross, had she really spent all this time thinking I was a festering asshole who'd let her down for no good reason? She had, hadn't she? "So I take it you've been cursing my name for the last five hours?"

She didn't say anything, which was pretty much all the answer I needed.

"Where've you been?" I asked, dragging my hand through my hair. "I've been going out of my mind."

"I was with my dad."

"You didn't take him to the game?" I hoped like hell she hadn't tried to do it all by herself. If so and something had gone wrong, I'd never be able to forgive myself.

"No. I spent the afternoon with him at the home. We sat in the courtyard and listened to the game on the radio. But I didn't have any cell service there, so I didn't see any of your messages."

I ground the heel of my hand against my forehead, feeling like complete shit. "You have no idea how sorry I am. I just—fuck, I need to see you. Please. Tell me where you are and I'll come to you."

"I'm a block from your building."

"You are?" I grabbed my keys and ran out of my apartment, not bothering to lock it behind me.

"I didn't check my phone until I got home a few minutes ago. As soon as I heard your first voicemail, I started walking toward your place. Please tell me you're there."

"I'm on my way down," I said, jabbing the elevator button impatiently. "I'm coming to meet you."

"You don't have to come down. I'm almost there. I can see your building."

"Too late, I'm already on the elevator." *Annnnd* I was barefoot, I realized as I stepped onto the cold metal floor. I'd forgotten I wasn't wearing shoes when I ran out of my apartment. Fuck it. Too late to fix it now. "I'll meet you in the lobby."

"Donal, I—"

The call cut off as the elevator doors closed.

Shit! Fuck! Goddammit! Fuck these fucking cell phones. Weren't they supposed to make it easier to reach people? It was all I could do not to throw the cursed thing across the elevator.

I crossed my arms, watching the numbers decrease as the elevator plunged toward the lobby. Why did I have to live up so high? And why was this elevator so goddamned slow? Could we hurry it up a little, maybe?

And now it was stopping. *Perfect.*

Two women in their thirties got on. Dressed up for a night on the town by the look of them. High heels, tight dresses, lots of makeup. And here was me, barefoot and probably wild-eyed, with my daughter's teary makeup smears staining my untucked dress shirt.

They eyed me warily, giving my disheveled appearance raised eyebrows.

"Hey, how you doing?" I offered them a nod as I hammered on the door close button like I was playing Rock 'Em Sock 'Em Robots.

"It doesn't actually make it work any faster to push it a bunch of times like that," one of them said helpfully.

"Can't hurt to try though, right?" I countered with a strained smile.

They didn't try to talk to me for the rest of the ride down, and thankfully no one else got on. As soon as we hit the lobby, I rocketed off the elevator before the doors had even finished opening. My mom would just have to find a way to forgive me for not letting the ladies off first. I had urgent business to attend to.

I ran into the middle of the lobby and stopped, searching for Tess. It didn't look like she was here yet. My gaze jumped to the windows facing the street, and my heart about leaped out of my chest when I saw her walk past on her way to the door.

She nodded a greeting at the doorman as he admitted her. She was dressed for the ballpark, in jeans and a T-shirt with her hair in a sagging ponytail. There were tired shadows under her eyes and tense lines around her mouth. I couldn't tell if her face looked pink from being in the sun or from crying.

Just inside the lobby, she stopped and looked around. The second she spotted me, she started walking my way. My feet carried me toward her and we met halfway.

She blinked up at me like she didn't know what to make of me, her lips thin and pulled down at the corners. Now that she was closer, I could see how red her eyes were. She'd definitely been crying.

Her mouth opened, but before she could speak I swept her up in a ferocious hug. The breath whooshed out of her lungs as I lifted her off the floor and buried my face in her hair.

"I'm sorry," I mumbled, holding her as tight as I could without hurting her. "I hate that I did that to you."

"I know," she said, and I took heart from the way she wound her arms around my neck. She was basically clinging to me, which had to be a good sign, right?

Please let it be a good sign.

I could have stood there all night holding her like that, but after a few seconds she said, "Donal, put me down," and I let her slide to the floor.

No way was I letting go of her completely though. My arms stayed locked around her, holding her in place against me. All around us, people came and went through the lobby, but I only had eyes for Tess.

"Is Maddy really okay?" she asked anxiously. "What happened?"

"She's fine." My forehead sagged against hers as I exhaled what felt like my first unconstrained breath of this whole cursed day. "Some lady blew through a stop sign and hit her driver's side door."

"Jesus," Tess breathed.

"Luckily it was a residential street and the woman was going pretty slow, or it could have been a lot worse. It ended up just being a minor fender bender."

"Thank God."

"Not that I knew that when Maddy called me crying and said she'd been in a car accident."

Tess's hands moved in comforting strokes over my neck and through my hair. "It must have been terrifying."

"I had to go get her. She needed me."

"Of course you did. I'm just so glad it wasn't more serious."

"I wouldn't have missed today for anything less than an emergency, Tess. Please tell me you knew that." I searched her face, hoping to find absolution.

Her lips stayed shut. When she dropped her gaze to the floor, my stomach went with it.

"You didn't know that." My voice was as hollow as my heart felt.

Tess's arms tightened around me as she pressed her face into my chest. "I know it *now*."

"But you thought I'd blown you off for nothing." It didn't feel great that she'd assumed the worst of me. That she kept expecting me to fail her. "You spent the whole day thinking that, didn't you? Right up until a few minutes ago."

She nodded, clutching me harder. Like she was afraid I was going to disappear on her again.

"You must have hated me. I can't stand that." I dropped my face to her hair. It smelled like fresh air and hospital disinfectant. "Tell me what I could have done different, because I don't fucking know."

"Nothing. You didn't do anything wrong."

I wanted to believe she meant that, but it was hard when I'd seen the pain written on her face. "I hurt you," I said miserably.

"It's not your fault. I forgive you."

"Just like that?" I searched her eyes. "You're really not mad?"

"I'm done holding grudges. It's already kept us apart for too long."

Hearing her repeat my words back to me went a long way to smoothing the jagged edges inside me. I pulled her against me again, resting my chin on top of her head. "I'm still sorry I had to pick someone else over you after I promised I wouldn't."

"She's your daughter and she needed you. I'm always going to understand that. And you didn't pick her over me, you picked her emergency over taking my dad to a baseball game. If you were supposed to take Maddy to a baseball game and you found out I'd been in a car accident, what would you do?"

I squeezed her tighter, hating this hypothetical. "I'd break every traffic law in existence to get to you."

"There you go."

My hands found their way to her face. "I don't ever want to hurt you."

"I know that."

"Do you?" I was so used to being doubted I found it hard to believe.

She answered by kissing me. My whole body breathed out in relief as her petal-soft lips pressed against mine. Fiercely enough to let me know she meant it, even though her mouth stayed closed because we were in public and already attracting curious glances.

"Come on." I grabbed Tess's hand and marched her toward the elevators, needing to get her alone ASAP.

I punched the up button and pulled her into my arms again, unwilling to let even a few inches separate us while we waited.

We must have looked pretty intense, because when the elevator came, the guy who'd been waiting for it with us gestured for us to go on without him. "You take it," he said with a faint smile. "I'll catch the next one."

"Thanks, man." I gave him a grateful nod as I punched the number for my floor.

As soon as the doors finished closing, I pulled Tess into my arms and brushed my lips over hers. "Tell me you don't hate me."

"I *love* you." Her fingers slid into my hair, her body pressing hard against mine as our mouths slid together.

My hands fumbled over her hips, her hair, her throat, her face. Needing to touch her everywhere. None of it enough.

Hunger surged in my blood when her tongue parted my lips and stroked over mine. I let out a growl and pressed her back against the wall of the elevator, kissing her like my life depended on it. Telling her without words all the things I wanted her to know. *I love you. I need you. I can't stand the thought of my life without you. Please don't ever fucking leave me, because I might actually die if I have to give you up a second time.*

When my hand pushed under her shirt, she grabbed my wrist and tore her mouth away from mine. "Security camera. Someone's probably watching."

"Shit." We didn't need to be giving my building's security guys a free peep show. The last thing I wanted was some creepy rent-a-cop getting off on the sight of Tess. Only I was allowed to do that.

Setting my hands safely on her waist, I eased my hips back enough that I wasn't so obviously dry humping her. "Sorry. I got carried away."

"Me too." Her fingers brushed over the makeup smears on my shirt as her gaze wandered down my body. "You're barefoot," she said as if she'd just now noticed.

"I was in too much of a hurry to get to you to put on shoes."

Her smile made the air taste sweeter, like it had been touched by sunlight, rainbows, and ocean breezes.

When the elevator doors slid open on my floor, I steered her into the hall. We held hands all the way to my apartment, our fingers laced so tightly it felt like they were fused together. Only once we were inside did I let go in order to throw the bolt behind us.

While Tess toed her shoes off, I sagged back against the front door with a groan. "What a fucking day, huh?"

Her smile faded as she looked at me. "I should have had more faith in you. I shouldn't have assumed the worst."

"Tess," I said softly, moving to take her in my arms. Her breath hitched as I pulled her close. "I shouldn't have given you a reason to assume the worst."

"You didn't. That's the thing." Her eyes closed as our noses rubbed together. "I keep trying to protect myself because you scare me so much."

I went still, my chest growing tight. "I scare you?"

"My feelings for you scare me. They're too big. It's overwhelming sometimes, how much I need you. And terrifying, because what happens if I lose you?"

A mixture of relief and elation flooded through me. She needed me. This strong, brilliant, *capable* woman needed me and wanted me in her life. I was the luckiest guy on the planet.

"You're not going to lose me. I love you." I took her face in my hands, then sucked in a breath because she was so beautiful she made my head spin. "I'm not going anywhere. You can trust me on that."

"But things happen," she said. "Feelings change. People change. You told me yourself you thought your wife was the love of your life, but that feeling didn't last."

"It didn't last because I let it die. I took it for granted, assuming it would always be there. I didn't do anything to nurture it or deserve it. I didn't fight for it, just like I didn't fight for you back in high school."

God, how I wished I'd been braver. And smarter. And tried harder. I should have told Tess how I felt about her back then.

My thumb caressed her cheek. "I'm not going to make that mistake ever again. I've spent too much of my life taking the people who are important to me for granted. I'm not going to lose you like that again. Now that I've got you, I'm going to fight like hell for us."

"Even if you have to fight me sometimes?"

"If that's what it takes, then yeah, I will. Gladly." I grinned, and her lips twitched in response. That little almost-smile sent a shower of happiness sparking through me. "You know there's no one I like fighting with more than you."

Her laugh stitched the broken pieces of my heart back together, cured my exhaustion, and soothed away all the tension in my muscles.

"So we're okay, right?"

"Yeah," she said, reaching a hand up to smooth my hair. "We are."

"Good." I picked her up and headed for the bedroom.

Her legs wrapped around my waist, but when she started kissing me I got so distracted I nearly missed the doorway.

"Ow," she complained when I readjusted course a little too late.

"Sorry," I mumbled as I licked into her mouth.

Apparently kissing Tess made my brain malfunction and destroyed my ability to navigate my own apartment, because we hit the bed sooner than I anticipated and tumbled onto the mattress in a graceless heap. There was a lot of laughing, and then more kissing, followed by a period of extremely inefficient and clumsy undressing. Finally, after much longer than it should have taken, I managed to crawl on top of her and properly enjoy the slide of her smooth, soft skin against mine.

"I love you," she said, gazing up at me as I held her hands above her head.

"You better." I moved my mouth to her ear and whispered, "You're stuck with me now, and you're never getting rid of me."

EPILOGUE
TESS

"Is that it?" Marie asked as I strolled through the door of her office carrying a gift box. "Oooh! Let me see."

Smiling proudly, I set the box on her desk. I was finally done with Erin's baby blanket, and Marie had made me promise to bring it in before I wrapped it so she could see the finished object.

She got to her feet and lifted the lid on the box. "Oh wow." Reverently, she unfolded a corner of the blanket and ran her fingers over the stitches as she examined the edges. "You did a great job weaving in all your ends."

"Thanks for your help with that." I'd brought the work in progress to the office a couple of times when I got into trouble to beg for Marie's help.

She waved off my gratitude. "I love the addition of the crochet border."

"All the credit goes to Dawn for that. She's the one who suggested it and taught me how to do it."

Dawn and I had finally gotten together two months ago to catch up over those drinks I'd proposed. She'd opened up about the medical issue that had been weighing on her the first time I'd visited the store—and was thankfully resolved now—in addition to filling me in on the latest developments in her love life.

Turned out, she'd recently started dating an old high school crush as well. Apparently, they'd reconnected while serving on the thirty-year reunion committee together. Go figure.

I'd talked to Dawn a few times since as part of my resolution to work harder at cultivating friendships. I was even thinking of signing up for one of the knitting classes at the store. Even though I had Donal now, it was good to branch out. You couldn't have too many friends, after all.

Marie refolded the blanket and tucked it back inside the gift box. "You really picked it up quickly. Clearly, you're a natural-born fiber artist. When are you giving it to Erin?"

"For her thirtieth birthday next month." It seemed fitting, since I'd originally intended for her to have it on the day she was born. I'd debated giving it to her at her baby shower, which was happening two weeks after her birthday, but decided to get her a nicer gift for that instead. Donal and I were going in together to buy her one of the big-ticket items from her baby registry.

Erin and I had been seeing each other regularly—a coffee date here, a lunch date there—and getting to know each other better. The exact nature of our relationship still felt like strange and uncharted territory, but we were making it up as we went along.

Donal and I had finally met Erin's husband, Mark, last month after he'd finished his overseas contract. Erin's mother, Paula, had invited us all over for dinner. I'd been desperately nervous about it, but it had turned out to be lovely. Afterward, Paula had asked me if I'd help her plan Erin's baby shower.

It was clear by now that Erin considered Donal and I family and wanted us to remain a part of her life. Sometimes when I stopped to count all the blessings this year had brought, it took my breath away.

Six months ago I'd had no family at all to speak of, and now I had not only Erin but Donal too. Because of them, my extended family had grown to include all of Donal's family and Erin's as well. And soon there'd be a new baby to bring us all even closer together. By finding me through that DNA registry, Erin had brought so many gifts into my life that I almost didn't know what to do with all my good luck.

"Tess." Marie elbowed me as I closed the box containing the blanket. "I don't want to alarm you, but there's a very attractive man lurking outside your office with flowers and some kind of sign."

"What?" I turned around and laughed when I saw Donal peeping in the door of my office across the hall. Marie knew very well who he was because we'd had dinner with her and Matt twice in the last several months. "Oh my God, what is he doing?" I wondered out loud.

"I don't know, but I can't wait to find out," Marie said as she came around the desk for a better look. "Should I go get him?"

"No, I'll do it." The poor guy was gazing up and down the hallway with a dejected look on his face. No doubt wondering where I was.

Grabbing the box with Erin's blanket, I opened the door of Marie's office and leaned out. "Excuse me, sir. What's your business here?"

Donal spun around, his face lighting up at the sight of me. As I went toward him, he dropped down on one knee and held up his sign.

My name was written at the top in thick hand-drawn letters outlined with glowing Christmas lights poked through the poster board. Beneath it was a poem, written in colored markers, with stars and planets decorating the edges.

Star light, star bright, first star I see tonight.

Wish you may, wish you might

Be my date on ~~prom~~ reunion night.

The word "prom" had been crossed out in red with "reunion" scrawled above it.

"What exactly is happening right now?" I asked in bemusement.

Donal proffered the bouquet of flowers with a flourish. "Teresa McGregor, will you be my date for our thirty-year high school reunion next month?"

"Is that glitter?" I asked, still marveling at the sign.

He got to his feet and looked down at it proudly as he came toward me. "Maddy, Jack, and Erin helped me make it. Promposals weren't a thing when we were in high school, so I recruited assistance from the younger generation to make sure I did it right."

"I don't understand." I hugged the box I was holding to my chest as I smiled up at him. "It's just a high school reunion. You didn't have to make a big production out of it." I hadn't even thought he wanted to go, since he'd always seemed so unenthusiastic about the reunions in the past.

"I think it's adorable," Marie said beside me. "Hi, Donal."

"Hi, Marie. Thank you. I think it's pretty adorable too."

I leaned up to give Donal a quick kiss before hooking my hand around his arm and towing him toward my office. "I'll see you later, Marie."

"You kids have fun!" she called out.

"I can't believe you did this," I said as I closed the door and deposited Erin's blanket on one of the extra chairs.

Donal held the flowers out to me. It was a bright-colored bouquet of yellow roses intermixed with pink and orange daisies. "Since I never got to take you to prom like I wanted, I thought maybe we could use the reunion as a do-over."

I looked up from admiring the flowers. "What did you say?"

He turned his back to me and propped the sign on the chair behind the box holding Erin's blanket. "I never told you this, but I'd been intending to ask you to prom before everything between us went sideways."

"Really?" I said, staring at him in surprise.

"I was crazy about you." He turned around finally, letting me have his eyes, which were so bright they could have lit up all the buildings in Chicago. "I wanted you to be my girlfriend, Tess. I didn't want to hide our relationship. I wanted to give you my class ring and have you wear my letter jacket while we walked through the school hallways together holding hands. I was trying to work up the courage to tell you that." His expression turned rueful. "I just wasn't fast enough."

"Donal." I tugged him into my arms and stroked his jaw as our lips brushed together. "I was crazy about you too."

"You haven't answered my promposal yet."

"Hang on." I arched an eyebrow as I pulled back to peer at him. "Didn't you swear to me you *weren't* trying to get a do-over on missed opportunities from high school?"

"Just because that's not the main reason I want to be with you doesn't mean we can't have some fun reliving the old days."

"I'm sorry, did you just refer to our high school reunion as *fun*? Because the Donal Larkin I know has always hated having to deal with reunions."

"Maybe I've changed my mind." He brought my hand to his mouth and rubbed his lips over my knuckles. "Or maybe the only reason I disliked them before was because it was too painful having to face the woman who'd gotten away."

That probably shouldn't make me feel like gloating, but it did. "And all this time I thought you didn't care at all."

"Tell me the truth. Before you found out you were pregnant, if I'd asked you to be my girlfriend and go to prom with me, what would you have said?"

"I would have said yes. In a heartbeat."

His lips curved in a smile that still made me want to swoon. "And yet you haven't said you'll go to the reunion with me."

"Of course I will. I'd love to."

"Whew," he said, his eyes crinkling. "I was starting to get nervous."

"No you weren't."

His lips lightly touched mine in a chaste kiss. Which was right and proper since we were in my office, but I really wanted more.

"What's your afternoon look like?" he asked, letting go of me before we got too friendly. "Any chance I can convince you to knock off work and play hooky with me?"

"You don't have to get back to the office?"

"Nah. I can skip out if you can."

My heart jumped happily. "Give me five minutes to send a couple emails and I'll be ready to get out of here."

The theme our high school reunion committee had chosen for our thirty-year was "Night at the Movies." They'd decorated the hotel ballroom with posters from old eighties movies and made centerpieces out of popcorn tubs and candy boxes. Someone had even crafted some handmade cardboard standees of iconic actors and pop stars from back in the day for people to pose for photos with. I suspected most of it was the brainchild of Dawn's best friend Angie, who'd taken over the committee from me.

I had to admit it was clever. I also knew from past experience with reunion planning that the nice hotel they'd chosen for this year's venue was going to gouge them on table, chair, and linen rental. Furthermore, even though the drink prices at the cash bar were outrageously inflated for the watered-down well drinks they were serving, the margins here were so thin I doubted the committee would recoup their costs. Most likely they'd end up either having to beg for additional donations or planning some kind of fundraiser to make up the budget shortfall.

Honestly, it was a relief not to be involved this time around and just be able to sit back and enjoy the reunion for a change without having to think about budgets or deposits or any of the other things that might be going wrong. Angie had done a good job, even if she'd done it differently than I would have. I decided to make a point to find her later and tell her so.

As I sipped my white wine, I glanced at my watch and then toward the door. No sign of Donal yet, but it was fine. In a stunning new twist for me, I wasn't the slightest bit worried. He'd warned me he had an important meeting with a big client this afternoon that might go late. I knew he'd get here as soon as he could.

The two of us were getting better and better at all this open communication and managing expectations stuff. It just went to show you were never too old to grow up and learn new things.

The DJ started up a Tone-Loc song, and I smiled as I watched a few more of my old high school classmates dash for the dance floor. The drinks had been flowing long enough that the party was starting to liven up.

My gaze traveled over the familiar and not-so-familiar faces around the room. I'd talked to a few old friends already, but there weren't many people I'd been that close to here tonight. Other than Dawn, of course, but she was on the reunion committee and was busy with her volunteer duties, as well as her new boyfriend.

I still found it weird that she was dating Mike Pilota now. I'd thought he was kind of a jagoff back in high school, but he seemed to have matured since his football player days and turned into a pretty great guy. Good for Dawn. And Mike. Donal and I had hung out with them a few times, and they seemed really happy together.

A couple of women I vaguely remembered from marching band approached me and started up a conversation. After a few minutes, they dragged me over to another, larger group of band nerds. I sipped my drink, nodding along with their nostalgic chatter and joining in with it occasionally.

Roxette's "Listen to Your Heart" started playing, which was one of the songs from the mixtape Donal had made me. Instinctively, I looked toward the door just in time to see him walk in. He couldn't have timed it better if he'd tried.

The room seemed to get lighter as soon as Donal entered it. It always felt that way, wherever we were. His presence made my life brighter. I hadn't even realized how dim my world had gotten until he'd dropped back into it and shined his light on everything.

His eyes scanned the ballroom, and when he found me he broke into that dazzling smile I loved so much. He started forward, but only made it a few steps before he was accosted by a couple of old friends.

I watched him accept their hugs impatiently before muttering what looked like an apology and heading in my direction again. Several other people tried to call out to him or flag him down, but he ignored them all, his steps unwavering until he reached me. The band folks I was with hailed him exuberantly as he stooped to kiss my cheek.

"Sorry I'm late," he murmured just for me, his lips lingering near my ear as his nose pushed into my hair. "I hope I didn't keep you waiting too long."

"Not at all," I assured him. "But I'm glad you're here."

As he turned to acknowledge the friends I'd been talking to, Donal's hand smoothed up the back of my dress until his fingertips found bare skin at the top of my zipper.

"Sorry guys, but right now I have to borrow Tess so we can dance to this song." His gaze homed in on me again, his eyebrows rising slightly. "If that's okay with you?"

"Of course."

With a hand on the back of my neck, he steered me away from the group, relieving me of my empty glass and depositing it on a table on our way to the dance floor. As soon as we got there, his arms wound around me, and I clasped my hands behind his neck as he tugged my hips flush against his.

"Careful," I murmured as I turned my face up to his. "People will think we're a couple."

"I fucking hope so." One hand slipped down to boldly squeeze my ass as we swayed to the music. "This is my do-over, remember? I want the whole school to know we're together."

"If you're planning to ask me to homecoming, the answer is no. One high school dance per decade is all I can handle these days."

His smile was as brilliant as the disco ball throwing off glints of light around the room. "You're saying I shouldn't get my hopes up for the Sadie Hawkins?"

I smiled back, my chest filling up with a loose, easy feeling I was still getting used to but knew now was happiness. "I still can't believe you actually wanted to be my boyfriend back in high school."

"What did you think I gave you that mixtape for? I wasn't exactly being subtle."

"I always thought you didn't want a serious girlfriend."

"I didn't want anyone *else* for a serious girlfriend because I was completely hung up on you. No other girl could compare."

"And yet you said nothing."

"I gave you a mixtape of love songs, woman."

My smile turned teasing. "Does Bon Jovi's 'Bad Medicine' really count as a love song?"

"Hell yes. That song is seriously fucking romantic."

"'She Drives Me Crazy' by Fine Young Cannibals? That one feels like an insult."

He grinned. "You did drive me crazy. Still do."

"And that Def Leppard song with the music video about the serial killer? What did you expect me to make of that?"

His eyes widened in mock offense. "Have you ever listened to the lyrics to 'Photograph'? Don't let the awesome guitar shred fool you, that's a straight up love song."

"See, now if it had been 'Pour Some Sugar on Me' I might actually have caught on."

"Don't think I didn't consider it." A lascivious smirk curved his mouth. "But I was trying to be classy and romantic in my awkward teenage boy way."

I stroked my fingertips over his jaw. "You always seemed so cocky and confident. It's hard to imagine you being too timid to tell me how you felt."

"I didn't think you felt the same way. I was afraid you wouldn't want me."

"I did want you."

His blue eyes shined with tenderness. "You've got me now. I'm all yours, McGregor."

I knew he was. What a privilege, to have a piece of this man's heart. I didn't even mind that he'd stolen such a big chunk of mine. I knew he'd take good care of it. We'd take care of each other.

"I'm thinking of getting a tattoo to that effect," he said. *"Property of Tess McGregor."*

"Where exactly would you put this tattoo?"

"Maybe I'll let you pick where it should go."

My eyebrows lifted. "Dangerous. I'm not sure I can be trusted with that much power."

"I trust you completely." He fit his mouth to mine and slid his tongue past my lips, kissing me senseless despite all the people around us. Someone wolf-whistled, but I hardly noticed. All that mattered was kissing Donal.

When he finally finished, I was weak in the knees and breathing heavy. Thank God he was holding me up.

"Sorry," he said, grinning down at me. "I got carried away."

I snuggled closer and laid my head against his chest. "Me too."

ABOUT THE AUTHOR

SUSANNAH NIX is a RITA® Award-winning and *USA Today* bestselling author who lives in Texas with her husband, two ornery cats, and a flatulent pit bull. When she's not writing romances, she enjoys reading, cooking, knitting, and watching lots of sad British mysteries on TV.

Sign up for Susannah's newsletter: https://www.susannahnix.com/newsletter

---

www.susannahnix.com

Facebook: https://www.facebook.com/susannahnix/
Goodreads: https://www.goodreads.com/susannah_nix
Twitter: https://twitter.com/Susannah_Nix
Instagram: https://www.instagram.com/susannahnixauthor/

Find Smartypants Romance online:
Website: www.smartypantsromance.com
Facebook: www.facebook.com/smartypantsromance/
Goodreads: www.goodreads.com/smartypantsromance
Twitter: @smartypantsrom
Instagram: @smartypantsromance
Newsletter: https://smartypantsromance.com/newsletter/

ALSO BY SUSANNAH NIX

Chemistry Lessons Series

(STEM Heroines)

Remedial Rocket Science

Intermediate Thermodynamics

Advanced Physical Chemistry

Applied Electromagnetism

Experimental Marine Biology

Elementary Romantic Calculus

King Family Series

(Small Town Siblings)

My Cone and Only

Cream and Punishment

Starstruck Series

(Movie Stars)

Star Bright

Fallen Star

Rising Star

Standalone

Maybe This Christmas

For the most up-to-date book list, CLICK HERE

ALSO BY SMARTYPANTS ROMANCE

Weight Expectations by M.E. Carter (#1)

Sticking to the Script by Stella Weaver (#2)

Cutie and the Beast by M.E. Carter (#3)

Weights of Wrath by M.E. Carter (#4)

Common Threads Series

Mad About Ewe by Susannah Nix (#1)

Give Love a Chai by Nanxi Wen (#2)

Key Change by Heidi Hutchinson (#3)

Not Since Ewe by Susannah Nix (#4)

Lost Track by Heidi Hutchinson (#5)

Educated Romance

Work For It Series

Street Smart by Aly Stiles (#1)

Heart Smart by Emma Lee Jayne (#2)

Book Smart by Amanda Pennington (#3)

Smart Mouth by Emma Lee Jayne (#4)

Play Smart by Aly Stiles (#5)

Lessons Learned Series

Under Pressure by Allie Winters (#1)

Not Fooling Anyone by Allie Winters (#2)

Out of this World

London Ladies Embroidery Series

Neanderthal Seeks Duchess by Laney Hatcher (#1)

Well Acquainted by Laney Hatcher (#2)